BEFORE THE GODS...

After a frantic but all-too-brief expansion that resulted in the creation of the First Terran Empire, mankind now lies divided and stagnant, lost in the depths of the First Dark Age.

The "Gates"— mysterious portals left behind by some ancient and long-vanished race, interconnecting the Seven Worlds of Man— stopped functioning nearly six hundred years ago. As a result, those worlds settled by humans have been cut off from one another entirely.

Now whispers have reached the ears of General Constantine Baranak of Majondra that the Gates may soon reopen. The general has resolved that if and when that happens, his armies and his starfleets will be the ones to subordinate the other human worlds and restore the Empire of Man.

But in a galaxy where the cosmic gods of the Golden City do not yet roam, other forces—alien forces—pull the strings, and their secret agenda may yet mark the human race—and all life in our galaxy— for destruction...

"Plexico is master of Space Opera."
–Pulp Fiction Reviews

The Shattering/Legions Saga
by Van Allen Plexico

BARANAK

STORMING THE GATES

A Novel of *The Above*

———

VAN ALLEN PLEXICO

WHITE ROCKET BOOKS

This one is for Mary Brown.

A stand-alone novel, this book is also the second volume in the "Above" series and is a part of the "Shattering" saga.

BARANAK: STORMING THE GATES (THE SHATTERING)
Copyright 2015 by Van Allen Plexico
Cover art by Mark Williams
Cover design by Van Allen Plexico

A White Rocket Book
www.whiterocketbooks.com
ISBN-13: 978-0692474822
ISBN-10: 069247482X

First hardcover printing: July 2015
First paperback printing: July 2015

0 9 8 7 6 5 4 3 2 1

The Above
(higher energy; slower movement)
Shortcuts (Paths) across spacetime

- Our Universe -

The Below
(lower energy; faster movement)
Realm of demons; the underverse

THE ERAS OF THE SHATTERING UNIVERSE

First Pax Machina

First Terran Empire

First Dark Age

Second Terran Empire

Terran Alliance

Second Dark Age

The Young Empires

Second Pax Machina

Shattered Galaxy

THE SEVEN WORLDS OF MANKIND

During the First Terran Empire and First Dark Age,
in order from the Earth outward, as linked by the Gates:

Earth
Original Imperial capital and most populous world.

Tolkar
Fortress and factory world.

Majondra
Second-most populous and wealthy world.*

Sarmata

Verghas
World ruled by expansionist military regime.

Trinity

Evergreen
Last-colonized, most sparsely-settled world.

Victoria
Primary moon of Majondra and home of the Baranak family.

DRAMATIS PERSONAE

The Baranak family,
in descending order based on age:

Louis (deceased)

Constantine, Commander-in-Chief of Military Forces of Majondra

Justinian, younger brother of Constantine and Second-in-Command of Majondran military forces

Aurelia, younger sister of Constantine and family liaison with the Church.

Octavia, younger sister of Constantine and Majondran government official.

Jerome, younger brother of Constantine, high-ranking military officer and twin brother of Alexius.

Alexius, younger brother of Constantine, high-ranking military officer and twin brother of Jerome.

Gaius, son of and military aide to Constantine.

Stephanie, youngest sister of Constantine.

Others of note:

Corindar Jeras, priest of the Church on Majondra

The Sister Superior, high priestess of the Church on Sarmata

Corinda Helaini, priestess of the Church on Sarmata

Jon Salas, Captain of the Majondran Navy ship *Marata*

Maxillus, Lord Steward of Majondra

The Immortals:

Istari, the Renegade

Elendi, the Mastermind

Orondi, the Oracle

Udasi, the Judge

Aleuvi, the Assassin

Yadrui, the Farseer

Dormor, former Hand

Kratok, former Hand

Hadog, former Hand

"It is more shameful to distrust your friends than to be deceived by them."
—Confucius

"As big as an elephant is, a whale is still larger. Everything's relative. Even gods have their spot on the food chain."
—Jim Starlin

"There are none of you, good doctors, could cope with my family anyway."
—Corwin of Amber

ONE

My father burned.

I watched in horror as the unearthly crimson flames consumed him. Within moments, his features were obscured by the awful intensity of the fire.

Desperately I fought toward him, despite the intense heat, casting about for anything that could beat back the flames. But I knew that it was too late, even before he toppled limply back into the burning remains of the tent. The cloud of smoke and debris that arose around him served as a macabre sort of punctuation to his struggles.

He was gone.

My world reeled under me, shifting off its axis. Now I was truly alone. My only ally swept off the board, all that remained were my uncles and aunts, those vipers. Cutthroats, backstabbers, religious fanatics and bullies. My family.

And here I sat, in that family's own armed camp, on the cusp of interstellar war.

War. I hated the very word. The idea, the concept, the thought itself. I was never cut out to be a soldier. I wanted nothing to do with battle. How was I supposed to deal with war, now that a war had landed in my lap?

In the past, I'd always had Dad to turn to. But no longer. Never again.

I dropped to one knee, running my soot-stained hand back through my hair.

How had it come to this?

It had begun, at least for me, scarcely an hour earlier, when my father, quite alive and brimming with confidence, stood poised to conquer all of humankind.

The message arrived that he had called a secret meeting in his tent. Obediently I gathered up my few belongings and hiked through the thick grasses of the moon Victoria to the location of his temporary command post. The sun was setting when I reached his tent, casting jagged shadows across the camp. No sign of my uncles, but other high-ranking officers including generals and admirals stood around waiting, some glancing up at me curiously as I approached.

And then I heard the words, just above a whisper.

"The General's lapdog."

I whirled, facing the man I knew had spoken them. Commander LaToy. A short, thick, muscular man in his late forties but appearing younger. He stood near two of his cohorts, two more who had never respected my father's rise to command or my own place within the service.

"You have something to say to me, Commander?" I asked.

He stepped forward.

"You heard me," he growled back. "You don't deserve to wear that uniform. The only reason you have it is because the General—"

I punched him.

It was swift, brutal. He had no chance to react, to move. My fist caught him in the jaw and sent him back into his two buddies, all three of them going down in a heap.

LaToy, back on his feet instantly, charged towards me.

"That's it," he growled. "I don't care whose son you are. You can't—"

"Gaius."

16

The voice had come from within the tent. Everyone froze.

"Gaius."

I hesitated, glancing back at LaToy. He eyed me with hatred and bitter anger, which roughly corresponded to my own feelings for him.

"Daddy's calling," he hissed. "Time to pretend to be a soldier again."

"We're not done," I replied, before turning and moving towards the tent.

The flap opened slightly and my father's broad face appeared. Seeing me, he gestured for me to come inside.

"Close it," he said as I followed him in, and I did.

He seated himself in a folding canvas chair and leaned back, peering at me, taking me in. I did the same of him.

Constantine Baranak, he was. Older now than the way I tended to remember him in his absence, his face had grown lined and hard, sharp and tough, like the rest of him. His eyes still shone with passion and fierce intelligence, as they had for as long as I'd known him. Lank hair once blond but now gone silver-white hung to his shoulders. He wore a black uniform with little decoration save the gold stat bars and pips that indicated his rank. On the small table before him lay maps and charts, notes and holos that I assumed related to our upcoming campaign, whatever that might be—and I'd yet to speak with anyone who knew. As I waited, he steepled his fingers before his lips, breathed deeply, and motioned for me to sit, which I did.

An overwhelming sense of anticipation and excitement crept over me. I felt that, at last, I might be about to learn why he had gathered all of our world's military forces here, on the moon of Victoria, and what great crusade he intended for us to embark upon. As the supreme military commander of our homeworld, Majondra, he had ordered it so without the slightest explanation as to why. Now all our ships waited up in the sky above us, prepped and poised for battle, and all our soldiers camped and drilled across the surface of this moon.

And all of us, soldiers and generals and admirals and even me, his only son and assistant, wondered what terrible, unimaginable threat might possibly exist that could require such a mighty mobilization.

A couple of minutes must have passed, during which neither of us spoke. I knew well enough to wait, to allow him to begin the conversation. He would do so when he was ready, and not before. Sounds of practice rounds being fired and the rumble of heavy equipment came to us from far away, but in the immediate space around our tent, there was only an anxious, nervous silence.

Finally, when my nerves could scarcely take it any longer, the quiet was broken by the terse words of a guard outside.

"My lord Baranak. Corindar Jeras is here."

"Yes."

The tent flap opened and in came the priest I'd seen visiting my father on numerous occasions in the past. He was tall and thin, like my father, but with wavy reddish brown hair and a thick beard, and appeared to be somewhere in his fifties— younger than my father but probably twenty years older than me. His eyes flickered from my father to me, and I was somewhat taken aback by the burning intensity they held. He wore the deep red robe of a corindar, the highest level of priest on our world. The golden emblem of the Church of the Burning Stars hung on a chain about his neck.

"Jeras. Welcome. Sit, sit."

The priest nodded to my father and pulled up a chair across from me, such that we formed a triangle. He started to speak, but my father stopped him with a raised hand and reached for a small device lying on the table in front of him. Clicking it, he activated distortion screens around us. The sounds of his armies drilling outside faded into silence. Then he settled back into his chair again and focused his attention on the priest, waiting. I was already perching forward on the edge of mine, anxious for news.

"I came as soon as I could," Corindar Jeras began.

He smoothed his robe with his right hand as his left reflexively stroked his beard. His eyes moved back and forth from my father to me; his words, as they emerged, were hushed but seemed loaded with great import.

"They have done it," he said. "The breakthrough we believed was imminent—it has happened. Within the next forty-eight hours, the Gates will be fully operational again."

A broad smile spread across my father's face—not just happy, but almost predatory—and he laughed once, then again.

I sat unmoving, dull incomprehension slowly giving way to utter shock. I looked from one of them to the other, unable to believe what I thought I had heard. They could not possibly mean…the Gates?

Corindar Jeras turned to me then, his expression an odd mixture of amusement, piety, and—beneath it all—a strong sense that he was gauging my reaction, studying it carefully, looking for…*something*…in it. I did not know what that might be.

The moment passed. The corindar brought his hands up and clasped them under his chin.

"Praise to the burning stars," he intoned. "Our empire, so long severed, will shortly be restored. Our long night of isolation is nearly at an end."

Then he smiled at me, and winked.

"What do you think of that, eh, Gaius?"

I still couldn't quite believe it.

"The Gates? You mean…" I gestured vaguely at the tent's ceiling, attempting to indicate the sky above, the space beyond. "The Gates themselves?"

"None other," my father said, laughing. I had never heard him laugh so much in all the years before this combined. "Nearly six hundred years of isolation—about to end!"

Jeras nodded, saying to me, "My brothers and sisters in the Church have labored for generations to gain a fuller understanding of the Gates. While they still have not mastered the technology by any means, they have managed to find a way to reactivate them, at least on a limited basis."

"The Seven Worlds of Mankind have been severed from one another for too long," my father said. "We now possess the ability to reunite the old Empire, to allow travel and communications among the Seven once more. The age of darkness is over!"

I tried to let all of this sink in, but I found it too incredible, too momentous, to easily accept.

Roughly a thousand years earlier, the first of the Gates had been discovered, by accident, out beyond the orbit of Earth's moon. Passing through that mile-wide, invisible gate led, almost instantaneously, to a similar location near another Earth-sized planet—but this one located in a star system so far away from Earth as to be, for all practical purposes, unreachable by any other means.

Mankind rapidly colonized that planet, and named it Tolkar. The logistics of colonization were ridiculously easy, requiring little more than a trip from Earth to a little beyond the Moon. Very soon afterward, explorers found another gate near Tolkar. This gate led to a third planet, Majondra, which became my family's adopted homeworld. Then later a gate from there was found, leading to Sarmata, and then one from Sarmata to Verghas, and then from there to Trinity, and finally to Evergreen, the apparent end of the chain, last of the Seven. Humanity had discovered a remnant of ancient super-technology that allowed for the settlement of a series of inhabited worlds stringing out across the galaxy. For over five hundred years, the Seven Worlds grew in wealth and in population, and a mighty Empire arose, centered on Earth, governing and dominating all of them. At the same time, the Church of the Burning Stars came to be founded on Sarmata. With Imperial approval and encouragement, it dominated the spiritual life of most of a human race now spread across seven far-flung planets.

For five centuries, all went well—better than anyone could have hoped or imagined. The Seven Worlds prospered, the Empire prospered, the Church prospered.

And then the unthinkable happened.

The Gates, all at once, ceased to function.

My mind still reeling from the possibility of their being restored, I hit on something my father had just mentioned. "You said the Seven Worlds have been severed from each other. But we've never known that for sure—that it wasn't just our gate that stopped working. For all we know, we were the only ones cut off."

"We know it now," my father replied. He looked at Jeras, who nodded.

"Our holy technicians have been able to open the Gates enough to observe through them for a matter of weeks now—all the way out to Evergreen, at the end of the line. During that time, we have learned a great deal about our sister worlds."

Jeras looked at me and smiled.

"At last we know the answer to the question that has bedeviled us for so very long: What has become of our sister worlds?"

I waited, as anxious as anyone to learn the answer.

He spread his hands.

"Each of them lost the use of the Gates at the same time we did, some six hundred years ago. We have not been left behind, as we feared. All shared the same catastrophe—the loss of contact with all the others."

"And in the time since? What has become of them?"

"Each," he replied, "has suffered a different fate."

I frowned, leaning forward, hanging on his every word now. "How so?"

"The Imperial governments on each world swayed, and most toppled," Jeras said. "None emerged from the sudden crisis quite the same as it had been before."

My father was nodding.

21

"And so you see the problem, do you not, my son?"

He sat back, poured three glasses of wine, and passed two of them to us.

"What might seem to you at first to be a great and glorious day—the return of the Empire—will instead, in all likelihood, usher in complete chaos," he said. "A reopening of the Gates will find not seven brothers eager for reconciliation, anxious to submit to a single rule. It will instead, overnight, place seven utter strangers at one another's throats."

He sipped his wine, his eyes never leaving mine, measuring, judging my reactions.

"You're sure of that?" I demanded, feeling myself on unsteady footing.

"The Corindar and his Church would prefer it otherwise," he replied, smiling tightly in Jeras's direction, "as would we all, of course."

He set the glass down, lifted a stylus from the map table before him, spun it idly in his fingers.

"But I am a soldier, son," he went on. "I cannot afford to engage exclusively in wishful thinking, or rely on prayers alone. I have to prepare for the worst."

The Corindar nodded slightly to him, then looked back at me.

"It will not be some sort of nostalgic affection for a long-dead government that brings those seven back together in harmony," my father continued. "It will be the one world strong enough to assert authority over all the others, to bring each of them into line. If none can do this, we will surely find ourselves plunged into civil wars for years—decades—to come. Or worse."

My father, apparently having made his point, sat back and drank the rest of his wine in one long swallow, then set the glass aside, waiting.

Corindar Jeras was perched on the edge of his chair, looking at me anxiously, as if fearful that I had been told too much, too soon.

And then it started to make sense to me. I would have seen it earlier, except that part of me—most of me—did not want to believe it. In addition, I had been deluged with information from the time I had arrived on Victoria; with world-shaking revelations I had never expected to hear in my lifetime. But I could not overlook our current situation any longer, not in the light of what I had heard so far. I had to ask the question openly. I had to hear it directly and honestly from my father.

"This all ties together somehow, doesn't it? This is why our ships, our armies, are here, readying for action. You aren't just preparing for the potential of conflict. You're going to precipitate it."

I gestured broadly, to indicate all the activity that buzzed silently about us.

"This is no drill."

My father smiled at me, and then the full extent of it all came out.

"There must be a new order, Gaius," he said, slowly and deliberately, as if instructing a child. "Beyond our own world, only on Verghas and on Trinity has some semblance of the imperial government endured. But in both cases it has been corrupted and distorted beyond real recognition."

"So you intend to unify the worlds," I said, "by force."

And there it was, on the table.

"If necessary," my father replied after a moment.

"You plan to conquer them," I said. "All of them." I knew it was true as soon as I said it.

My father poured himself another glass of wine.

"Hopefully not all at once," he said finally. "That would prove much more difficult. Hence the secrecy."

None of us spoke a word for several seconds, as I continued to stare at my father, incredulous. Then I turned to the corindar.

"And you? The Church?"

He shrugged.

"The other worlds would not willingly join with Majondra to restore the old Empire," he said. "They would not submit to what they would perceive to be outside rule. The Church is in agreement with your father on this point."

"The Church?" I frowned at him. "The entire Church? Or just our own branch of it?"

The corindar hesitated, glancing at Constantine, then looked back at me, biting his lip for a moment, seemingly struggling for the right words.

"The…Church…is in accord," he said finally, almost painfully. "All of it. We… we have already spoken at some length with the leaders of the branches on all the other worlds, and…"

"And you all agree on this?" I prompted him. "You support military conquest?"

"We…the seven branches are in agreement with one another on everything. Everything." His mouth flattened into a thin smile, and he bowed his head. "The Church is restored. It is whole again."

My eyebrows rose involuntarily.

"How can that be? Surely…surely, in six hundred years, some differences must have arisen."

Jeras appeared even more pained, and looked plaintively at my father.

At that moment, the ground trembled violently. One of my father's electric lanterns fell from its shelf and went out. I bent down to pick it up, while the rumbling only increased. Seconds later, it faded.

A ship taking off, nearby, I realized. A big one—probably a troop transport. Not a hell of a lot Dad's distortion field could do to cover that up. And it reminded me, once again, of the sheer size of the force he had assembled here. He really meant to do this.

Rising, I set the lantern back on the shelf and looked over at him, waiting.

He frowned, glanced at the corindar, and made a quick dismissive gesture at me.

"The Church's internal workings aren't pertinent to what we're about, Gaius," he said. "We can address whatever specific questions you have on that score later."

Jeras seemed wet with relief.

I nodded, still trying to absorb all of what I was hearing. The ramifications, in so many different directions, were simply huge. What was I missing? Something…

"What of our own government?" I blurted out suddenly. "What of our regent, Maxillus? Has he approved all of this?" I paused a moment, thinking it all through. "Do you intend to set him up as a new emperor of all the Seven Worlds?"

Again Jeras looked nervous, his eyes darting back and forth between us.

"Maxillus is a non-factor," my father replied coolly. "He is nothing. He lacks the vision, the understanding, the capacity to seize this opportunity for all it is worth, and to prevent the terrible alternative, should we not push forward with all our efforts and resources at once."

"A non-factor," I repeated slowly. "How can that be? He is the regent!"

"Not anymore," Corindar Jeras said.

I looked at him, then back at my father.

"What?"

"Your uncle, Justinian, is moving against him now," Constantine said. "I made certain that the forces most loyal to him were here with us on Victoria, where we can control them. Justinian commands a large garrison back home that is completely loyal to us. To me. We should be getting word from him tonight. Once that is settled, and the Church has the Gates open, we will be completely free to act."

I blinked, stunned beyond words.

"Ah, yes, I was waiting to tell you," Jeras said to my father. "I made a discreet inquiry on my way here. The corindar at the capital said that all appeared to be going extremely well.

Maxillus's government is folding up, collapsing with scarcely a shot fired. This was roughly two hours ago," he added.

I gaped at them. I simply could not believe it.

"A coup?"

My father shrugged.

"It is not as if Maxillus is of direct lineage to the old emperors," he said. "The man has scarcely a drop of royal blood in him. His ancestors merely happened to be the highest ranking imperial officials on Majondra when the Gates failed."

Still surprised, I looked at the corindar.

"And you approve of this, too?"

He closed his eyes and nodded once.

"The Church does not recognize Maxillus's legitimacy, and he will find no support among my order. We agree that your father is the logical choice, the most effective leader to restore and preserve some semblance of the old Empire."

"I will do my best."

Jeras smiled and nodded to him.

"And the Church will bless you for these actions, Constantine."

"You're sure of that?" I shook my head. "They don't know you, father. They can't have learned much in so short a time. How can they possibly support you in so grave, so consequential a matter? I do not understand it, and thus I do not trust it."

My father paused for a moment, frowning, regarding me, and then he stood. The corindar and I both did likewise. My father turned to Jeras then and smiled. He moved to the tent flap and pulled it aside, ushering us both outside. The roar of spacecraft, aircraft, and ground vehicles all around washed over us.

"Thank you for the good news, my friend," he said to the corindar.

Jeras bowed.

"Bless you, Constantine. It will not be long now."

"Indeed."

My father watched as the priest shuffled away into the star-spackled darkness of the camp. Then he gestured for a junior officer to come over, and whispered a few words to the man that I could not make out. After the officer saluted and hurried away, my father turned back to me again, motioning for me to go back inside. He followed me in and closed the flap. The sounds fell away once more, and I became conscious of the fact that he had not yet turned off the distortion field around us.

"You said," he began, his voice deep but gentle, "that you do not trust the Church's actions."

I had worried about admitting something so radical, so blasphemous, to my father. But I could not back down from it. I straightened, moving to face him directly.

"Yes, I—"

"Good," he said. "Neither do I."

My eyes widened, and then the air went out of me as I felt myself relaxing. Then you haven't become their creature, I thought to myself, immensely relieved.

"But I—we—do need them on our side," he continued. "We need their support and their good will."

He walked back to his chair and dropped heavily into it.

"The operation is already underway. The orders have been given. The Gate here, above this moon, will be open before the night is over. The moment it opens, our forces will strike."

He gestured at the maps and diagrams before him.

"In general terms, once out the other side, we will make a feint toward Sarmata, but actually continue on through their gate and hit Verghas, which we consider the greater threat. Perhaps the greatest of all. Once the Verghasites are defeated, the others should prove much more manageable. Even Earth itself, if the intelligence we've received from the Church is accurate."

I nodded, looking over the papers.

"We are ready," he said, leaning back in his seat. "As long as there are no surprises."

"You trust what the Church has told you?"

"If I had not felt we could win either way, I would not have embarked on this operation," he said. Then he shrugged. "All of it has come to me via Corindar Jeras. And Jeras has been a friend for many years. I trust him completely."

"All right," I said, nodding. "But we don't know if the information they have given to him has always been accurate, or complete."

"What we could verify for ourselves has always proven accurate," he said. "Beyond that, though…"

He shrugged, then climbed to his feet again and moved around next to me, placing one hand on my left shoulder, speaking softly.

"And that brings me to you, son. I want you to look into them. Quietly, carefully, and very discreetly, I want you to investigate the Church."

His lips formed a tight, flat line as he studied me, my reaction. Apparently satisfied with what he saw, he continued.

"After tonight, if all goes well, you will have access to more than just our own branch on Majondra. Jeras claims the Church's views and policies and agendas are uniform across all the Seven Worlds. I agree with what you said before—we cannot take such a claim at face value. Even if the Church on Majondra does fully support us, we cannot be certain the other six branches will. Look into all of them. Find out what they are hiding from us."

He stood there for a few more seconds, then turned away and leaned against a support, waiting.

And there it was, I thought. My own role in his coup, in his campaign of conquest. For five years I had served only as his assistant, essentially doing his paperwork and keeping up with his appointments and the like. But now I'd been given an actual, meaningful job—and a crucial one.

The thought of it scared me to death.

As much as I hated men like Commander LaToy, often I feared that they were correct about me, when they whispered behind my back—or said things to my face. They all believed the only reason I held any rank at all in our military was due to the influence and power of my father, and outwardly I rejected such views utterly. In private, however, such doubts gnawed at me. Part of me longed to prove them wrong; to be given the opportunity to excel on my own merits. But another part of me honestly believed them. That part of me had hoped I might never be placed in a position where the truth about myself, for good or ill, would be forced out into the light.

Now it seemed I had no choice. My father was placing an awesome responsibility on my shoulders.

Now we would see what we would see.

I met his eyes again and nodded, and the weight of the heavens descended upon me.

"Alright," I said. And I resolved to do the best I could do.

He looked back at me and smiled, and it was a warm and confident smile, and that weight on my shoulders lightened ever so slightly. If he truly believed in me, how could I do any less?

My father surely read all of these thoughts on my face, and he probably knew my mind as well as I did—or better—in these matters. He simply returned my nod and moved to sit down again, pulling his maps out once more, dismissing me if I was so inclined.

I was not, not quite yet.

"There's just one thing," I said.

He looked up again, surprised.

"You said before that our forces were gathered here because you believed in preparing for the worst. But that wasn't true. You aren't preparing to react to something—you're acting yourself, launching that very conflict. I will of course support you and our family and our world. But understand that by doing this you are crossing a line here—the line of open war—and taking the rest of us with you. Whether we like it or not. I hope you know what you are getting us into. Because there is no going back."

My father looked back at me, pursed his lips, and nodded slowly.

"You are right, son. You are right."

"So you had better win," I said, smiling.

He laughed once, sharply.

"I intend to."

I nodded, then walked out of the tent and did not look back.

This momentous night was not over yet, though. In fact, it had scarcely begun.

I resolved to get moving on my assignment immediately, rather than waiting around on Victoria or Majondra to observe the start of the campaign. From this vantage point, after all, one merely would see our ships accelerating away through the invisible Gate, the moment the Church managed to activate it. The real action would be on the other side, when they attacked the unsuspecting and unprepared defenders of Trinity and Verghas and the rest of the Seven Worlds that lay along the line of Gates, stretching out across the galaxy.

My work would have to begin on Majondra, at least until my father secured the route through to one of the other worlds. I knew, though, without doubt, that my mission soon could take me well beyond my homeworld. I found I was anxious to begin the work. Frankly, I was relieved that my father harbored as great a suspicion of the Church as I did. And so I rushed across the darkened camp, heading toward the shuttle that had brought me to the moon earlier.

Hurrying around a parked personnel carrier, I bumped into a figure rushing back the way I had come. He stumbled and I caught him by the arm before he could fall. We looked at one another.

It was Jeras. He looked feverish, almost wild-eyed, his hair mussed and his robes somewhat disheveled.

"Oh, Corindar," I said. "I had thought you had already left the camp."

His eyes focused on me momentarily, then he looked away again. Sweat ran down the side of his face.

"No," he mumbled. "Not just yet."

"Are you alright?"

He stumbled to one side, and I was unsure whether he was having difficulty standing or was trying to get away from me. Equally concerned and curious, I grasped him by the upper arm again. He appeared to me as if he needed the support.

His eyes met mine again, this time in a flash of anger that passed quickly. He inhaled deeply and exhaled.

"I remembered some other business I have with your father," he said evenly then, pulling away from my grip.

"I see."

"Good evening," he said breathlessly, before rushing on into the night.

I nodded after him, started to continue on, then hesitated. Around me, the sounds of our shuttles and cargo vessels grew louder, as more of them launched into the night sky.

The Jeras I had always known was a careful, deliberate, fastidious man. If he intended to seek an audience with my father in that state, something had gone terribly wrong. And I needed to know about it.

Turning, I walked back in the direction Jeras had gone, in the direction of my father's command tent.

The rumblings all around grew even louder. It appeared as if most of our forces would soon be airborne, on their way up to positions near the gate, awaiting the time to strike.

I had just rounded the last corner and was about twenty yards away from the tent when I heard the scream, coming from inside it.

Jeras's voice.

Then my father's voice boomed out, the words indistinct but forceful, even angry. Obviously he had turned off the distortion field after I had left. As I reached for the flap, I could hear what they were saying.

"—do you mean, a trap?"

"I—I'm sorry, Constantine! I did not want to do this, but the others, the corim—"

I jerked the flap aside and took one step inside, then froze.

Jeras appeared to have my father pinned up against the far side of the tent. The corindar's clawlike hands were dug into my father's shoulders, and he exhibited strength I would not have thought he possessed.

"Father, what is this?" I demanded.

Constantine looked past the priest and saw me.

"Get back, son. He—"

Jeras became aware of me then, turning halfway to look back, and he cried out once more.

"No! You were not supposed to—" He gasped. "Stay back! I—"

His eyes, now crimson points of light, darted from me back to my father. The golden emblem of the Church, swinging out from his chest on its chain as he moved, flashed brightly, as if it held some sort of scarcely contained energies. His voice took on a plaintive, almost apologetic tone.

"I don't want to, I don't—"

His words dissolved into a keening wail—a sound itself instantly subsumed by an eerie, mechanical whine that seemed to be coming from his insignia.

I had had enough of this. Gritting my teeth at the unholy noise, I moved forward to grab him, to pull him away—

—and the flames burst forth, seemingly pouring from every part of his body, engulfing him instantly. His robe became a torch, but his body within burned even brighter.

My father! Still he was held in the unnaturally strong grasp, and the flames had already spread onto his clothes, his flesh. Gasping, he stumbled backward, and the corindar fell upon him.

Panicking, I attempted to move forward again, but the intensity of the flames only grew greater, the heat doubling and doubling again in the space of a second.

Their end of the tent was on fire now. The flames surged up the walls and engulfed the furniture, the papers, everything. The two bodies that had fallen to the floor were indistinguishable now, within the inferno. Rancid smoke filled the remainder of the tent, and I choked, trying to move forward, unable to do so.

Guards entered the tent behind me, bringing themselves up short as they ran headlong into the heat. They looked at me, but all I could shout was, "Out! Out!"

They listened, and we all shoved through the now-burning entryway and fell to the grass. It was burning now, too, and we had to scramble further away to keep from being engulfed ourselves.

Two of the soldiers grabbed jackets, blankets, whatever was available, and tried to beat at the flames, to no avail. The others called for help. Only a few seconds had passed, yet I knew, in that dull space before shock sets in, that my father was beyond saving. Anger and confusion welled deeply within me.

The tent collapsed into a formless mass, already mostly devoured. More soldiers ran up with extinguishers and turned them on the blaze, surrounding it and attacking it from all sides. The unnatural fire resisted, though, and it was more than a minute before the expansion of the circle of flame could be halted. Then began the job of fighting it back toward the center, which took more long, agonizing minutes.

None of us could approach the remains of the tent until the bulk of the fire had been extinguished. It was simply too hot, too deadly. Finally I rushed in, the ashy remains of the grass and the tent crunching and crumbling under my boots. The heat still was unbearable. Gritting my teeth, breathing shallowly, I searched for and found the spot where I believed my father and the priest had fallen. I leaned over, grimacing at the heat that still radiated upward, searching the ashes for any signs. At first I found nothing, but then I spotted a flash of red, partially obscured by ash, and dug it out. It was a jewel, a gemstone of some sort. I pocketed it and continued to search.

Then I found it.

A tiny piece of metal, half-melted and disfigured. It burned my fingers as I grasped it and lifted it closer

One of the rank insignia from my father's uniform.

There could be no doubt. He was gone.

Dazed, light-headed from the smoke and the heat and the shock, I looked around, seeing the looks of disbelief and confusion on the faces of our troops, seeing the ships still lifting off in every direction. The ships headed for the first battle of our great campaign. My father's great campaign.

And now he was gone. And his murderer, if appearances could be believed, was a member of the very Church that had endorsed our operation, indeed had paved the way for it. The same Church that had pushed him onto this path to begin with. That had provided our military forces with all of the intelligence we had on the others of the Seven Worlds.

Cold panic gripped my heart. If we could not trust Corindar Jeras himself, given his long, personal friendship with my father, then how could we trust anything the Church had told us?

Just what were we getting ourselves into—exposing ourselves to—with this war?

A moment later, I had my answer.

An alarm sounded from the command bunker nearby, and several soldiers around me pointed up, shouting.

The sky above, already sparkling with the tiny points of light that were our ships, had grown suddenly far more crowded.

Another fleet had arrived, as if from nowhere.

No, not from nowhere. From the Gate. I knew it then, without question. The Gate was operational. It was open now, and another force was emerging from it, in massive numbers. An attack fleet.

Our own ships had been caught flat-footed, prepared for an offensive campaign—a surprise attack of their own—not a defensive stand.

Explosions blossomed in the darkness overhead.

"Verghas," one of the techs shouted from the command bunker. "It's the Verghasites!"

We had been betrayed. Not just my father, all of us.

Cursing, I ran for the shuttle.

TWO

Hands shaking, still covered in soot, I fumbled at the straps and managed by the hardest to secure myself into my seat.

"Go. Go!"

The rumbling of liftoff shook the cabin. I closed my eyes and struggled to push my emotions down, to contain them, at least for now.

I was no renowned military commander, no master strategist like my father or some of my uncles. Dad knew—had known—my strengths, and had asked me to perform a service that he believed I could accomplish, and one that needed doing, now more than ever. My uncles and aunts could battle the obvious enemies of the moment, and could do so far better than I could. It fell to me to discover the identity of the deeper enemy, the real enemy, no matter where the answer lay. No matter how potentially blasphemous the answer.

I couldn't bring Dad back, but I had the mission he'd given me. For now all grief was set aside. It was time to act.

My shuttle roared into the sky above the moon Victoria. I lay back in the cushioned seat, trying to relax my body, but my mind worked feverishly, examining possibilities and probabilities. Very quickly, something occurred to me that had escaped my thoughts during all of the chaos of the preceding events. I leaned forward in my seat and clapped the pilot, Selvin, on the shoulder. My voice was ragged from the smoke, but I managed to make myself understood.

"Can you locate the corindar's ship?"

"Yes, sir," he replied, and quickly he brought up a tactical display of the vessels still parked at our camp. Most had already taken to orbit, but several dozen of different sizes and configurations yet remained on the ground. One of them flashed red.

"There it is, sir. Looks like they're just now lifting off."

"Indeed." I frowned. That certainly made them look guilty, or at least complicit in Jeras's betrayal.

It was a medium-sized transport ship, its hull a deep red and gold to match the Church's colors. Apparently in quite a hurry, its engines strained against the pull of the artificial gravity boosters active on the surface of Victoria—those devices that approximated normal Majondran gravity on the moon.

Jeras's ship was obvious now that I knew where to look. Activating the communications array, I hailed it.

If he heard my transmission, the pilot ignored us. The ship lifted out of the thick atmosphere of the Tagas Valley, where our base was located, and angled away from us.

I watched it, a frown developing on my face. The ship was moving closer to our fleet, closer to the invading Verghasites, closer to the massive firefight going on above Victoria. Even from this distance, I could identify dozens—hundreds—of spacecraft, from corvettes up to big battleships and carriers, on the Majondran side alone, along with what looked to be a roughly equal number of attackers. A long and bloody conflict appeared unavoidable.

I watched, frowning. Why would the Church ship possibly want to get closer to such a battle? The only thing I could think of was that perhaps they sought to lose us amid the confusion. I began to think that perhaps I should have waited and observed them a bit longer before hailing them. Now they knew someone was watching and wanting to catch up to them.

I leaned toward my pilot again. "Do we have any way of stopping them?"

"No, sir. We're just a shuttle—not equipped for combat at all."

I considered my options. The Church ship had stretched the distance between us, and would soon enter the sphere of the battle. If the other pilot thought he could lose us there, he might well be right. I had no desire to follow him into that mess.

Then it occurred to me: Why should I have to go into it at all?

I scanned the tactical readout for a few seconds, then made my selection and flipped the communicator back on. Keying in my personal security codes and overrides, I waited.

It did not take long.

"This is Captain Jon Salas of the *Marata*, Lord Baranak. How may I be of service?"

I nodded to the holo display and greeted the captain. "I hate to drag you away from the battle, even for a few moments, Captain," I said. "But this may be just as important. Do you see the Church-registered shuttle at…" I consulted the tactical display and read him a series of numbers.

He glanced to one side, where the edge of a wide, three-dimensional holo display floated in midair. Then he looked back and nodded. "Hard to miss, sir."

"I need you to lock that ship down, Captain."

He raised his eyebrows. "Lock it down?"

"Minimize the damage, keep them alive if you can—but don't let them leave the area."

"Ah. Yes—certainly, sir." He blinked and hesitated a moment. "A *Church* ship, sir?"

I had expected that question, that doubt. Devotion within the very conservative ranks of the Majondran military ran at least as deep, probably deeper, than the population of my homeworld as a whole.

"*That* Church ship, yes."

He must have quickly set any reservations aside, which I appreciated, because he nodded and said, "At once, sir."

The captain turned away again and spoke to one of the techs seated nearby on the bridge.

I waited, anxious. The Church ship had gained velocity and would soon be deep within the swarm of battling spacecraft.

"We should have them for you in a moment, sir," Captain Salas reported.

I allowed myself to relax a bit, glad to hear that the discipline of our military forces could trump even Church indoctrination. Then again, he scarcely could have objected. All I had asked was that he detain the ship, not destroy it.

A bright flare of light at that moment drew my attention away from the holo and to the viewport. Ahead of us, a crimson beam of energy speared out from the *Marata*, just barely missing the Church ship. A warning shot, clearly. Only a tiny difference in firing angles and the smaller vessel would've been vaporized into an incandescent cloud.

A second later, that's precisely what happened: the ship exploded.

My jaw dropped.

I leaned closer to the tactical display, making sure I had seen what I thought I had seen. It was painfully apparent. Our quarry was no more.

Leaning back and looking at the holo, I could see that Captain Salas was just getting the word of what I had witnessed firsthand. He didn't appear any happier than I felt.

Shouting, nearly screaming at the display, I got his attention. My already-rough voice nearly cracked as I choked out the question.

"*Who ordered that ship destroyed?*"

The captain blanched visibly in the display.

"Sir, I…I do not know! I gave no order to the gunners. My orders were directed to Lieutenant Genz, to lock them up in tractor beams."

I glared at him. Part of my brain hovered on the brink of fury. Another part, trained and conditioned over most of my life, stepped back, observing our exchange dispassionately. That part carefully studied the man's expressions and reactions, seeking any additional information that might be gleaned.

"So am I to understand, Captain, that your gunners are free to fire their weapons at any time they please? Free to blast ships out of space whenever they feel like it?"

The captain looked horrified.

"No—no, sir! Not at all."

"Then how did that just happen?"

The captain started to reply, apparently thought better of it, and managed an, "Excuse me a moment, sir," before whirling around and barking at his subordinates.

I waited, the anger welling up again despite my efforts to control it.

After several seconds, the communications officer approached the captain. She spoke a few words to him that I could not overhear. Then he turned back to me.

"No order was given to fire, sir. In fact, gunnery reports they only fired the one warning shot, and it safely missed." He shook his head. "It must've been a stray shot from the battle."

I cursed, angrily and vehemently. My only lead was gone. I turned away from the holo display and brought my right hand up to my short, blond goatee, stroking it absently, thinking. Several moments passed during which no one came up with any additional information sufficient to be worth disturbing me. Then my reverie was broken as Captain Salas spoke up.

"My lord," he said, "perhaps the ship wasn't actually destroyed."

"What?" I turned back to face him, where he floated there in miniature in the cloud, and crossed my arms. "We saw the ship explode, Captain."

"Perhaps that was what we were meant to think we saw," Salas replied. "I'm running a high-intensity scan now..."

I waited impatiently, curious what he was getting at and desperate enough for any hope that I was willing to entertain even the most far-fetched of ideas.

"There," he cried, standing in the display and pointing to a readout screen that was not part of the image I was seeing. "It was a ploy. They didn't explode."

"What are you talking about, Salas?" I demanded.

The captain manipulated the controls aboard his ship and suddenly I was seeing a tactical display of our immediate area of space above Victoria. He pointed to a faint trail of dots.

"They slipped away while we were focused on the explosion. There's the ion trail their engine is leaving behind. It must've been slightly damaged."

I was confused. "But—the explosion—!"

Salas shook his head. "An old trick. Likely they released a big cloud of fuel just behind them—between us and them, to be precise— and ignited it. Then they slipped away in the confusion."

Nodding now, I pressed Salas. "Can we follow them?"

"A simple thing," Salas said. He manipulated controls and grinned. "There. They went around the bulk of the fighting and..." His grin vanished. "...and passed through the Gate."

"The Gate?"

"Yes, my lord. Definitely. The trail leads directly to it and vanishes."

Groaning, I leaned back in my seat and stared up at the section of sky where I knew the gate hid, invisible but now so powerful and important. The canopy of stars and constellations surrounded us, the moon Victoria still a massive mottled shape at our backs and the blue-white swirled orb of Majondra, only homeworld any of us aboard had ever known, a large and insistent presence above and to port. A shimmering nebula of many colors swirled along, snakelike, in the background. Most disturbing of all, in the vast gulf of space between Victoria and Majondra, wave upon wave of dull-gray and olive drab warships from Verghas poured through that invisible gateway, colliding with wave upon wave of defending ships rising from our bases. Streaks of hard light and glowing tracers of harder projectiles crisscrossed the shrinking distance between them, and an ever-increasing proportion of that sector became filled with explosions, streamers of smoke and debris, wreckage, and above all the dead.

Why was this happening? How had the Verghasites known the Gates were about to open? How had they had time to construct so vast a fleet, poised to strike at a moment's notice, even more quickly that my father's ships could react? And why had Corindar Jeras killed him—right on the cusp of the war?

And how would the fighting come out? What good would it do to solve the mystery, only to see my world overrun by the enemy and the answers rendered meaningless?

I shook my head. The war was not my concern at the moment. I would pass on word of what had happened to my uncle, Justinian, and his brothers and sisters. They would pick up the fallen baton from Dad and lead us to victory.

I had a different task before me. For the moment, only I knew that something more sinister than a simple attack on our command structure was afoot. The only thing I could do was to chase down my only remaining clue—the Church ship. No matter where it ventured. And so I made up my mind and issued the order: "*Marata*—pick us up. I'm taking command."

"You're commandeering our ship, my lord?"

"That is correct, Captain Salas. We have a new mission. We are going through the Gate."

+ + +

We docked our much smaller ship with the *Marata* and I ordered us through the Gate before my crew and I had even had time to climb out. By the time I reached the bridge and strode in, taking a spot to stand alongside Captain Salas in his center seat, the *Marata* was plunging forward, the starless circle of the Gate expanding to swallow us up.

No one aboard knew first-hand what to expect. We had all seen historical recordings and descriptions from some six centuries previous, but to actually live through the experience of almost instantaneously stepping across a vast portion of the galaxy; it was a singular moment that could never be closely approximated by a holo recording or a poet's hand.

We tumbled through a nightmare tunnel of light and dark, color and void. The seemingly stable fabric of reality twisted and spiraled and shredded around us and the spot in the galaxy we had occupied moments before became a spot many, many light-years away, while the spot we now filled formed into reality before us.

The *Marata* shot back out into reality as the stars reemerged, though in all-new configurations. Before us hung the brown-green limb of Sarmata, fourth world out from old Earth in the chain of newly-awakened Gates.

The crew were all astonished, and again I had to remind myself that this was something entirely new for them, as it was for me. I was fairly certain no one aboard was six hundred years old and could remember the last time this had been possible.

But we would have no time for awe and wonder until the job before us was accomplished. Relieved that the sky here wasn't filled with thousands more Verghasite warships, en route from their own world to ours by way of this world's Gates, I barked out, "Find the trail," and watched as, one by one, the officers and tech crew pulled their eyes away from the main display and forced themselves to get back to work on the myriad tasks of running a spaceship—now having become, for the first time in so long, a *starship*.

"Your uncle is on the line, my lord," the communications officer said, ending my musings. I knew exactly which uncle the young woman was referring to; there was no need for further names or titles. So—he had called me before I could call him. And he'd found me remarkably quickly.

I accepted an earpiece from the communications officer and thanked her, found a spare 2D monitor I could borrow, then opened the channel. "Justinian," I said. "I was just about to call you."

"Gaius. Where are you?"

The voice was deep, resonant—just as I remembered it. I hadn't chatted with Dad's next-eldest sibling—and now, presumably, our new leader— in a while. He appeared to be standing in a camp very similar to the one we had just taken leave of on Victoria, but the sky was different. I took that to mean he was on Majondra itself. Soldiers hustled and bustled here and there around him and there was a general sense of urgency verging on outright chaos.

"It's Dad," I began. "He—"

"Yes, I know about that," he snapped, cutting me off. "We'll discuss it—and mourn—later. Right now, I need to know where you are, and what you're doing."

"I've taken the *Marata*," I said. "We're on the other side of the Sarmata Gate."

"The Sarmata Gate?" Justinian's astonishment was evident. "What in the name of the Holy Church are you doing there?"

I quickly sketched the chain of events that had led us here. Then I tossed in mention of Dad's orders regarding the Church—and not trusting it. I concluded with my plans to track down the ship and thoroughly question its crew.

A long pause, then, "Very well. Do what you must. I wouldn't presume to contradict Constantine's final orders to you. And I don't see anything the Church has done at this stage to earn our favor. Your Aunt Aurelia won't like to hear of such talk, but I won't say anything for now." He stroked his smooth chin, glanced at displays off to his right, and looked back. "I'm down with the armies planetside, attempting to rally the remains of Maxillus's forces and deal with whatever Verghasites have managed to land. Only a few have gotten all the way through so far, thankfully. Jerome and Alexius have control of the fleets," he said, referring to his two younger brothers. "Aurelia is nowhere to be found; she's off seeking spiritual guidance on it all, I'm sure." He looked annoyed as he said that last part. "Octavia and Stephanie—" He waved a dismissive hand. "So—I can spare you for a brief while, but I will need you back here soon."

I nodded. "Understood."

"But know this," he added, leaning forward into the camera, his expression still carrying with it no small traces of his frustration and his near-desperation. "On that side of the Sarmata Gate, the entire Verghasite navy is between you and any help I could provide. As long as you're over there, there's little or nothing I can do for you."

I nodded again. "We will be okay. Safer, in fact, than you might think—because, from here, it appears you're correct that the *entire* Verghas navy is engaged with you—because there are no signs of them here. They must have slid right through Sarmata airspace en route to attacking us, and they've poured everything they have into that."

"Terrific," Justinian murmured. "I suppose it would've been too much to ask that the Sarmatans resisted them on the way—or had something to throw at their rear guard." Silence for a moment as he appeared to be deep in thought, then, "Alright, fine. The *Marata* is officially assigned to you for the duration. Stay out of trouble, stay alive, find out what you can, and get back here as quickly as possible. If we're all still alive in twenty-four hours, we will gather at the palace on Victoria." He sighed. "And we will go from there."

I nodded.

"Understood. See you then."

I cut the link and sat back, thinking.

My other two uncles would probably go along with Justinian, follow his lead, at least for now. I could not imagine either of them venturing much beyond his orders, especially during a crisis. The same held true for the women of our clan. Depending on how things worked out, though, there could be trouble ahead. My father had possessed the gift of managing the various relationships within our family, of keeping most of my aunts and uncles on decent terms with one another. Could Justinian do this? From what I knew of him, I doubted it. He was a decent enough general, but not a great diplomat. I hoped I was wrong. I did not want to imagine my family winning the war only to fall to internal squabbles turned violent.

"We have reacquired the trail, my lord," the captain reported, disrupting my thoughts. I glanced over at him and nodded.

"Very well. Can you tell where it leads?"

"Down to the surface of Sarmata. To their capital city—or, at least, what was their capital six hundred years ago." He spoke a few quiet words with a bridge tech, then added, "We're accessing their data nets now and updating all of our records."

"Good," I said. "That's one thing we can contribute when we get back home."

"As expected," the captain said then. "There's a Church complex outside of the city. That's where they went."

Nodding at this not remotely surprising bit of news, I quickly issued orders for my regular crew to return to our shuttle. "We're going down, Captain," I told Salas before vacating the bridge. "Stay up here and keep an eye on things. Let me know the instant anything changes."

The captain saluted. "I can send another shuttle along with you, my lord," he suggested. "With a contingent of at least two dozen Rangers."

I pondered the idea, then shook my head. "No. We may need the cooperation of the Church officials here—assuming killing my father was a rogue operation and not official Church policy. And of course we do represent the first official contingent from Majondra to make contact with this world's Church leaders in nearly six hundred years. Leading a platoon of heavily armed Rangers into the Grand Corindar's sanctuary probably wouldn't go far toward establishing a good working relationship moving forward."

The captain offered a sliver of a smile. "I take your point, my lord," he said.

"Still," I added, "I wouldn't object to said Rangers sitting aboard a shuttle, ready to launch at a moment's notice, in the unlikely event we might need them."

"Of course."

Satisfied, I turned and departed the bridge. A veritable mountain of problems lay before me, but the only one that truly concerned me at the moment was finding the priests that had worked with Jeras and putting some extremely pointed questions to them.

It turned out the trail indeed led down to an area just outside of the capital city—an area dominated by a vast and ornate complex of white stone buildings surrounding a rectangular, man-made lake that gleamed like topaz in the afternoon sun. A spire some five hundred meters tall reared up from the center of the waters, and at the top of it shone the circular emblem of the Church of the Burning Stars.

"Nice temple complex they have here," I muttered. Glancing over at the pilot, I asked, "No one has challenged us yet?"

The pilot shook his head. "No communications whatsoever, my lord—though I started signaling the Church complex the moment we started down. And nothing much in the way of air traffic." He glanced at me, puzzled. "It's as if the whole planet is deserted."

I didn't like the sound of that. "No answer at all?"

He shook his head.

I leaned forward, staring out the viewport, slowly shaking my head. "Could the Verghasites have killed them all before they attacked us?" And then, before anyone could answer me, I provided myself with a sort of reply: "There's no damage, no signs of conflict."

"Pretty strange," the pilot said.

"Too strange," I agreed. I chewed my lip for a few seconds, then motioned to the co-pilot. "Ask Captain Salas to go ahead and send out the Rangers."

"Aye."

We moved into a slow circle over the complex.

"Any sign of the ship itself?"

The pilot hesitated, then pointed. I followed his gesture to where he indicated through the viewport. A tiny gray smudge slowly resolved into the late Corindar Jeras's ship. It sat almost dead center in the grassy field that filled the space between the main building and the artificial lake.

"Odd choice of parking spots," I observed. "They must have been in quite a hurry. Can't imagine the Church was happy about it."

"Maybe they knew we were chasing them," the pilot said.

I looked at him. "Did they? Could they have?"

He shrugged. "Possibly."

I considered. If the Church officials weren't out throwing a fit over Jeras's ship landing there in the middle of their landscaping, they weren't likely to care much if we did the same, I reasoned.

"The ship with the Rangers will be here in two minutes," the co-pilot informed me.

"Very well. Then take us straight down beside the other ship and we will go from there."

The pilot nodded once and manipulated the controls of our small vessel.

The expanse of immaculately maintained lawn had been cut into a representation of the Church's emblem, seven stars in a circle, wreathed in flame. At the base of the emblem stood the cathedral that formed the foremost structure of the compound. The seven towers comprising its façade loomed at least a hundred meters above the lawn, each of them reflecting a different architectural style; presumably, representative of the styles of the Seven Worlds, before the closing of the Gates had cut each off from the others. Behind that edifice, the lower shapes of the administrative and support buildings trailed away into the distance.

Waiting by the hatch, I hopped out as soon as we touched down. The grass, thick and fragrant, swallowed up my boots. Motioning for the others to remain onboard, I jogged across to where Jeras's ship rested, its engines off but smoke still rising from its exhaust ports. I stared at the ship for several seconds as I felt the anger—the rage—rising up from within me. I could see my father in his tent, and I could see Corindar Jeras. I could see them both erupting in flames. The look on Dad's face would haunt my dreams for the rest of my life—or so I believed at the time.

I pushed the all-too-recent nightmare images away and drew my sidearm. Slowly I circled the ship, moving to my right, until the entry/exit hatch came into view. It stood open. I halted and stared. The ship's occupants had disembarked in a hurry. A big hurry. They hadn't even bothered to close the door behind them.

A whoosh of air brought my attention above and behind me and I looked back. Another ship, this one bearing the emblems of my own government and navy, was settling to the lawn on columns of vectored thrust. A heavy troop transport shuttle. I waved.

Hatches snapped open and the Rangers filed out briskly. They wore dark blue jumpsuits with brown leather belts and boots. Each wore a red commando's beret and carried a heavy rifle. Their sergeant came up to me and saluted. Then he eyed the Church buildings warily.

"What's this all about, if you don't mind my asking, my lord?"

Many of our planetary troops were religious. Our planetary regent, Maxillus, had always encouraged it, to foster obedience and devotion. These men probably were nervous about brandishing their weapons on the Church's grounds. I sincerely hoped they could overcome that feeling, if the situation called for it.

"We're just going to have a look around, Sergeant," I said. "The place actually appears to be deserted."

This seemed to satisfy him well enough, and he returned his attention to his soldiers.

I glanced back at the cathedral as the troops formed up. The place indeed appeared vacant. No one moved on the tops of the towers. I frowned.

I started across the lawn and had gotten within a few yards of the massive main doorway when it swung slowly inward of its own accord. I stopped, waiting, but no one appeared, so I continued through and inside. The room was dark, and it took my eyes a moment to adjust.

"Did you have a fire on your ship?"

"What?"

Puzzled, I turned toward the voice.

A woman in the brown robes of the Church stood just inside the door to my left. She was of medium height, and I could make out tanned skin beneath the hood that completely covered her hair and most of her face. I recognized the emblem of a junior corinda dangling on a chain about her neck, the red gemstone glittering at the center of a golden starburst.

"Your clothes," she said, approaching. "You look like you've been through a fire."

I looked down at myself, saw what she meant. My blue uniform was dingy, streaked with soot, and my hands didn't look much better. I'd already forgotten what the fire and its remnants had done to me, back on Victoria. And that brought back other memories I preferred not to dwell upon.

"Things have been a little too busy to worry about it," I said, causing her to frown.

"What do you—?" she began.

"Where is everyone?" I asked.

She opened her mouth, closed it again.

"I am Sister Halaini, assistant corinda," she said after a moment's confusion. "Who are you? Where are you from?"

I touched a point on my belt and a holographic image appeared in the air between us, showing my credentials.

She drew back her hood and stared, first at the credentials, then at me. Her hair was dark and her features somewhat Polynesian.

"Gaius Baranak," she read. "Commander. Special Assistant to Lord General Constantine Baranak." She looked up. "Never heard of him."

"My father," I said. "My late father. Which is why we are here, in a way."

"You aren't from Sarmata," she gasped, recoiling, stumbling back a step. Her eyes, widening now, never left me. "You've come here from one of the other worlds. Through the Gates."

"We have indeed," I said with a nod. "From Majondra."

She walked forcefully past me and out through the doors onto the front area. She looked around almost frantically, seeing the Rangers patrolling here and there. She clutched at her Church emblem on its chain. "You've come to take over. To conquer us."

"Not at all," I replied quickly—ignoring the fact that, yes, that had indeed been part of my father's original plan. That plan had not survived first contact with the enemy; the question I now faced was, exactly who was that enemy?

She appeared extremely dubious of my denial. "Then why are you here?"

"Following a lead," I replied. I gave her a quick and basic summary of the events that had led us to her world and her cathedral, omitting the part about why our forces had been gathered on Victoria to begin with.

When I finished, she shook her head.

"We are the Holy Church," she said, her voice indignant. "We harbor no assassins." She folded her arms across her chest, grasping her golden insignia with one hand, and glared.

"Are you certain of that?" I asked. Turning, I pointed back to the abandoned Church ship sitting parked in the middle of the expanse of grass. "It's empty now. They had to have gone somewhere. And they chose to flee to this facility."

Her expression clouded. "I have seen no one arrive," she snapped. "In fact, quite a few of our own have disappeared this afternoon." She gestured around at the empty courtyard and the open doors; the only people visible were my own Rangers. She frowned then, and I began to wonder if she had until now appreciated just how deserted her church facility was.

One of the Rangers caught my attention. He held a small sensor device. "My lord," he said, "she has sent a signal. I just detected it."

I faced her, frowning.

"I have called for the Sister Superior," she said before I could ask. "Perhaps she can better answer your questions."

I didn't reply to that. We stood there a few moments, waiting, while the Rangers continued their search. At one point a sergeant approached and informed me, "No signs of the people from the ship, my lord. We are continuing to scan."

"Very well."

"What is this?"

We all looked around as a new figure strode out through the cathedral's main doorway.

"Who are you people? How dare you bring armed soldiers onto Church property?"

It was a woman, that much was clear enough. Though almost entirely covered in a brown cloak and robes like Sister Halaini, she was taller and stronger of build. She whipped back her hood to reveal angular features and long, black hair. Her eyes were cold and blue and drilled through me as she approached.

"I am the Sister Superior," she announced. She gave her name, as well, but I immediately forgot it and did not remember it again until much later. "What is going on here?"

I attempted to calm her, to little effect. "We are from Majondra," I explained, "and are chasing the accomplices of a murderer."

Her expression altered only slightly at that. "And you believe these—accomplices—have come here?"

I nodded toward the ship we'd tracked.

The Sister Superior and Sister Halaini exchanged looks.

"What have you told these men?" the Sister Superior demanded.

"Nothing," Halaini replied, now appearing defensive for the first time. She hesitated, then, "They have also asked where the rest of our people have gone. And, to be honest, Sister Superior, I have been wondering that same thing myself. The Church grounds appear far more deserted than I was expecting, and—"

"Silence," the bigger woman barked. "Such information is not to be shared freely with infidels who—"

"Infidels?" I stepped forward. "We—"

I was interrupted by a high-pitched whining sound that rapidly escalated in volume and intensity. It seemed instantly familiar to me, though I couldn't say how or why. The two women looked at one another again, clearly puzzled. I glanced over at the sergeant; he was working the controls on his sensor device but shaking his head to indicate he couldn't tell what was happening.

Then I remembered precisely where I'd heard it before.

Stepping forward, my eyes flicked from the golden symbol dangling from the Sister Superior's neck to the one worn by Sister Halaini.

That one. The red jewel at its center glowed like a tiny star. And the whining sound had become almost intolerable.

Reaching out, I snatched the symbol from Halaini's neck and hurled it across the broad, smooth, gray-streaked marble floor of the cathedral's front patio area. The golden star skidded to a halt, the jewel now almost blindingly bright.

"Wha—how dare you—?" Halaini was saying, outrage filling her voice.

The golden symbol exploded, flames flashing out in a two-meter radius.

We all covered our eyes and some stumbled back.

A second later, it was done. The golden insignia was gone and only a large black smear remained on the marble flooring where it had lain. Smoke swirled lazily above the spot.

Sister Halaini gawked, first at the spot, then at me. After a couple of seconds of stunned silence, she found her voice. "How—how could you possibly have known that was going to happen?"

"It's not the first time I've seen it," I said. "In fact, it's the reason I'm here."

She blinked back at me but had nothing to say. Her eyes kept flicking over to the black smudge on the marble and she swallowed with some difficulty.

The Sister Superior recovered and moved forward, stepping between us. Her expression had transformed from one of shock to anger and I quickly gathered that she had concluded it was all some elaborate trick of mine.

"You are fooling no one," she growled, her ice-blue eyes drilling into mine. "You are trespassers and heretics and I want you off the grounds of the Church immediately!"

I started to answer her one way, then changed my mind and instead merely said, "Or else what?"

The eyes flared brighter. "Or else... I will summon our security forces and have you all arrested. Or worse."

"By all means, do so, lady," I said with an overly affected polite smile. "Summon away. I'd love to have a talk with your security forces. Or your administration. Or, for that matter, another corinda or corindar." I leaned in toward her, my voice dropping but intensifying. "Because, to be honest, sister, you and your friend here are the only human beings we have encountered since passing through your gate."

She opened and closed her mouth, blinking rapidly. Turning suddenly, she looked back at the big cathedral building that towered behind us.

"Tell me the truth for a change, sister," I said to her. "Where has everyone gone?" I paused. "Or—do you not even know yourself?"

She turned back to face me and now her expression of haughty defiance had melted away, replaced by a confusion very similar to the look worn by her subordinate. She started to say something, but the high-pitched wail returned.

She looked down at the golden insignia that hung before her breasts, then up at me. Her brows were knitted.

"It must be some trick of mine," I said, reminding her of her words to me mere seconds before. "So that means there's no point in taking it off. You're perfectly safe."

The whining noise rose into the extremely uncomfortable range and a bright light began to flare from the stone set into her insignia. She was staring back at me, now wearing an expression that I found completely inscrutable.

I smiled. "That's it," I said, "just keep doing nothing. You'll prove me a fraud any second now."

"Sister Superior!" wailed Halaini. "Please!"

The sound was deafening.

Furiously, the corinda grasped the chain about her neck, whipped it over her head, and hurled it across the open space. It landed only a short distance from where the first had hit the marble, but by then it was already flaring like a tiny sun,

56

flames jetting out in every direction. By the time it landed, it was a blackened husk that crumbled to dust as it hit.

She looked from the second, newer black spot to me and snarled.

"You're welcome," I said with a slight bow. "Now—as for the others you were going to call for us?"

At that precise moment, others did actually arrive—though not the type that either she or I would likely have preferred. Instead of fussy bureaucrats or spit-and-polish soldiers, the figures that rushed out as a side door swung wildly open wore cloaks and hoods, very much like the corindas, but they carried exotic items that very quickly revealed themselves to be weapons. Slugs and streaks of hard light erupted from the attackers and came our way, and I barely managed to pull the sister superior down before she could be riddled with bullets and laser holes. As we hit the hard flooring, I noted from the corner of my eye that the sergeant of my Rangers had done the same with Sister Halaini.

I tried to pull the two women to cover but there was none to seek. We were exposed out there on the marble patio area before the cathedral. Our only hope was that enough of the Rangers were still close by.

They were. They hit back immediately. Gunfire rang out from both directions—unfortunately, with the two women and myself stuck in the crossfire. As we lay there, trying to put ourselves on as intimate terms as possible with the floor, I counted some dozen of the robed attackers. I had my handgun out and wanted to shoot, but I was concerned that I would only succeed in drawing their fire in our direction and getting the two women—to say nothing of myself—killed. So instead I shouted orders to the sergeant, who was also pinned down nearby, and he in turn relayed them on to the others.

The robed attackers quickly concealed themselves behind the massive stone base of an equestrian statue that stood a couple dozen meters from us, and from there they traded gunfire with the Rangers. For their part, my men were blasting away, blowing gaping chunks of stone and decoration off the front facade of the cathedral and various limbs off the statue. But they couldn't quite get an angle on the bad guys themselves.

I had just about made up my mind to take to my feet and rush them from the side—likely a suicidal gesture at best—when a roaring sound came over us. I followed it with my eyes just as a wall of wind swept in, buffeting us. It was the troop transport. The pilot had lifted off and was swinging it in toward us. I grinned; I knew what that meant.

"Surrender now," came the voice of one of the Ranger officers on board, amplified over the vessel's external address system. "Surrender or we will kill you all."

"I hope not," I shouted above the roar of the transport's vectored thrust, for anyone who cared to hear. "I'd like to question somebody else before we're done here—and these guys seem to know more than our ladies do."

The robed attackers continued to fire back, undeterred by the warning. This lasted for perhaps four more seconds, and then the ship's main anti-personnel cannon erupted.

High-caliber slugs slashed into the stone statue base, shattering it into clouds of dust. A second later, the ship's fire lashed into the enemy soldiers, cutting them in half. There's no telling how much longer the carnage would've gone on but, as it happened, the question became academic.

They must have all been wearing those same golden insignia. The combined whine was deafening. The flash was blinding.

"Hold your fire," I shouted, climbing to my feet and running toward their former position. I knew precisely what I'd find, but I was hoping against hope that at least one of them hadn't burned up yet.

No such luck. They were all gone. Utterly incinerated. The space behind the statue base was a vast black smear, still cooling, smoke swirling above it.

I cursed.

The two women raced up behind me, took one look, and turned away.

I had nothing to say. There was no way the sister superior was going to try to blame my men for what had just occurred. Much as the two corinda didn't want to admit it, the true cause of what was happening here was all too obvious now. It was the Church, not we strange invaders, that was killing—or attempting to kill—its own representatives.

"So, what will you do now?" the sister superior asked once order had reasserted itself and her junior companion had settled down. "As you can see, there is no one else left here."

"You really do not know where they have gone?"

"I do not," she said. "I was in my office for the past two hours, working. No one said a word to me about an evacuation, and I heard no alarms."

"Nor did I," added Sister Halaini.

I nodded. It appeared our fugitives had made good their escape—but they'd inadvertently led us into a bigger mystery.

"Sergeant," I yelled, "have your troops take one last look around, see if they find anything suspicious."

He came up to me, looking puzzled.

"Suspicious, sir?"

I shrugged.

"More enemy agents... assassins... hidden bombs... you know, anything out of place."

I glanced at the two corinda.

"Those things would be out of place here, wouldn't they?"

Each of them glared at me but said nothing.

The search proved as fruitless as I'd expected. I was mulling over the possibility of continuing it when the decision was taken from my hands. The comm link built into my belt beeped in my earpiece, and I keyed it open. It was the copilot of my shuttle.

"My lord," he said, his voice nervous, "I'm getting reports of three Verghasite destroyers coming this way, fast. They just passed through the gateway from Majondra. We might want to make ourselves scarce, just in case. It could get hot here in a bit."

I nodded, though he couldn't see me.

"Do you have them on the sensors yet?"

"Not yet, my lord," he said.

"Alright. I'm wrapping things up here now. I'll be out there shortly."

I cut the link and called to the sergeant.

"Go ahead and get the men back out to your ship," I told him. "There may be trouble on the way."

"We like trouble," he replied, grinning, but he turned and issued the orders to withdraw from the facility.

"What is it? What's wrong now?"

I looked around and realized that the sister superior still stood nearby. She had her hands on her hips, frowning.

"You two might want to clear out," I told her. "There are enemy ships coming this way."

"Enemy? We have no enemies, save the Church's enemies," Halaini said almost automatically.

"You can tell the Verghasites that while they're looting the building and cutting your throat," I said, starting for the shuttle.

Halaini gasped. "They—they will do that?"

"I don't know," I said. "But if you remain here you will surely find out the hard way."

I was partway across the grassy lawn now. Rangers moved past me, tromping to where their own ship was now parked, much closer to the cathedral. The sergeant barked impatient orders to the few still inside the building.

"You're giving up, then?" the dark-haired woman called after me. "First sign of trouble and you and your soldiers bolt?"

"You no longer want to find these people you say were complicit in your father's murder?" the other one added.

I scowled and came up short. Turning back, I faced the two women; they had been hurrying along in my wake. Now they stopped, too, appearing startled, and we confronted one another there on the lawn of the cathedral.

I actually paused and considered what the two of them were saying. I mean, the sister superior was grossly and unfairly exaggerating the situation in specifics, but in general, she had a point. I was leaving, and leaving without any answers.

I groaned in the back of my throat, frustrated, because I didn't feel I had any choice in the matter. Had it only been me and perhaps the Rangers on the line, I'd have stuck it out. After all, if I abandoned the search here, I might never find the people who had been aboard Jeras's ship. But it wasn't just the Rangers and me. There was also the *Marata* up there in orbit, waiting on us. The ship I'd commandeered and thus placed in the line of fire here. I owed something to all those men and women, too.

Cursing, I issued the final recall order.

"Then you must take us with you," the sister superior said when I was done.

"Take you with us?" I was incredulous. "I thought you hated us. Infidels, remember? Barbarian invaders."

"The situation has changed," the dark-haired woman said. "Our own Church has tried—more than once now—to kill us. I find I have no choice but to admit that. Meanwhile, you and your ship have been delivered to us."

"Delivered to you? That's not exactly how I would characterize—"

Her ice-blue eyes twinkled as she ignored me and kept going. "You are here, and in a position to be of service. I am therefore fully prepared to retract the things I have said about you."

"You haven't said that many things about me, honestly," I noted.

"Well..." She paused, and the eyes twinkled again. "I definitely thought them, at least. But I'll take them all back— if you'll take us off this world."

How could I refuse an offer like that? I bestowed upon both ladies my most ingratiating smile and bowed. "But of course. You are welcome to come along." I thought for a moment, then added, "I may have lost my leads that brought me here, but perhaps you two will recall something that will help— given time, of course, and the comforts of guest berths aboard the *Marata*."

"My lord, we must depart now," the sergeant called to me.

I nodded. "Off we go," I said, gesturing toward the shuttle.

The two corinda raced through the grass toward my ship. The Rangers clambered aboard their own transport. Engines roared to life. Thirty seconds later, we were all airborne and headed back up to Sarmata orbit.

"Where are we going?" the sister superior asked once we had docked with the *Marata* and I had personally led them to their quarters.

"Beggars can't be choosers," I attempted to point out—but the sentiment did not go over well with my two new guests. So I followed that with, "The family estate on Victoria."

The two women took this in and nodded.

"You'll like my family," I added with a wink before I left them alone in their new cabin for a time. "They're just about as murderous, lying and duplicitous as your Church."

I shut the door behind myself before they had the chance to find anything heavy that they could throw.

THREE

It occurs to me that perhaps I should pause here and explain to you, as we stand on the edge of infinity and stare out at the great cosmic rupture and the energies pouring forth from some other unimaginable realm, that I am no great wordsmith. I am no poet, certainly no scholar—save in perhaps the martial and military arts, at least by training if not by preference. My strengths lie in those years of training, in my strategic and tactical knowledge, and in my good right arm. If you're desirous of some lyrical account of what transpired, I recommend that you look elsewhere, for that is not something I can supply. All I can tell you is what I said, what I did and what I witnessed; what brought me and those around me to this place and this time, here on the edge of infinity.

So now, as the Fountain gurgles and hisses and erupts behind me, and I gaze out at this universe not my own, and as I feel my old identity and my old memories and my old self slipping away and being replaced by something...newer? Larger? Perhaps—only perhaps—greater? I make this and only this promise to you: I will speak truth. Artistic or no, I cannot say. But this is what happened; that much is certain. That is what I will tell you.

So we took our leave of Sarmata with our two new passengers in tow, and I was of two minds about the wisdom of bringing them along. My need for information—for any possible leads, now that all others had dried up—prevailed, and thus they came with us. The voyage back up to and through the Sarmata Gate was uneventful, though we did suffer a few close calls once we passed through to the Majondra side, where the battle between the forces commanded by my uncles and the fleets of Verghas yet raged, if in somewhat reduced state for the moment. Soon enough, however, we arrived in low orbit around the Victoria moon and I, along with the two corinda and a couple of Rangers serving as personal guards, boarded the shuttle for the trip down.

The family palace—the one on Victoria, not the much grander one down on Majondra itself—was a somewhat impressive structure, even by the standards of the wealthiest and most powerful members of our society. It had been originally constructed at least four generations before, by the first of my forebears to claim a portion of the moon's surface for our clan. Located in the foothills of a mighty mountain range that ran the width of one of the two major continents, great snow-capped peaks towered above it, lending it grandeur beyond even that provided by its architecture. It sat at the farthest end of a short, narrow-necked peninsula that broadened out tremendously as it went, with gently sloping lawns and carefully-tended arbors all around, blending into a forest at the mainland. Broad towers and slender minarets danced along its upper reaches.

We brought the shuttle down and landed in one of the cobblestone courtyards that swooped out in lazy curves from the western side of the edifice. Three other shuttles, all bearing the official seals of our family, rested nearby—so I wasn't the first to arrive.

The soldiers patrolling the courtyard saluted as we strode by, and I returned the gestures. As we passed them, though, I wondered what they might be thinking. Their loyalty to my father had been absolute. With him gone, they had likely transferred that iron-clad devotion to Justinian. As for little old me? That remained to be seen.

Into the palace we went, through the tall, iron-bound doors set into the western wall. The two ladies accompanying me looked around, wide-eyed, and I wasn't surprised, for the Victoria Palace was at least as impressive as their own cathedral. Majondra was a wealthier world than Sarmata, or it had been before the Gates closed. Our structures were older and, for the most part, grander.

A black-uniformed soldier I recognized as bearing the insignia of Justinian's personal staff met us just inside and saluted crisply. "The General requests that you and the other members of the family gather in the second floor library in one hour," he said.

"I will be there," I replied with a nod.

The man hurried away, presumably to deliver my response, and I turned to face the two women squarely. They still seemed somewhat taken aback by the splendor of our surroundings.

"I believe our first order of business should be to find something to eat and drink," I said. "Does that meet with your approval?"

The smaller one—Halaini, I remembered—looked to the other, whose name I had not yet recalled. She nodded. "That would be appreciated," she said. The other made a face the meaning of which was not readily apparent to me, but she did not object, and I took that as a positive.

And so we adjourned to the kitchens and helped ourselves to whatever we could find, consisting in the main of some cold roast beef and cheese and a particularly nice Shiraz, after which we separately engaged in the timeless tradition of "freshening up." This was particularly necessary in my case, as I still bore the ashes from the fire. Even thinking of that brought with it pain, and I found I couldn't wash myself fast enough. The mirror revealed a man who appeared much older than my own thirty-two years, thanks to the soot that permeated my hair and goatee. The shower was welcome, and a change of clothes afterward helped, too—I donned a thin, long-sleeved, golden-mesh deflector suit shirt with the family crest on the left breast, black pants and boots, and a broad black belt.

I met the ladies back in the main hall afterward. They looked considerably refreshed as well, and I had to remind myself that they, too, had endured something of a trauma this day. I had questions for them—questions unconnected to the ones about my father. The Church was up to something, and I intended to find out precisely what.

I greeted them and complimented them on their new attire. Servants had located sets of spare clothes, likely cast off by one or more of my aunts, and the two corinda had accepted them reluctantly but with good graces. We exchanged brief pleasantries until one of the guards informed me that the hour had nearly expired. I thanked him and we made our way in the direction of the second-floor library.

We entered the great hall and strode across its cavernous space. Its ceiling was vaulted, with great dark wood beams curving up toward the heavens. Very large and mostly faded tapestries hung along both walls, depicting scenes either real or imagined from my family's history. At the far end a second-floor balcony projected out, with one broad, curving stairway leading up to it from our level. Beyond the balcony on that upper level stood broad oaken double doors set into the back wall—the doors that led into the library.

As we walked I glanced up at the balcony and noticed two figures standing in the shadows of its far right corner. One of them appeared to be wearing the uniform of our world's military; the other I couldn't make out at all. The dim light of the balcony glinted on something, though; either metal or glass, it seemed—and a lot of it. The second figure took notice of us and visibly reacted. I still could see nothing but the outline of a very tall man. And that strange glinting, as from all over. Both figures quickly moved deeper into the shadows, and at that moment we passed beneath the balcony and I lost sight of both of them.

Frowning, I stopped in my tracks. The two women accompanying me realized a moment later that I'd stopped and turned back to look at me, curious. I motioned for them to wait. Something felt wrong about what I'd just seen. It was nagging at me, at the back of my brain. I turned and moved back out far enough that I could see atop the balcony again. Two figures were there, sure enough, but they were two of my uncles—Jerome and Alexius—and they were clearly visible and recognizable, standing in the light, near the railing.

I lingered there, staring up at them for several seconds, wondering. Could they have been the two figures I'd seen at first? It didn't seem possible. One of them, perhaps, but the other had been much taller, skinnier, and there was that odd glint...

Before I could say anything they both moved away from the railing and I heard the double doors open and close.

"Are you coming?" hissed the sister superior. She and Halaini were still standing impatiently at the foot of the stairs, looking extremely annoyed.

"Yes, I—I am coming." I paused and ran through my memories of what I'd just seen one more time. Something was not right. I was sure of it. I could feel it.

"You say that," the corinda replied after a few more seconds of my immobile introspection, "and yet there you still stand."

I snapped out of it, laughed politely at her remark, then led them up the stairs.

No one was present there on the balcony—no one to see me, and no one to see the two corinda. As far as I knew, only a few members of the household staff had laid eyes on them thus far, or even knew of their presence. This gave me a thought. I turned to them and ran my hand over my chin, then,

"Would the two of you mind waiting in the small sitting room next door?"

"You don't want us to go in with you?" blurted Halaini. She paled. "Are we in some danger here?"

The sister superior regarded me with a frown but withheld her judgment for the moment.

I offered both of them what I hoped was a reassuring smile. "Not at all. However—I believe you'd be more comfortable there, and you would be near at hand when I need to call you in to describe what you saw and to verify my testimony, or if one of the others wishes to question you."

After initial concerns the two women acquiesced with grace. Expressing my appreciation for their understanding, I led them to the small but comfortable room, made certain they had access to refreshments and knew where the nearest restroom was, and left them there.

Around the corner then and to the library. The two broad oaken doors parted as I neared them, and I was greeted by the broad, smiling face of my Aunt Aurelia, who stepped aside to usher me in.

The eldest of my three aunts, she had been something of a confidant of my father, though she and I had never been particularly close. I had always respected her deep affinity for the Church, her devotion to it, but it had always made me somewhat uncomfortable, and never more than now. I resolved to bear her beliefs and allegiances in mind when speaking with her.

As if reading my mind, she smiled, the corners of her eyes crinkling. She wore a richly embroidered sea-green dress with tiny red and white gemstones set in patterns upon it. She wore her thick, red hair up, held in place by jeweled combs. Her lips were blood red and her eyes ice blue.

"Gaius," she said. "I am pleased to see you."

I smiled a tight smile and returned the greeting, then looked around the room, taking it all in.

The library was high-ceilinged, paneled entirely in dark wood where the wall was visible behind the many shelves of books and other forms of media. Half a dozen dark, overstuffed chairs sat positioned around the interior space, and a long, broad table that looked to weigh tons filled the center of the room. A small fire burned in the fireplace across from me.

"We will talk privately later," she said quietly. "I know you must be anxious to make the rounds."

Not particularly, I thought—and she knew this, too—but I smiled again and nodded, and walked past her.

At first I thought only two others—my younger uncles, standing beside the table—occupied the room. But, as my eyes adjusted to the room's dim lighting, I realized someone else had arrived before me.

In a broad corner chair, nearly lost in its depths, sat a small, slender woman with short, black hair and pale skin. She wore a long, black skirt and sleeveless black top that revealed both her arms, one of which featured a spiraling tattooed line that trailed down from her shoulder to the back of her hand. Silver rings sparkled on most of her fingers and a small, starburst tattoo shone on her left cheek, below vibrant green eyes. In her lap lay a marbled silver and black cat, while another, all of silver, curled about her feet. Seeing me, the faintest of smiles touched the corner of her mouth, then vanished.

Stephanie. Youngest of my three aunts in age—at twenty-five, even younger than me—and perhaps the most enigmatic. What I knew of her, I liked. Mainly that consisted of a studied disinterest in our family's politics and ambitions. Where her interests did lie, I had no idea.

I nodded to her, and continued across to where the twins, Jerome and Alexius, stood.

Glancing at me, they both seemed to size me up at once, measuring my worth in a mere instant. They did this every time we met, and had since I was a child, to the point that I scarcely reacted anymore.

Jerome, the elder by about ten minutes, stood about an inch taller and appeared twenty pounds lighter. Beyond that, they seemed identical, though they were only fraternal twins. They both wore Majondran dress uniforms of navy blue with lots of gold pips and stat bars, and both had shaved their heads. Their eyes were blue, like Aurelia's, and indeed they shared the same mother with her. My father and Justinian had shared a common mother, dead these many years, while Stephanie's mother was a much younger, dark-haired woman who still lived, and could be seen from time to time, bustling about the estate. My own mother had been very blonde, a trait I shared, and thus I had rarely if ever been confused for a brother to one of my uncles or aunts.

I greeted the twins and received gruff acknowledgements in return. They had a map spread across one end of the table and seemed to be arguing over something related to it, sprinkling in sharp gestures and rebukes. They always did this, and it never escalated to actual conflict. Separately, I got along well enough with each. Together, everything became a competition, and I found them intolerable. It was simply the way they were.

I came very close then to asking them who the mysterious and very tall individual had been—the one I'd seen on the balcony. Something nagged at me, though, holding me back, and I decided to hang onto that little tidbit for later, when it might yield better results and do the most good.

I leaned between them, frowning down at their map, only to find both of them ceasing their bickering and looking at me, their brows furrowed. I started to say something when the doors banged open and we all looked up, startled.

My eldest uncle, Justinian, strode in. Tall and regal in bearing, he resembled my father, though somewhat thinner. One might even say "gaunt." Four years younger, he actually appeared older than Dad, his face lined and his hair thinning.

He wore the dark blue regular uniform of the military rather than a dress outfit, probably in order to send some sort of subtle message to the twins in their finery. I noticed that a commander-in-chief insignia like the one previously worn by my father now rode on his chest.

That didn't take long, I thought to myself. *Maybe he had it in his pocket all this time, waiting for the opportunity to put it on.*

Justinian inserted a data crystal into a receptacle on the table, as Jerome rolled up the paper map over which they had been arguing. A three dimensional image of our homeworld, Majondra, shimmered into existence above the tabletop, spinning slowly.

"We're all present, then?" Justinian asked, scarcely looking up.

"Where's Octavia?" I asked.

The others looked at one another.

"I couldn't reach her," Justinian said. "I've been trying since yesterday."

The twins shrugged. Aurelia shook her head.

No one seemed terribly concerned, so I let it go, filing it away for later investigation.

"Here is our strategic situation," Justinian began. He pointed to a cluster of red dots between Majondra and the moon we now occupied, Victoria. "The Verghasites caught us by surprise, no doubt about that. We were arrayed for travel, for attack, not for defense. Some hit Victoria. Some even made it close to here—to the palace." His mouth formed a tight line. "But we held. And, in the past few hours, we've pushed the bastards back."

There was a murmur of agreement from Alexius and Jerome.

My eldest uncle moved his hand over the controls and the image zoomed in to a point in space behind the Verghasite fleet.

"The Sarmata Gate is here," he said, pointing to an empty area nearly surrounded by enemy vessels. "They're guarding it with their very lives now, of course."

"We smash those ships," Alexius growled, "we gain access to the gate. And then we hit Verghas itself."

Jerome nodded grimly. "Just as we originally planned." He gestured airily with his right hand. "This all becomes a mere distraction—a delay."

"That fleet of theirs is not inconsiderable," Aurelia said. "Can we 'smash' it so easily?"

Alexius smiled at his elder sister.

"Their advantage is gone," he said. "Now it comes down to ability, to skill. They can't match us."

Aurelia gave her little brother a sweet, brief smile, then looked at Justinian.

"Is it so easy as that?" she asked.

He frowned, running a hand over his long chin.

"Not so easy, but it will be done. It must."

"I had no real problems passing through the Sarmata Gate," I pointed out. "Either direction."

For a moment no one spoke, but everyone was plainly looking at me.

"That's where you've been?" Jerome exclaimed.

"You've been to Verghas?" Alexius said at almost the same instant.

"What? No—not at all," I quickly answered. "We didn't go beyond Sarmata itself."

Things turned chaotic for a moment, with the twins demanding tactical and strategic information—number of ships we passed, formations, configurations, and so on—and Aurelia seeking to glean whatever Church intelligence I could provide from my brief visit to their cathedral on Sarmata. At last Justinian brought the whole crazy proceedings to an abrupt halt, shouting, "Enough!"

The others stopped chattering and looked up at him, cowed.

"There will be time for such things later," he said. He turned to focus on me and his eyes burned intensely. "My only concern is that you made it there and back again still in one piece."

I spread my arms and smiled. "As you can see," I said, "none the worse for the wear. Though we did run into trouble at the Sarmata cathedral. A bit of gunplay."

"The Verghasites were there?" Justinian asked, turning and regarding me fully.

"Of course they were there," Aurelia said. "One of their first actions would have been to neutralize a rival branch of the Church."

"It wasn't the Verghasites," I stated. "We never even saw them. It was a whole group of corindar. Locals."

Aurelia appeared most troubled by this news. She sat up straight. "You're sure they were priests?" she asked.

"They came from inside the cathedral," I replied. "They wore the robes and the golden insignia." I snorted. "And they were extremely well-armed."

"Did you bring back any evidence? Photos, genetic—"

"They burned," I answered quickly, cutting her off. I didn't want to have to think about the fire again. "Just like Jeras and Dad. Nothing was left."

Aurelia's expression at that little revelation was inscrutable.

"I don't know about your theory that the Church is divided, sister," Jerome interjected after a moment's silence. His tone was belligerent.

Aurelia rounded on him. "What is that supposed to mean?"

Jerome shrugged. "A priest from our own world killed Constantine. The Church let the Verghasites attack us through the Gates before telling us they were operative. A bunch of corindar on Sarmata attacked Gaius. Sounds like they're pretty well unified to me. It is almost as if they were never separated."

Anger flashed in Aurelia's eyes. She stood. "What are you saying, brother?"

Jerome met her look with one of his own, stepping forward, jaw out. "I am saying the Church appears to me to have a single objective in mind, regardless of world—at least, that they've revealed thus far."

"And what would that be?"

"The destruction of this family."

Aurelia took an involuntary step backwards, blinking. "That—that's insane," she managed after a moment. "The Church has always supported our family."

Jerome laughed. "They appear to have abandoned that position." He paused, then, "Even as they abandon *all* their positions, quite literally," he added with a smirk.

Aurelia said nothing to that, merely looking back at him with obvious hostility.

"What do you mean, Jerome?" I asked. I was curious but was also hoping to distract at least one of them before something was said or done that couldn't easily be retracted. Of all times, we needed everyone together now, with Dad murdered and the Verghasites on our very doorstep.

"Tell him, dear sister," Jerome said. "Tell him why you can't simply contact our friends of the Church on our own world."

Aurelia glared at him.

I waited, very curious about this.

"Because they are all gone," Justinian said after my aunt failed to respond. He moved between them—better late than never, I thought as I watched him. If he was going to serve as the patriarch of our clan now, he needed to pick it up a bit.

Then the import of what he'd revealed hit me. "Gone?" I asked, frowning.

Both Justinian and Jerome nodded. "Just as you described of the priests on Sarmata," Justinian said. "All of them vanished, as if they'd never been there—and no signs of how or why or where they've gone."

"Your allies flee at every turn, sister," Jerome jabbed.

Aurelia reddened. She said nothing, instead merely turning away and reaching for her glass of wine. She lifted it, glanced quickly at Alexius, frowned, and turned her full attention to her drink.

"Let us not be unkind to our sister," Alexius said then, clasping his twin on the shoulder. "A faithful friend of the Church she might be, but she cannot be held responsible for their actions—however bizarre and inexplicable they might be."

This seemed to mollify Jerome somewhat, and after a couple of seconds he allowed the tiniest of nods.

"I did not call us here to bicker like children," Justinian declared. He was clearly annoyed, and I suspected it was not just at the behavior of his brothers and sister but also at his own inability to dominate the room the way my father once had.

"Proceed with your business, then, brother," Alexius said, "so that we might all return to our pressing concerns."

Justinian shot him a look but let the insubordination pass. He moved away from the rest of us a short distance and then turned back to face us, regarding us with a stern expression and waiting for us to settle down, like some professor before an unruly classroom.

"In addition to coordinating our actions," he said at last, "I wanted to be certain each of us is primarily engaged in activities that most benefit the family, and our world."

No one commented. We were all genuinely curious as to where he was going with this.

"I must prepare our forces for our counterattack," he said. "Jerome, you and Alexius will continue to lead our defenses in the meantime."

The twins both nodded their agreement or their acceptance—not necessarily the same thing, of course. I was curious which it was.

"Aurelia, the Church seems to me a lost cause at this point." He paused, possibly to field what we all felt would be an inevitable retort, but she said nothing. Somewhat surprised, he continued. "Therefore I believe your efforts would be best spent at the capital, working with the regent." He paused again, pursing his lips. "Helping him to make the right decisions, with regard to this war..." He smiled. "...And this family."

Aurelia closed her eyes and breathed for a few seconds, and we all awaited the explosion. Instead, she surprised us all for the second time in as many minutes. "I will do that thing," she said, "and Stephanie can accompany me."

I for one had almost forgotten my youngest aunt was even in the room. I glanced back at her as she was nodding.

"Fine," said Justinian. Then he looked at me.

"I have a job," I said quickly.

"I am giving you a new one."

"I won't have time to do both," I said.

"You won't do both. You'll do the one I'm giving you."

"No."

Justinian froze, staring at me. "No?"

I was growing warm. "Dad gave me my mission. It was the last thing he did before he died."

"But he did die."

"But his orders stand," I said, a bit angrily. "I'm sorry, Justinian—I respect you and recognize your right to lead us now, but Dad's orders still trump yours."

"Even from the grave?"

"Even so."

Justinian seemed poised to argue—or something worse—when Aurelia turned to me and interjected, "Gaius, I don't know what the point would be of investigating the Church now. As you've been told and have seen for yourself, the corindars and corinda have all vanished. To whom will you put your questions? Whom will you interrogate? And—given the current state of affairs—what difference would it all make in the long run?"

76

I started to point out that, at least to me, discovering why our own Church had murdered our top military leader on the eve of our planned attack on our enemies seemed a perfectly reasonable and timely objective—a question that desperately needed answering. Furthermore, I would have added that not all the corinda were gone—that I had brought two of them back with me from Sarmata and they were waiting in an adjoining room, in fact. Both of those points I opened my mouth to utter, but then something in the back of my mind intervened and kept me from saying any of it. Call it what you will; intuition, suspicion, or just knowing more about my aunts and uncles than perhaps even they were aware I knew... But I was overcome with a sudden and unshakeable sense that I should keep the two ladies' existence a secret for at least a little longer. And so I instead simply said, "We don't know what I will find. Why don't you leave that to me to determine?"

"Hold on, now," Jerome interrupted. He got out a few words about all of us needing to follow orders before his twin stepped forward and halted him with a gentle hand on the shoulder. Jerome trailed off and glanced back, puzzled.

Alexius smiled, first at him and then at the rest of us. "I agree with Gaius," he said. "He should have the opportunity to finish what Constantine ordered him to begin."

I watched the two of them, knowing from a lifetime around them the subtle signs I should look for. Sure enough, Alexius cast his eyes quickly at Justinian and then back at me, his brows knitted, as his twin looked on. Jerome blinked, seemed to understand, and nodded. "Yes—yes. I spoke hastily." He half-bowed towards me. "My apologies, Gaius. Alexius is quite right—as are you."

Any normal person would have missed it entirely. But we of our family were anything but "normal." I got it, and got it very clearly. They were challenging Justinian's absolute authority and also attempting to drive a wedge; to open a rift—or widen the one that already existed—between him and me. I took that to mean they were not thrilled with Justinian as supreme leader and would be looking for any occasion to undermine his authority and weaken his hold over the rest of us. Wonderful. With our family, the politics never cease, and never cease to nauseate me.

In this case, however, they worked in my favor, and so I wasn't going to raise a fuss. I turned back to Justinian, waiting to hear what he would say.

He was not happy, obviously. He was frowning at the twins and reddening. Before he could issue any sort of response, however, dear Aunt Stephanie tossed in a grenade.

"May I ask why Justinian is our leader now?"

He turned sharply her way. "What?"

She hadn't risen from her chair, and the marbled black and silver cat in her lap didn't stir. She merely cocked her head to one side, her bobbed black hair falling that way, and said, "Gaius is the son of our late commander. Should leadership not devolve to him, rather than to you, brother?"

He simply stared back at her, astonished.

It always struck me as funny when Stephanie referred to Justinian that way—as "brother," as though they were equals. Certainly it was technically true, given that everyone present—everyone except me, of course—had shared the same father. But Stephanie was less than half Justinian's age—and a good seven years younger than me, even—her mother a much younger woman who had come along years after their father's first wife had died.

Justinian sought to gather his thoughts, blindsided by this point as he had been. Stephanie merely gazed back at him, a faint and almost sweet smile playing about her blood-red lips.

"We are not a hereditary monarchy," Jerome interjected. "Constantine was no king, and there is no crown or throne for Gaius to inherit. It doesn't work that way."

"How does it work, then, brother dear?" Stephanie asked, the very picture of innocence.

"It works like this," Justinian said over-loudly. "It works that I am now in charge. Unless, that is, Gaius wishes to challenge my command." He looked directly at me.

"Not at all, uncle," I said, raising an open hand in gesture of submission to his authority. "You are clearly the man for the job. I have no ambitions along those lines whatsoever."

Justinian regarded me for a couple of seconds, appeared satisfied, and nodded. He turned to Stephanie. "Will that do for now? he asked her.

My youngest aunt shrugged, her Mona Lisa smile still in place. "If Gaius is agreeable with the state of affairs, I am."

I frowned slightly at her words. Where was this even coming from? Since when did little Stephanie take a part in the family's maneuverings? And since when did she care about my position in the unofficial family hierarchy? Despite the fact that her argument had been intended to benefit me— or perhaps because of it—I was extremely puzzled.

"It's a shame dear Octavia is missing out on this performance," Aurelia stated then. "I'm certain she would have a pithy comment or two that would take each of us down a peg."

"She'd make some idiotic remark that would insult at least half of us and only serve to drag this business out even longer than it already has been," Alexius growled. He took a cigar from a box on a side desk, lit it, and strode back over to the big table. Then he jabbed at the holographic display with the burning end, like a pointer, as he spoke. "This still shows Verghasite fleets here and here. I thought we'd beaten both of them back." He turned to Justinian. "Are we certain we have the most up-to-date intelligence on what the enemy is doing?"

"I believe so, yes," Justinian replied defensively.

They started into a back-and-forth about the state of our military intelligence services and their appalling failure to anticipate the Verghasite attack. I tuned the whole thing out and was privately working out how I could extricate myself from this increasingly distasteful meeting when Stephanie demonstrated to all of us that she wasn't yet out of grenades.

"I've had serious reservations about this entire plan ever since Constantine first brought it to our attention," my youngest aunt said.

The room quieted again. My three uncles slowly turned and practically gaped at her.

"*You* have?" Alexius said—and he most emphatically placed the emphasis on the first word, not the second.

"You take issue with elements of our military strategy?" Justinian asked.

Stephanie made as if to utterly ignore their condescension. "Strategy? Hardly," she said. "My issues are of a different nature. To wit: Why are we doing it at all?"

"Doing what?"

"Attacking the other worlds."

Justinian blinked but said nothing. Alexius leaned in and stated, "They did attack us first."

"That was happenstance—or something more," she shot back. "Don't treat me like a fool. We were planning to attack them first—all of them, if necessary. That's common knowledge. The fact that the Verghasites got the jump on us doesn't change that."

The three men simply stared back at her, wide-eyed. For my part, sitting off to the side and watching, I merely wished I'd brought popcorn. It was fascinating to me; the job of needling my uncles had in the past fallen mainly to Aunt Octavia, but in her absence Stephanie apparently now wished to fill the role. She was doing so, all right—and topping anything Octavia had ever managed.

"What makes us—we of Majondra—any worthier, any more suited to do this—to rule the Seven Worlds," she was asking, "than any of the others?"

"You cannot seriously be asking this," Justinian said.

"Humor me."

Justinian frowned. The twins looked to him, deferring. He shrugged.

"Very well. The reopening of the Gates, in Constantine's opinion and in ours, posed the risk of plunging all seven planets into chaos. We had no way of knowing what sort of regimes had arisen on any of the other worlds. We, however, have kept the old empire alive, through the Regent Maxillus and his family, and through the actions of our own family, supporting his all these years."

Stephanie nodded once, as if accepting this and encouraging him to go on.

"We of Majondra have the power, the stability, and the wherewithal to restore the old empire very quickly and with as little violence and bloodshed as necessary—something we don't know about any of the others. We have the forces at our disposal to prosecute such a reunification war and bring it to a successful conclusion quickly, before events can spiral out of control and hurl all of humanity into chaos. To accomplish that goal, however, our late brother felt it necessary to strike quickly, before any warlords or other tyrants that might have seized control of the other worlds during the last six hundred years managed to attack us or one or more other of the Seven Worlds and spark a general conflagration."

He looked up, meeting Stephanie's eyes.

"Constantine understood this," he said. "The rest of us do, as well. Do you?"

The marbled cat leapt from her lap with a loud and angry sound that might have been directed at Justinian.

"And a 'successful conclusion,'" Stephanie said, "would be—what? You as the dictator of all the human race?"

"A successful conclusion would be for humanity to hold together and resist the darkness, resist anarchy and mass destruction," Justinian snapped back. "We are in a unique position to see that this happens, and I will not stand aside and watch the Seven Worlds descend into darkness if I have the ability to prevent it."

He smiled a grim smile, pointing to the holographic display over the table.

"And I do."

"You hope," she said, matching his smile. "Don't you think the Verghasites are preparing another wave of attack, even now?"

Justinian's eyes narrowed. He glanced over at the twins, then back to my aunt. "I'm certain they are. But we will defeat them." He paused, then, "What is your alternative, *sister*?" He said that last word with a heavy dose of venom. "That we simply surrender? That we roll over and allow the Verghasites—or one of the other worlds—to conquer us instead?"

"I believe you are conflating offense with defense," Stephanie observed. "The alternative to being conquered is not necessarily conquering everyone else. There are many shades in between."

All three of my uncles started to reply angrily to that, but I'd had enough. I stood and raised my hands, interrupting all of them. "I think I will call it an evening, ladies and gentlemen," I said. And before anyone could compose an entreaty for me to remain, I quickly exited the library.

How much longer would they remain in there, arguing and accusing and questioning one another—all to no real purpose that I could discern? All evening and into the night? There was no telling. But I was done with it.

Then I remembered my two guests, kept waiting all this time. I hurried over to the side room where I'd left them and, sure enough, they were still there. The younger one, called Halaini, was actually asleep in a large, overstuffed chair. The other—the sister superior, whose name yet eluded me— looked up from a book as I entered and offered me a not-particularly-welcoming look.

"I apologize for the delay," I told her. "My family can be somewhat... long-winded."

"Do they wish to speak to us now?" the corinda asked.

"Um... no," I answered, smiling weakly. "In fact, they don't even know you two exist. And I now believe we should endeavor to keep it that way for the present."

The corinda's frown deepened. "And why should that be?" she demanded.

"It is a fair question, my lady, and one that I cannot fairly answer at this time," I replied. "Call it a hunch."

"A hunch?" She appeared quite skeptical.

"I know my family," I said by way of explanation, "and I believe we should leave it at that. Please—trust me, at least for now."

Halaini was awake now and the sister superior quickly caught her up.

"So what would you have us do—wear disguises?" the sister superior asked.

"In fact, that would be a good idea," I said. "Fortunately, you are already provided in that manner."

The two looked down at the borrowed clothes they wore as if seeing them for the first time. Meanwhile I sincerely hoped the servants had long since fed their old Church robes into the incinerator.

"I will conduct you to guest quarters near my suite," I told them. "It would be advisable for you to try to remain out of sight, at least for now."

"Are we your prisoners?" the older woman demanded, not quite angrily.

"Not at all," I said. "But we have a mutual interest in getting to the bottom of the mystery we confront, and I don't feel that interest will be well served if certain members of my family learn of your existence and of your presence here."

"Which members?"

I shook my head. "I don't know. Yet. But I aim to find out."

"But otherwise we can leave if we choose?"

"You can," I said, "and in fact I will see you conducted to whatever location—within the limits of current feasibility—you desire."

"Meaning we cannot return to Sarmata."

"Not at present, no," I said. "There's something of a small war happening between this moon and the Sarmata Gate at present. We were fortunate to get through before."

The older woman said nothing but did not seem entirely convinced. The younger one was frowning deeply.

"So, in short—you are not my prisoners," I said, "but I believe we can be allies in the hours and days to come, if you are willing to work with me and follow my advice. Not my orders," I reiterated, "my advice."

The two women exchanged looks, then both nodded.

A short time later I had them comfortably situated for the night. An older housekeeper who had been particularly close to me since my childhood agreed to see to their needs and unlocked two very nice adjoining bedrooms for their use, along with giving me her promise to be discreet about their presence.

From there I made my way to my own rooms, pulled off my boots, and dropped heavily onto my bed without even undressing. My body was sore and weary, but my brain was still racing along as frantically as ever. I lay there for all of five minutes, staring up at the ceiling, before I was convinced I wouldn't fall asleep any time soon. So I rose and, boots again in place, strolled back out into the hallway.

The palace was quiet and mostly dark, it being well past dinner time now. Fearing that I would inadvertently run into one of my uncles or aunts and get pulled into another long and undesired conversation, I made straight for the nearest exit. That put me out near the stables and so I made a snap decision to stroll that way.

Entering the old wooden building, I nodded to Voras, our blacksmith, who labored at the far end of the stalls. He returned the gesture, as did his slender, wiry assistant, Goran.

Moments later I found my feet had led me straight up to my current favorite horse, a tall chestnut called Comet. The thought struck me, then: why not a ride? Surely a quick lap or two around the palace would leave me ready to hit the hay and sleep for a week—something I felt was not particularly advisable in the current situation, but likely necessary for my own sanity.

After reacquainting myself with Comet I mounted up and we set out, no real destination in mind. The sun was already below the horizon but there was enough artificial lighting around the palace that we could see where we were going. We passed through a well-landscaped grove and down into a shallow valley at the end, moving at barely above a walk. That was when I saw it.

I had no idea what it was. At first I thought it was a man—perhaps a groundskeeper or maybe even one of my uncles out for a walk. But then it moved, and it did not move like a man. Not at all. It was taller, thinner; *spindly*, one might say. The dim light glinted here and there on its clothes or its armor, or whatever it wore.

I brought Comet up short and kept him quiet as I looked and frowned and tried to discern exactly what I was seeing.

A black horse stood nearby, unmoving. I thought I recognized it from our stables but wasn't certain. After a few moments the strange figure approached the horse and in a surreal, supremely acrobatic springing motion leapt into the saddle. It landed almost weightlessly, so that the horse did not react at all.

I watched this transpire and I wondered. What, exactly, was I seeing here? Was I experiencing some sort of waking dream, brought on by a combination of sleep deprivation, trauma, and general anxiety?

Now mounted on the dark horse, the figure started to move away, seemingly not aware of our presence. Through the grassy valley the horse and rider went, and I urged Comet to follow—again, quietly.

Fortunately my mount was up to the challenge; he trotted along stealthily, and we kept a decent distance while always having our quarry in view.

Around a bend and through another grove we went, past a small brook that gurgled along, detouring quickly past a bed of small rocks I was certain would crunch at our passing and give us away. For a moment I feared I'd lose sight of the figure, but I never did. And he never looked back.

Into a flat plain of sparse but richly-leaved trees we passed, and through it, and out the other side, emerging into a bare stretch where the grass gave way to a densely-packed sandy surface. Fog swirled around us as from nowhere and Comet grew somewhat spooked, as did I. This went on for some time, during which I barely managed to keep the strange being we were following in view. The ground, now virtually invisible at Comet's feet, leveled out and became perfectly flat. On we went, our quarry clopping along, clearly in no particular hurry, remaining just at the limits of visibility ahead. Then at last the clouds parted and a dim light shone down and the trees reappeared. Now, though, they were all of an entirely different variety, many with bright purple blossoms and surrounded by pollen-bearing pods littering the ground—and that ground had traded hard-packed sand for short, yellowy grass.

I realized then that the sun had somehow risen again and was now off to the right as we trotted along. A full understanding of just how bizarre that was didn't come to me for several seconds, so distracted was I by the changes to the vegetation. Then I looked around, blinked, and gasped.

How could this be possible? How could the very sun have moved—have come back up, less than an hour after it had set for the evening? How could the trees have changed so much? For that matter—how could gravity itself now feel slightly stronger?

I looked back around behind me. The forest stretched as far as I could see, up a gently sloping hill. Of the palace there was no sign whatsoever.

My head reeled. I felt as though I might faint. Comet didn't seem particularly happy, either, and I soothed him even as I sought to calm myself. I thought about it—about what could have possibly happened.

There was only one possible answer, as insane as it might sound.

We were no longer on Victoria.

We had been transported to a completely different world.

FOUR

The building was all of crystal, shot through with strands of pink and purple, much of it transparent or at least translucent. Great shards reared up from the ground at various angles, none of them directly upright, and together they blended to form a jagged domelike structure, there amid the strange forest. The spindly being I'd followed from the palace—and, I had to admit, from Victoria itself, to wherever this was—had tethered his black horse just outside and passed into the crystalline dome via an arched entrance just ahead.

I resolved to follow. As ridiculously foolhardy as that sounded, I was determined to discover what this was all about. Frankly, I was sick of not knowing what was going on around me, from the behavior of the corim of the Church to the Verghasite sneak attack to dad's murder to this eerie being who had just inadvertently led me from my home to this alien place. I had to have answers, and soon, or I feared that not only would we lose the war, but also that I would lose my very sanity.

Tethering Comet to a tree in a spot camouflaged with undergrowth, where I was hopeful he would avoid easy detection, I crept along the path my quarry had taken. Fortunately the black horse was busy chewing on the grass and ignored me entirely. Soon I reached the arch and hesitated just outside it. What, I asked myself, if the interior of this place was filled with more of these creatures—and they were hostile? What if something notified them the moment an intruder entered?

Then again, what other options did I have? If I went back to the palace to gather troops and to better arm myself, could I find my way back here again? For that matter, was it even possible to return to the palace? I could no longer see it in the direction we had come. How was I supposed to find it?

Too many questions, and none of them immediately answerable—except perhaps by the being I had followed here. I shook my head, drew my pistol and walked through the arch.

First came a sort of entryway with several passages leading in different directions from it. I could see some distance down each of them and quickly I realized the interior of the dome was a maze of tunnels that wound round and round with seemingly no pattern or rational intent. It felt a bit like what I imagine being shrunk down and tossed into an anthill must feel like. Fortunately, it appeared to be deserted; I could neither see nor hear traces of anyone. Unfortunately that included the one I'd been following.

I chose the wide passageway directly opposite the entrance and padded slowly down it. A crunch up ahead, coming from around a sharp corner, and I halted, then backed up a few steps. Someone was coming. The walls were extremely uneven due to mainly being formed from angled pillars of crystal and I moved until I'd pressed myself into a narrow alcove formed by a crease between two of them. There I waited, pistol up and ready. Seconds later the strange figure I'd been following strode by. He didn't look my way and didn't slow down.

What to do? Jump out and accost him, demanding information? Follow him again? I wasn't certain. As I wrestled with different approaches and plans, his footsteps faded and disappeared.

At that moment a fear seized me: What if he had represented the only way back home? Then again, I reminded myself, I had no way of knowing where he was going now. What was the likelihood that he was headed back to Victoria? To the contrary, he might well have led me to some even more remote locale. Perhaps one where the atmosphere wasn't this breathable.

So I forced myself to calm down and wait. I would find a way back home, I told myself—but on my terms, once I'd thoroughly investigated what was happening here.

Stepping out of the alcove, I hurried down the corridor in the direction from which the being had come and rounded the sharp corner. Then I nearly stumbled and fell.

I had entered a room—a room filled with pinkish light. The walls and ceiling were composed of the same crystal shafts that comprised the building's outer construction. What seized my attention, however, was what filled much of the space at the center.

Banks of equipment of some sort—boxy and white and made of metal and plastic and entirely out of place here in this crystalline funhouse—surrounded a silver metal slab which rested on a single matching leg at the center. The slab was at least two meters wide and more than twice that in length and it was tilted at a slight angle back. Strapped onto it—bolted to it by metal brackets at wrists and ankles and waist—lay a man, or something like a man yet not one.

It was another being like the one I'd followed. He wore none of the glittering glasslike armor that the other had possessed; instead he was clad in gray rags that looked to have been violently torn and burned in places. Something that might have been dried blood formed splotches here and there. His features were narrow, angular, sharp. He was not as tall as the other but just as slender and spindly. His skin was pale and milky; his eyes were closed. As I neared him I could hear a soft groaning sound escaping his too-thin lips.

What was this? Had the other been torturing him? Was he a prisoner? Or perhaps merely a patient, receiving particularly onerous treatments for his own good? It was hard to tell which.

Before I could formulate a question or even clear my throat and introduce myself, his eyes snapped open and he stared directly at me.

I somehow resisted the impulse to leap back, though my pulse grew rapid. I felt my pistol tight in my grasp, then considered and holstered it. I raised my open hands in what I hoped was a universal signal of peaceful intentions—not that he was in a position to threaten me, restrained as he was. It simply somehow seemed the appropriate thing to do.

He said nothing, merely staring at me, and so after a few seconds I approached and executed a somewhat formal bow. "Hello," I said. "Um—can you understand me?"

The other didn't open his mouth, but a moment later I could somehow hear what must have been his response anyway. The words were unintelligible to me but they resounded within my mind.

The effect was somewhat startling and I must have stumbled back a step or two again. Waving my already upraised hands I called out, "Wait, wait—I can't understand—"

The voice in my head changed slightly, changed again. Then suddenly I could understand it.

"A human. Well. This is unexpected."

He was speaking directly to my mind. That certainly took me aback. That and the fact that he was an alien. And that I likely stood on some other world, far away from my own. And that I had ridden a horse rather than a spacecraft to get here.

Yes, when I truly put all the activities of the day thus far in proper perspective, hearing his voice within my head didn't rank up there with the most startling developments. I resolved to worry about all those things at a later date, when the situation was not nearly as pressing.

I looked back at the alien and smiled. "Then may I ask whom you were expecting?"

"Oh, no one," his silent voice replied in my head. "I had resigned myself to the idea that I would be quite alone until my tormentor returned again."

Tormentor? "You are being tortured here, then?"

A soft chuckle, actually out loud, from his thin lips.

"In a manner of speaking," he replied, now communicating verbally and with no discernible accent. "In several manners, actually."

"Why?"

Now his lips turned upward in a true smile, though clearly filled with tinges of pain and regret.

"For being the point of greatest resistance," he said. A pause, and I could feel his presence within my head grow stronger for a moment. Then, "For being the sand in the gears. The spanner in the works."

"You took those phrases from my mind, didn't you?"

"I did. I wanted to be sure you understood my meaning, and they seemed colloquial and apt."

"I'm not at all sure I appreciate you rummaging about inside my mind."

He said nothing for a moment and I waited, studying him. Then, "You are quite right," he said. "Quite right. Perhaps I have lost my sense of appropriateness, of proper boundaries, during my long period of incarceration here."

I nodded. "I can see where that could be possible."

Another pause, this one slightly uncomfortable. He continued to stare back at me, unblinking. It began to give me something of the creeps. At last he smiled weakly and said, "Might I inquire as to how a human came to be here?"

"I followed someone. Your jailer, I suspect."

"Ah." A pause. "Followed him from...?"

Now it was my turn to offer a smile. And that was all.

After a few seconds he frowned, realizing I wasn't going to volunteer every scrap of information I possessed simply for the asking.

"So," he said, trying a different tack, "will you be getting me down from here, then?"

I reached up and stroked my goatee, thinking. He continued to stare at me.

"I imagine that would be to your advantage," I told him, "but I don't know that it would be to mine."

"How now?"

I smiled and spread my hands. "I do not know you. Nor do I know the causes of your incarceration here. Perhaps you were put here for very valid reasons, by proper authorities. Dare I go against their judgment? And if so, for what reasons?"

He looked back at me for several seconds before his expression slowly changed. A sly smile appeared; it was almost seductive.

"I can see that you are a cautious man. That is good. Very wise. Very healthy."

I shrugged. "I try to be."

He nodded that long, slender head.

"I believe that you can be of some use to me."

I chuckled. "Afraid I'm terribly busy at the moment." I hesitated dramatically. "But... if *you* were of some use to *me*..."

He looked somewhat shocked for an instant, and then angry. The look passed within a very brief moment, however.

"I believe we could be useful to one another," he said, the smile returning as quickly as it had evaporated. "An arrangement promising mutual benefits, as it were."

"I'm listening."

"Free me from this infernal captivity and I will show you the way back to your home."

I gave him a look intended to indicate that I was considering the offer, though I was not.

"No," I replied at length. "I think I will go roaming about this place on my own. It looks capable of holding my interest for some time." I shrugged. "When I tire of it, I'm sure I will find the way home eventually."

"I am sure that you will not," he said. "You will require a guide."

"Will I?"

His laugh was soft and staccato. "Furthermore, I will grant you the one thing you most desire."

"Would you now? And what might that be?"

"The opportunity to gain revenge on those killed your father."

My expression slowly morphed from one of curiosity to one of anger. "I will tell you this only once more," I said, my voice very low but filled with menace. "*You need to stay out of my head.*"

His smile broadened. "I did not take that information from your mind, Gaius son of Constantine. I did not have to." He laughed at my surprise. "Oh yes. I know who you are now. And I know what you want above all other things." He chuckled softly. "And I can help you get it."

Suffice to say I freed him from his restraints and helped him down. He moved very slowly and stiffly at first, like an old man wracked with arthritis. His condition concerned me in that if we were to travel on foot at the speed he appeared capable of moving, we might never reach Victoria. Conversely, though, I was at least able to relax and not overly concern myself that he might attack me. He could scarcely move at all, much less threaten physical violence.

You might think me foolish for choosing to—trust him? No; I never trusted him. Never. Not even at the end, after he went into the machine and... No, I digress. It was not so much that I trusted him but that I was willing to give him the opportunity to demonstrate the truth of his promises. Remember—at this point I was lost on an alien world and the final strands of the web I had been trying to unravel since that horrific moment in my father's tent were slipping through my fingers. This strange being represented the best—the *only*—chance I had to make any progress toward finding my father's killers.

He discarded his old, stained clothes and donned a shining tunic of royal blue with red and gold trim, an eight-pointed silver star on the chest. His pants were of similar material and were dark gray. He'd retrieved those items from a drawer after I'd helped him down.

We immediately set out, negotiating the maze of passages I'd passed through before, and emerged back onto the grassy lawn. An orange-yellow sun hung directly overhead now and it beat down with remarkable intensity. The grass and flowers and trees around us fairly vibrated with color and brightness. It was all very nearly too much, and I found myself squinting, raising a hand to shield my eyes and wishing I'd brought sunglasses along—though I could only laugh at the notion that I would have felt the need to bring sunglasses on what had begun as a late-night ride.

My companion's movements picked up a bit once we were out in the sunshine and he began to stride purposefully through the grass. I could tell then that he was not nearly as tall as the first of his kind—the one who'd led me there— though he was still a bit taller than me. I followed along after him, curious about a great many things.

Reaching the outer edge of a glen of trees, he stopped and knelt down, then leaned back his head and closed his eyes. I watched this transpiring with no small amount of puzzlement. A few seconds later he opened his eyes, smiled, and returned his head to its proper angle.

The horse burst through the brush with such a suddenness that I nearly fell over backwards.

The strange being reached out his right hand, palm open and facing upward, and the horse came to him immediately, sniffing at him. It was black as night and beautiful as a new dawn, and it was not the one the other alien had ridden on the way here. It looked at me briefly, showed no apparent interest, and returned its attention to him. He stroked its nose and spoke a few words I couldn't understand to it.

"You have a horse?" I asked, taken aback. "An Earth horse?"

"I do."

"Where did you get it?"

He shrugged, his attention remaining on the horse. He stroked its nose and smiled wanly at it.

"Pardon me," he said, "but I have to reacquaint myself with him. I've been held here quite a while." He looked the horse over, then smiled again. "At least it appears they have been taking care of him during my incarceration."

I shook my head. "I don't understand. You are aliens. Why would you keep horses from Earth?"

"We have no beasts of this sort on any of our worlds. And we have found them to be perfectly suited for our needs— for walking the Paths. In addition to generally traveling at the quickest rate we prefer for transitioning through dimensions, they seem to possess an unerring sense of sudden danger along the way. Far better, and with much better reaction speed, than any mechanical device we could construct and carry along. Eddies and sudden twists and vortices in the dimensional currents; weak spots in the walls of the cosmic passages; hidden traps. When it comes to the Paths, they have a natural nose for danger, and a talent for avoiding it. And so we keep them, and we breed them for better and better senses of this sort."

I just stared back at him and at his black beauty and I shook my head again. "Horses. Huh."

At that, and in defiance of his previous infirmity, he fairly leapt onto its back, in a move almost identical to what I'd seen the other do, back on Victoria. Again the horse scarcely appeared to notice.

"Shall I summon one for you?" he asked.

I shook my head. "Mine's over here somewhere..."

I retrieved Comet—I hadn't been gone long enough for him to get grouchy towards me—and mounted. "Where to?" I asked.

"To a place where you can find some of the answers you seek," he replied. With that, the dark horse set out across the grass.

Comet trotted ahead. I encouraged him and soon enough we rode along just behind and to the alien's right.

"What is your name?" I called to him.

"I no longer have a name. My name was stripped from me by my fellows. All I retain now is the term of scorn they bestowed upon me: Renegade."

I frowned. "That won't do. What was your name before?"

He looked away for a moment, as if considering whether he wanted to answer me at all. At last, in a barely audible voice, he said, "Istari."

"Pleased to make your acquaintance, Istari," I said formally. "I am—"

"As I indicated before," he snapped, "I know precisely who you are."

I bit my tongue and said nothing, instead looking around at the landscape through which we passed. And I frowned. More grassy slopes, more odd trees, and now a narrow glen—but no fog, no swirling lights. None of the strange indicators I'd encountered and passed through on my previous journey. Though I fully expected a sharp, non-informative reply, I started to question him about this. Before I could do so, however, he brought his horse to a halt and raised a hand. I drew up beside him and reined in Comet.

"There," he said, nodding to his left.

I looked and there beheld something I had not noticed from when we'd entered the glen until that moment: a tree, gnarled and obviously ancient, with long, low-hanging branches. Just beyond it, nearly hidden amid rocks and bushes, I could make out the dark entrance to a cave.

I looked back at him and saw that he was pointing directly at the cave mouth.

"That's not the way I came here," I said.

"It is not," he replied. He continued to point. "Yet it is where you must now go."

I blinked. "Why? What will I find in there?"

"Answers."

I frowned. "Answers? To who is responsible for killing my father?" I squinted at the cave mouth, but couldn't make out a thing beyond its opening. "I'll find answers in *there*?"

He smiled at me and the smile was sly, almost mischievous. "Perhaps. All sorts of answers may be found within that cave. It may be that the ones you seek are among them." He shrugged slightly. "Or not. There is only one way to know."

I continued to regard him for another few seconds. Then I climbed down from Comet, led him over to the ancient tree, and tethered him.

What did I have to lose? My world was upside down. My uncles and aunts were busy leading an interplanetary war against our enemies and obviously had little use for me in that. My father was dead. Along with him, I realized then for perhaps the first time and with a shock, I'd also lost my purpose in life up to this point. For in truth my career till then had consisted of assisting him, serving him. What did I have now?

The answer, at least in the short term, was clear: I had my mission. I sought retribution. Call it justice or call it revenge. Whatever. I didn't care. All that mattered to me now was finding the reason for his murder and exacting rough payment from those who had ordered it. This lead—this alien and whatever he was involved with— represented my final remaining avenue of investigation before I would have to simply give up. I resolved to pursue it even at the risk of my own death.

I looked at the alien, Istari, once more. He continued to stare at the cave while utterly ignoring me. It was as if I didn't exist, other than as a piece on the game board, to be manipulated. Perhaps that was all that I was to him.

Fine. I wasn't terribly concerned with what he thought of me, as long as cooperating with him led me to the information I sought.

I reached down, loosened my blast pistol in its holster and strode forth, passing through the opening and into the darkness of the cave.

Scarcely had I passed through the opening before complete darkness surrounded me and swallowed me up. The entrance itself didn't entirely vanish, but as I glanced back over my shoulder it seemed to recede to the point that it was now far away in the distance, as though it would take quite a bit of a walk to reach it and leave the cave. This made me feel extremely uncomfortable and I turned, facing back in that direction. I contemplated leaving immediately.

Then a warm breeze blew past me, gravel crunched, and a voice echoed out of the void at my back: "Greetings."

"Who's there?" I called, turning. My pistol was out and in my hand.

Only darkness, all about me.

"Who are you?" I demanded. "What do you want?"

"You have a strange manner," the voice said after a few seconds. It was smooth and low, deep and rich, and it held an unmistakable edge of menace. "You come uninvited into my home and seek to interrogate me. Is this what passes for civilized behavior among your kind?"

The warm air wafted by again, as from the bellows of some mighty forge. It smelled sour. I began to suspect that it might be breath.

"You are quite right," I said, still searching the darkness, hoping my eyes would adjust faster and give me any indication of who—or what—I was dealing with. "My apologies. I did not intend to intrude or trespass."

"Then why came you here, if not intentionally?"

"I was directed here by a—by an acquaintance," I said. "I was told I might find answers."

"Ah," the voice said. "Yes. That is entirely possible. Or," it added after a brief pause, "you might find something else. Other things entirely."

"Perhaps I am supposed to ask you my questions?" I said.

The warm air again, pungent and moist. My nose wrinkled involuntarily and I turned my head slightly to one side, seeking to avoid breathing it in.

"You could," the voice said. "I would not object in principle." A pause, and then, "Of course, understand that if I do not like your questions, you will not be leaving my domain, my world. You will be... *consumed.*"

This took me aback. Not the threat—that seemed almost *de rigeur*. But—"Your world? This world I've come to—it belongs to you?"

"*This* world. Here. This *pocket universe*, as I believe the Dyonari call such things. It is my world."

I had no idea what any of that meant. I looked around and could see nothing but darkness. Even the cave mouth had now vanished. "Ah, yes." I nodded, and I'm afraid the sarcasm was clear in my voice as I added, "And a lovely world it is."

"Talk like that will lead to the consumption I referenced in my previous utterance."

"Sorry."

"Yes, yes. Now—the questions, eh? I will allow... *two*, to start. More if I feel so inclined after those. And if you have not yet been consumed."

What was this creature? How could it possibly answer the questions that plagued me? It all seemed ludicrous. And yet, so did everything else that had occurred in the time since I'd taken Comet and ridden into the night. Again—in truth, what had I to lose?

I nodded in the darkness. "Very well." I kept the blast pistol ready as I searched my mind for the most efficient way to ask my single question. But—what *was* my single question? Could I whittle everything that plagued me about Dad's demise down into a lone query? For a moment my thoughts were a jumble, and I could hear impatient-sounding gravel-crunching from a short distance away. Then my thoughts snapped almost miraculously into clear focus, and I decided upon the single thing I felt I most needed to know—the one question that could hold the key to unlocking all the others. I looked up into the darkness and said, "Why was my father killed?"

I anticipated counter-questions such as, "Who exactly was your father?" or "How the hell should I know? I'm just a creature living in a cave-slash-pocket universe." But the voice uttered neither of those things. Instead it issued no sounds whatsoever, for a time long enough that I began to suspect it had slunk back into the depths of its cave—its mini-universe, if it was to be believed. I was just about to give up and begin walking in the direction I hoped led back to the entrance, when it at last broke the silence.

"I cannot say with absolute certainty, but in all likelihood it was because he might actually have succeeded."

I believe I took an involuntary step backwards; certainly my jaw dropped open. Blinking rapidly, I closed my mouth and sought words. At last I found a few.

"Succeeded in what?"

The creature—if creature it was—issued a sort of groan. "Are you *sure* you want that to be your second question? Because I find it boring, and it will probably be your last."

"No—*no*, not at all," I said quickly. "I was simply musing out loud. I have a better second question, of course."

"Ah. Excellent."

"Just give me a moment, if you please."

"By all means."

And then I faltered and mentally cast about—for of course at that moment my mind became a blank canvas and I an artist bereft of all paints and brushes.

"Who was responsible for my father's death?"

I blurted it out quickly, without putting a great deal of thought into it. Simply put, it was the single question I most wanted answered, whether by some faceless creature in the dark or anyone else. If asking it cost me my life, then so be it.

Even as I was speaking the words aloud I could hear the crunching of gravel underfoot drawing closer and smell the rancid breath of my host, now almost overpowering. I aimed my gun in the direction of the sounds and prepared to fire.

The crunching stopped.

"You don't know? It was Corindar Jeras. I thought you were present at the event."

Now I was growing frustrated. I wanted to ask him how he knew that—how he could possibly be privy to that information. But I dared not—he might take it as an official question and decide it violated his bizarre and inconsistent rules for our discourse. Still, I was too deep in it now to fall back on false politeness or feigned courtesy. "Well, yes, I know that he did the actual deed," I said, my impatience clear in my tone. "But he was just the catspaw. Who was the mastermind? Who ordered him to do it?"

A long pause, silent save for the sound of heavy, labored breathing. Then, "I cannot answer that question specifically," the rumbling voice said, "but I could tell you more than enough to set you on a direct path to those ultimately responsible. I really could."

"That would be—"

"But I won't."

"What? You won't?"

A slight chuckle that grew; the fetid wind wafting from his direction dissolved into staccato snorts. "No, I believe it would be far more amusing if you were to instead direct that question to your new friend outside."

"My new friend—?"

"Quite right, my mistake. You called him 'an acquaintance,' I believe."

A light in the darkness: I stared at it and saw that it was the cave opening, visible once more. As I watched it grew in size and in proximity. Soon it was only a few strides away. The green of the glen shone beyond.

"Wait," I said, not moving. "That's it? We're done?"

"We are done. You may go."

"But—"

"But? I expected you would be relieved. Most who venture within my realm never even get to utter a second question."

I was frowning, and now the light from the cave mouth made that apparent. "Then why are you letting me go?" I asked, conscious that I had essentially been reduced to whining and not terribly concerned about that fact at the moment. I turned my back on the opening and gazed in the direction of that grating voice but, despite the light now trickling in from the outside, I still couldn't see anything. Not a thing.

And then I realized I had just asked another question. I braced myself to be rushed.

"Because it gets very boring in here sometimes," came the singsong answer, in lieu of violent death. "And while extending our conversation further might provide some small measure of entertainment, I'm not entirely convinced you're up to it."

"That's very likely true," I said.

"Yes. You do strike me as rather danger-prone. And, see, I think you're sort of interesting and I've decided that I would feel bad about things if you were to get yourself consumed. Besides," the voice added, "I think you hold the potential for greater entertainment value if I let you continue."

"Entertainment value?" Now I grew angry. "You see me as merely an actor in some drama, staged purely for your amusement?"

"Of course," He replied. "All of your kind. The Dyonari and the others as well. And I must say, you've been something of a disappointment thus far. Yet still, you may live. But try not to disappoint me again. I'll be watching."

I had no idea how to respond to that. I didn't even understand it, for the most part. The desire to lash out violently, in words if not in actions, seized me, and I had to remind myself—forcefully—that this creature likely could slay me in an instant. At least, that was the impression he liked to create. I did not feel like testing that theory if I could avoid it. So I breathed in and out and said, "I appreciate the help. Or what little you have provided."

"What did you expect? Most who enter this place leave by way of my digestive system. I have at least pointed you in the direction to find your answers."

"But that's what Istari said when he sent me in here. He told me you could provide the answers."

"*That* guy?" A snort. "He is a liar. A traitor. A renegade. I wouldn't believe much of what he says."

"But you would have me direct my questions to him. How can I believe his replies?"

"*Believe* him?" Another laugh. It was absolutely blood-chilling. "Oh no. I never said anything about *believing* him."

"Then what—?"

"You don't have to ask him anything point blank and I certainly wouldn't believe anything he told me directly. But that doesn't mean you cannot cause him to lead you to the truth. That's a completely different thing."

I took this in and thought about it. "And how exactly do I do that?"

"That constitutes a third question—at the very least—and I've already stated that you don't get another. Fortunately for

VAN ALLEN PLEXICO

you I didn't find it boring enough to make me reevaluate my position."

I felt strongly at that moment that I should cut my losses, be grateful for my life and take my leave—before my temperamental host changed his mind again.

"Understood," I said. "Thanks for everything. Sincerely. And goodbye."

"You got it, kid," came the deep, rumbling voice one last time. It was growing fainter as he spoke, as though he were moving away from me at rapidly increasing speed. Back down into the darkness. "Good luck. And hey– do try to make the rest of this thing entertaining, okay? I'll be watching."

My new acquaintance might have been an alien, but there was no mistaking the expression on his face when I reemerged from the cave: surprise.

No—shock.

He recovered and covered quickly, but I'd seen it. It had been all too clear: he'd never expected me to come out of the cave again. He'd sent me in to die.

I briefly contemplated possible actions I might take in response to that fact, but ultimately discarded each of them. I still needed him to show me the way home, after all. And if the entity in the cave had told the truth, I also needed him alive to answer those questions that hadn't been answered yet—in other words, nearly all of them.

"I told you," I said to him, gesturing towards the cave mouth, "that was not the way back to Victoria."

"My mistake," he replied with a nod.

"Very much so."

Istari was now regarding me with an expression I couldn't quite read. The surprise was still there, but perhaps some measure of respect, as well. Then again, perhaps I was only imagining that part. Wishful thinking.

106

"Well," he said. "The Watcher in the Warp must've been quite taken with you."

"That's his name? Interesting fellow. We had quite a little conversation."

"Did you?" He sprang up onto his horse and then looked at me sidelong. "About what, might I ask?"

"Several topics. You, for one."

This seemed to rattle him, if only for an instant. That was twice in less than a minute that I'd shaken him up. I found it a pleasant feeling.

"And what did the Watcher have to say about me?"

"Good things, good things—for the most part," I replied.

"Oh?"

"At least, from my perspective."

I retrieved Comet. He seemed a bit agitated. I stroked his side as I turned back to Istari.

The alien seemed even more agitated than Comet.

"Give me an example," he said.

I gazed into his dark eyes and grinned. "He said you had the answers I seek."

Istari darkened. "He is a—"

"A liar?" I interrupted him. "Funny—that's what he called you." I chuckled. "You can probably guess which of you I assign greater credibility."

He made another facial expression I couldn't read.

As I assumed we were about to travel again, I climbed onto Comet. Then I looked back at Istari. He had turned his gaze to the cave and was frowning.

"Are you a Dyonari?" I asked.

He turned sharply and looked at me, hesitated, then nodded his head once. "The one in the cave used that term, did he?"

"Yes."

Istari pursed his thin lips, then nodded. "That is what my people are called."

His dark horse began to move, slowly circling around Comet and me. As he traveled, his expression changed once again—at this point I could practically feel him evaluating and reevaluating me, his opinion morphing continuously.

"Perhaps," he said after a few seconds of silent inspection. "Perhaps you could be the one I seek, after all."

"The one you seek?"

His horse halted directly in front of me.

"That is how I came to be in the state in which you found me, restrained and tortured. I did not approve of the plans or actions of my associates, and they did not approve of my objections or my counterproposals."

"I'm going to need to know a lot more about what you and they were up to before any of that will make sense to me."

"All in good time," he replied. "But know this much for now: I had a vision."

"A vision."

"Yes. A clear view of a possible future. We of my kind experience these on very rare occasions. And with the vision came a voice."

"Okay," I said, waiting, my expression neutral.

"A voice from the aether. It came to me some time ago, back when all was well and I was working quite happily and contentedly alongside my brethren. It told me that, quite simply, I was on the wrong side of history. That the activities that my associates and I were engaged in were wrong. And it instructed me to travel to your moon of Victoria, where all would be laid out for me; all that would happen in the days to come. And all that I must do."

"And you believed this voice?"

"I did and I do."

"Why?"

"Because it was my own voice."

This took me aback. But after everything else I'd experienced of late, it didn't seem so far-fetched. "I see," I told him.

"The voice also said that one would come—one whose destiny is written across all time and space. A destiny too great, too large to be contained in a single lifetime. One to whom I would not be worthy to wash his feet."

"Interesting," I observed. The wheels in my mind were turning now.

He continued to gaze levelly back at me.

"And you believe I am that person?" I asked.

For a second he didn't move, didn't blink. Then he looked away. "I seriously doubt it," he said. "But the Watcher obviously found you worth leaving alive. That tells me something." He didn't look back at me as he added, "You might at least be useful."

I nodded. I resolved to leave it at that for the moment. "So," I said. "What now?"

He made a gesture that might've been some sort of alien shrug. "Now? Now we storm the Gates."

FIVE

A *sword?*"
I was staring at Istari the Renegade wide-eyed, attempting to process what he had just said.

"We have to retrieve a sword?" I asked again.

"Just so." He appeared to think for a moment, then, "It will be extremely dangerous. You must be prepared for the possibility of agonizing death."

I stared back at him and slowly shook my head. "A sword. A sword is the thing we need most. What in the Seven Worlds have I gotten myself into?"

Moments earlier, the alien I had freed from captivity had decreed what our first order of business would be— "That is," he'd added, "if you do wish to work together to solve both your problems and mine."

"Yes," I'd replied. I'd felt it represented the best and perhaps the only opportunity I had left. "We are in agreement. You help me find those responsible for my father's death, and I'll do whatever I can to help you against your enemies."

"Very well," Istari had said. He'd coaxed his dark horse forward at a canter, and I aboard Comet had followed. "Our first order of business is to retrieve a weapon—the single most important weapon in the galaxy. The one weapon with which we can track down, reach, and if necessary kill our

111

mutual enemies. No matter where in this cosmos they hide—
or in any other."

That had gotten my attention. I'd looked at him. "That sounds impressive. What sort of firearm are we talking about?"

He'd offered the faintest of smiles, then looked away. "Why, it is no firearm at all," he said.

"Then what—?"

"It is a sword."

Thus my exclamation previously described, which brings us up to date.

"How," I asked after I had managed to calm myself a bit, "Can a mere sword do the things you are describing?"

"It is no 'mere' sword. It is ancient." He met my eyes as our two horses carried us along. "Older than your species. Likely older than mine, too. It must go back at least as far into the past as the Machine itself."

"The Machine?"

He chuckled and looked away again. "Another time," he said. "This galaxy is a vast and ancient place, filled with wonders and terrors in equal measure—about most of which your kind remains blissfully unaware. Let us not needlessly add to your already formidable list of things you must quickly learn."

I swallowed that comment without reply, instead considering the larger problem. "If this weapon is as powerful as you say, let us go back to Victoria, so that I might gather a regiment of my family's troops to help us secure it," I suggested.

"There is no time and less need," Istari snapped. "Udasi the Judge, my jailer whom you followed here, made the mistake of speaking aloud in my presence his destination after leaving my prison—as well as the fact that the one he will be meeting, Elendi the Mastermind, is currently in possession of the sword." He grinned, and the look of it actually sent chills down my spine. "I therefore know the current location of the sword. I also know they and it will be there for but a short time. After they depart that place, it could be anywhere in the multiverse."

"I see," I said, though I wasn't at all certain I did.

"Let us move with greater alacrity," he added. "Too much time has been wasted."

And whose fault is that, I wanted to ask—but I kept my mouth shut and encouraged Comet to pick up the pace.

We rode on without further conversation for a short while; no sounds came to us but the clop-clop of the horses' hooves. I watched with interest as the terrain around me changed and morphed slowly. Fog drifted in, very similar to what had engulfed me on my journey from Victoria. It enshrouded us and produced a tunnel effect, with the two of us traveling down its center. This reassured me somewhat for I took it to mean we were actually journeying between worlds, rather than this being another case of my companion attempting to trick me, as he had done with the cave.

Crosswinds struck then, whipping into us from right to left. Before I could so much as express my surprise aloud, the temperature plunged. Frost formed on my extremities. Around us, the swirling colors darkened in sinister fashion and lightning strobed on either side.

"Faster," I could just hear Istari crying, though he was scarcely two lengths ahead. "Faster!"

Comet scarcely needed encouragement on that score. He galloped.

Still the storm around us intensified, sheets of rain like tiny daggers jabbing my face and hands. My golden metal mesh tunic provided little in the way of insulation; I was growing damned cold. My breath was a cloud quickly whooshed behind me, gone.

The black horse was really moving now. We fell behind. I had to be quite persuasive with Comet to keep him close on the black beast's tail. We moved at breakneck speed, the tunnel of fog streaking by all around. It twisted and turned and rose and fell as we went, to the point that I felt I'd climbed aboard some ancient roller coaster. A mix of bright and dark colors streaked past within the swirling depths. I ignored it all and urged my mount to ever greater speed.

Through gaps in the fog I could just make out images—strange vistas and even stranger inhabitants of those vistas. I believe I saw a wooden windmill, juxtaposed a moment later with a building that floated over a broad, forested plain. A squadron of aircraft flew past on my left hand, and a battalion of tanks rumbled by on my right. Explosions, excursions and all that. Comet flinched repeatedly and I worried that his nerve would fail. Still we pressed on.

And then it was over. The clouds around us parted and dispersed. The lights and colors faded and vanished and I could see solid ground beneath Comet's feet again. Istari reined in his horse and I did the same. He hopped down and I followed.

We stood on a desolate, wind-swept surface—and quickly I saw that it was a cliff, projecting out over rough seas. There was no sun to speak of, though some sort of pale light just managed to illuminate the surroundings. I turned away from the drop off and the waters and saw another cliff face there, leading up into the dark skies. We therefore stood upon a shelf, a stair step, a horizontal interruption in the diagonal, almost vertical wall, located some indeterminate distance down between one drop and another.

Before the cliff in front of me was a geodesic dome, all of white, perhaps twenty meters high. I was reminded of historical pictures I had seen of igloos, although this was considerably larger. Also, it did not appear to be made of ice.

There was nothing to which we might tether our horses. Istari moved in front of his mount and caught its attention. He looked intensely in its eyes and spoke a few words in a language I could not understand. The horse stood still, not moving a muscle after he was finished. Then he came around to Comet, presumably to repeat the act.

"Wait," I said, stepping between them. "You aren't harming them, are you?"

"Certainly not. But we can't have them wandering over the edge."

I considered, then nodded and moved to the side. He repeated the same trick and Comet became a statue.

"Hurry now," he said. "Time is of the essence. Also, we will need the element of surprise."

I drew my gun and followed his long, lean form toward the dome. Seeing no obvious entrance, I wondered how he planned for us to go inside. My unspoken query was answered a moment later as he reached up and touched his fingertips to the smooth white surface, sliding them slowly across it. Directly in front of us a black rectangle formed. A second later, the section of wall that had filled the rectangle vanished, leaving a doorway leading inside.

"Idiots," Istari remarked. "They haven't changed the locks in all this time." He passed through it without a backward glance. Frowning, I hurried along after him.

Of course he would know how to get inside. He was part of whatever this was—or at least he had been, before his compatriots had kicked him out. The Renegade, indeed. I needed more information from and about him, I knew. More answers. He'd deflected me thus far by pleading urgency, but that excuse was wearing thin.

We had traveled a fair distance into the structure. He wasn't running, but his stride was so long that I had to almost jog to keep pace with him. We passed along a winding corridor and at last emerged into a broad, circular interior space with a high ceiling.

What I saw there gave me pause, to say the least.

At the center of the big room, massive rectangular-shaped pieces of some sort of very advanced equipment stood in a semicircle, connected to one another by bundles of thousands of thin, translucent cables. At the middle of the semicircle was a low platform or table, and a dozen articulated metal-

and-plastic arms sparkling with lights along their angled lengths moved like the legs of some gigantic insect trapped in the ceiling. Bright beams of coherent light stabbed out from the tips of each arm at regular intervals, striking something on the table.

None of this, however, was what startled me.

No, what truly startled me was the strange, humanoid figure that stood next to the equipment, operating its controls.

He appeared to be a man, at least in terms of gender. Not so much in terms of species.

Also, he was utterly bald, wore a skin-tight, shiny red metallic suit that covered him from knees to mid-waist, and stood at least three meters tall. And his skin was all of gray.

Another alien. Another *kind* of alien. I shook my head. This had been quite a day.

As we entered, the giant looked up and stared directly at us, with eyes so dark and piercing I was certain they looked through my own flesh and scrutinized my soul. I felt my stomach dropping in the general direction of my feet.

Those eyes did not linger upon me for long. They snapped toward Istari and locked on him.

"Dormor, my old friend," my companion called, raising a hand in greeting.

The gray giant did not respond. He merely continued to stare intently at Istari.

We were now halfway across the open space separating the room's entrance from the giant and the equipment. Istari had not slowed in the least.

"Where is Udasi?" he added, looking to one side and then the other.

The giant allowed us to approach for a few more steps. He still had not moved. Then his expression soured and he began to stride toward us. It was bizarre and almost surreal; he seemed to move in slow motion, and yet he covered ground very quickly. His massive hands came up, fingers working.

Just as the two of them reached one another, Istari side-stepped, pivoted and swung around beneath the giant's grasp. Springing back up, he placed a slender foot against the giant's back and kicked.

Nothing happened. The giant was simply too big, too heavy.

The big creature whirled about and the loglike, meaty arms lashed out again. This time they succeeded in seizing Istari by the upper arm. Still silent, the giant flung my companion across the room. He hit the floor and rolled to a stop; he did not immediately rise again.

I swallowed then, because the big creature was now looking directly at me.

I attempted a smile and nodded his way. "Greetings," I said, already placing one foot behind the other to prepare for a hasty retreat.

The giant took a step my way and I responded by taking two quick ones in the same direction, preventing the distance between us from shrinking. Sweat trailed down my cheeks and itched my goatee. I was acutely aware of the blast pistol in my right hand but I seriously wondered about its ability to stop or even slow such a creature.

Istari was beside me again, then. I hadn't heard him rise or approach. He danced into my line of sight and this time he raised both hands as he addressed the giant.

"Dormor," he began, "hear me out. My conflict is not with you or your kind. You know this. It is with Elendi and the others. They wish to harm the humans, for no reason other than fear. You know this to be the wrong path to follow. Surely you, a former Hand, can see—"

The gray giant had heard enough, I guessed. He charged, this time backhanding Istari and sending him sprawling again. It was a remarkable thing to watch. He seemed to move slowly over all, yet when he finally committed to a movement, his individual motions and gestures were sharp, quick, like lightning. And brutal in their effectiveness.

I wasn't sure what I should do. Istari wasn't moving—this time he seemed incapacitated. Should I shoot? Would it matter? Should I flee? Even assuming I could escape this being's pursuit, how would I get off the ledge?

I scampered over to where Istari lay, figuring he was still the best bet we had, given the circumstances.

He lay still as death, though. His previously pale skin looked positively snow-white now. I grasped him and shook him and said all sorts of vile things, but he didn't rouse.

Then time ran out. The giant lunged and only by the narrowest of margins did I evade his grasping hands. I brought my gun up to fire but his meaty paw swatted out and knocked the blast pistol from my grasp. Out of the corner of my eye I saw it smack the ground and snap into at least two pieces. I cursed.

Istari must have awoken at that precise moment, assuming he hadn't been playing dead all along. He leapt to his feet directly between the giant and me and he struck with a lightning chop to the sternum that actually seemed to give the big creature pause.

The giant backed off a step, but then he took his turn and swung with a tight but broad punch that barely grazed Istari. That was still enough to send him stumbling back. The two locked eyes again and charged.

I took advantage of the fact that neither was paying me the slightest bit of attention and I ran toward the equipment at the center of the room.

The segmented silver arms continued to move in rhythmic fashion, low above the table, blinding beams of hard light flashing from their tips—and now I could see what they were engaged in cutting.

It had once been human; of that much I was fairly certain. Given its current state, though, I couldn't tell much beyond that. Not even race or gender.

I felt as though I were going to throw up. I looked away swiftly, even as the smell washed over me. What were they doing here, in this facility? I couldn't begin to imagine, but my animosity toward the big gray alien had just magnified itself by a factor of a hundred at least. Probably more like a thousand.

Turning back the other way, I saw the giant had Istari in a sort of stranglehold, and appeared on the verge of ripping his head off. Frantically I looked around for a weapon; something that could possibly be effective against a creature of that size.

Nothing.

Except, perhaps...

I leapt onto the table, doing my best to ignore the grisly evidence that lay upon it, and grasped the nearest silver arm. It didn't want to be redirected from its programmed course and I had to strain mightily but after a couple of seconds I managed to angle it upwards. The beam shot wildly across the inside of the dome and struck the far wall, scoring it black. The robotic appendage fought me like a wild fire hose but I wrapped both of my own arms tightly around it and directed the shimmering orange beam over and down, over and down...

The gray giant bellowed incoherent rage as the hard light sliced into his left shoulder. I ignored him and waved the beam into him again. He screamed and released Istari; I was relieved to see that my companion's head was still attached, though he slumped forward and lay still.

The giant scrambled to his feet and came at me, murder in his eyes. I'd forgotten how quick the big monster was, because it never looked like he was moving very fast. But he ate up the distance between us in an instant, and the only thing that saved me was managing to get the robot arm pointed back at him. Its beam gouged him in the abdomen and he stumbled to a halt. As he looked down at it, the beam punched all the way through and erupted out his back. He looked back up at me then and bellowed again.

I had no sympathy for him—none before, and certainly not after having seen what lay on the table at my feet. Plus I feared he could still easily kill me.

He charged again.

I waved the beam in and sheared off his left arm just above the elbow.

This seemed to take him aback. He halted and stared at the smoking arm where it lay on the floor. Then he looked up at me, dumbfounded.

I waited to see what he would do next. I figured he'd come at me one more time. He seemed a pretty determined sort.

He didn't disappoint me.

He charged one more time. I brought the beam up and sliced into his right leg. He stumbled, bellowing again, and dropped to the floor as the leg sheared off inches below the knee. There was little blood from any of his horrific wounds; the beam cauterized as it cut.

Surely that would do it. I released the arm—it continued to fire away— and hopped down from the table. The giant lay on his stomach, mumbling words in a language I couldn't understand. As I neared him, gazing down at what was left of his massive form with a mixture of continued outrage and disgust, he contracted inwards, into a ball. I frowned at this. What was he doing?

He sprang. How he accomplished this, I could not tell you. He crossed the space between us like a snake striking and his remaining hand closed about my ankle before I could react. He yanked me down and then his bulk lay upon me, crushing me. I stared up into black eyes filled with cruel hate, and I cursed myself for my foolishness in approaching him before I'd finished him off—before I'd made him more closely resemble the thing on the table.

Holding me down with the weight of his body, his good arm came up, fist poised to smash down into my face. I grimaced as he screamed words in an alien tongue.

And then there came a bright orange flash and his head separated from his shoulders and tumbled away.

The big body slumped forward, lifeless and still and completely covering me.

I couldn't breathe. I mean, I was unexpectedly still alive and that was all well and good, but I had no time to consider what had happened or how. I was being crushed to death and suffocated.

Managing to draw one of my knees toward my body, I kicked upward and kept pushing, and after a few seconds of this I'd managed to move the gray bulk just enough that I could draw a shallow breath. I gasped and drew up the other leg and shoved as hard as I could with both. Lord, but he was heavy—and now nothing but dead weight. Absurdly at that moment I wanted to laugh at the thought that he'd have been even heavier if I hadn't just sliced a few pieces off of him. But I couldn't draw in enough air to attempt such a thing. So I kept pushing.

Then help arrived. Someone was pulling at him from behind. Very quickly my upper half was uncovered as the giant's bulk slid down, and then it was a matter of extracting my lower half. Seconds later I'd done it and lay on my back, staring up at the dome above me and breathing as if I'd just run three marathons, back-to-back.

A tall, slender form moved into my field of view and looked down at me.

"Thanks," I said.

"No," Istari replied. "Thank you." He held something aloft for me to see. The gray giant's head. "You continue to surprise me, human."

I stared at the gruesome item he was clutching like a prize and shook my head, laughing almost maniacally. "The feeling is mutual, I assure you," I told him.

He wasn't seriously...

Yes. Yes, he was.

Istari had been rummaging around inside the banks of electronic equipment that half-surrounded the surgical table for several minutes, while I kept the giant's headless corpse company. Now, as I looked on, he pulled a sheaf of wiring loose from one of the cabinets and spooled it out until he reached the severed head, which he'd set upright on the floor nearby. Carefully he separated the bundle of wires and then, after studying them very briefly, he began plugging them into the flesh of the head in various spots.

"Can I ask what you think you're doing?" I managed, feeling queasy all over again. He of course ignored me.

Once he'd inserted about a half-dozen of the stripped ends of the wires into the head, he moved around to stand directly in front of it. He stood there, stock still, for several seconds before lowering himself to the floor and sitting lotus style, staring back at it. Slowly he closed his eyes and he began to mumble strange words in an alien tongue.

"You don't seriously expect to be able to communicate with—" I began.

"Silence," he barked, not opening his eyes or otherwise moving.

Anger filled me but I restrained myself. Idly I wished I possessed a sword; likely I would have employed it at that moment to render him in a similar state to the giant. So perhaps it was for the best that I didn't have one.

Several seconds passed and my annoyance grew. Finally I opened my mouth to speak—but, even as I did, sparks erupted from the back of the big gray head where the leads penetrated the gray flesh.

Istari's eyes snapped open.

A second later, so did the giant's.

I might have jumped a good half-meter off the ground. It was extremely unsettling.

Istari spoke up louder now and, though he continued to speak in a language I couldn't understand, it rapidly became clear that he was directing a stream of questions at his former associate. The head merely stared back at him silently, sullenly at first, and so the questioning became louder, more intense.

I realized then that up until that moment he hadn't actually been speaking out loud to the head. He'd been using his silent mental speech, and apparently its intensity was so great as to enable me to hear it as well, as a sort of bleed-over. But now he was actually talking, his mouth working furiously as he enunciated the alien speech.

My head throbbing, I moved back a step or two.

Istari's eyes were wide and angry now and he practically barked at the head. As he spoke, I noticed an electricity in the air and the hair on my arms stood up. The temperature in the room dropped and frost formed on the floor around us, spider-webbing its way toward me. My breath was a white cloud that shrouded my face.

The giant's features twisted with what looked like scarcely-contained rage. But—what could he do against such indignity? He was merely a head.

The gray lips parted and he spoke. No actual words came forth, but I could hear him nonetheless in my mind. His voice as I perceived it was deep, rumbling and though I understood not a syllable of it, I could tell that it was shot through with hate.

I will spare you some of the grisly details, but you must know the gist of how this transpired. The interrogation went on for several minutes more. Each time the giant spoke, sparks shot out from the points of contact with the wires Istari had implanted in the back of the gray cranium. Flames leapt to life and began to spread over the head's surface. The eyes melted from the inside and little orange tongues of flame danced in the empty sockets. When the mouth opened, it was a glimpse into hell. By the end, Istari was demanding answers from a blazing, blackened, misshapen mass. It was all quite horrific.

I stood between them, my eyes flicking back and forth from the flaming skull to the seated alien. I couldn't decide which of them disturbed me more.

Istari blinked and looked up at me, as though coming out of a trance. Slowly he rose and I helped him fully to his feet.

"Did you learn anything useful?" I asked. There were other things I wanted to ask of my strange companion but I held them back for now.

He allowed that very faint smile of his to reappear briefly on his lips, and he chuckled softly. "Oh yes," he said, his voice very soft, very faint, to the point that I had to lean in to make out what he was saying. "Most of it was useless. Things I already knew. And of course the babbling, the pain—as was to be expected."

A sour look crossed my face at this.

"But, toward the end," Istari went on, "he could not hold back the singular item I most sought."

"That being...?"

"The destination of Udasi the Judge, after he left this place. Udasi, my erstwhile associate among the Immortals." He chuckled again, louder. "Udasi, who carries with him the sword."

SIX

Not again," I insisted. "No. We need help before we go blindly charging off across the galaxy again."

We were mounting our horses on the narrow cliff outside the dome. Istari had walked up to each, spoken a few alien words and snapped his fingers, and they'd come back to full wakefulness as though nothing had happened. I'd briefly examined Comet and he'd seemed none the worse for the experience. So I climbed aboard and we started off behind Istari yet again.

"Are you listening to me?" I called, when it became apparent that my pale, slender companion was not.

"I am not certain you have understood what has transpired thus far," Istari offered by way of reply. "As before, time is of the essence. Everything that transpired here, everything we endured and all that we accomplished means nothing if we do not take advantage of this actionable intelligence."

"This 'actionable intelligence' seems to me to be giving us a good place to go to get killed," I replied. "We were extremely fortunate to survive against our big gray friend back there. Now you want to push our luck?" I shook my head. "We can't do this alone."

"We can and we will," Istari said. "The entire purpose of fighting him was to interrogate him and gain the information I

125

now possess." He looked back at me, his voice rising for the first time since I'd first encountered him. "Would you simply walk away from our mission now?"

"I don't want to walk away from it, but I'd like to feel that we have a chance against whomever or whatever we have to face next."

"We will have a chance," he said after a moment's pause. His tone softened back to the way it had been up until now. "I have learned where Udasi the Judge has gone with the sword. I know what he is doing there. And I know how to ambush him. The risk to each of us is miniscule."

I didn't reply to that but I may have snorted derisively under my breath. I didn't trust this guy in the slightest. And "our mission" as he called it was really only *his* mission. My only interest in it was doing my part in our alliance—no, that sounded too friendly; call it a mutual assistance pact, at best—and in helping him acquire an item he had repeatedly assured me would be of tremendous value in completing *my* mission afterward.

That was, of course, if I still lived at the completion of *his* mission.

The fog and the lights returned as our horses carried us along across the barren landscape. We moved at first along the cliff, parallel to the wall of steeply-sloped mountain on our right and the drop to the sea on our left. Soon, though, both cliff face and drop vanished into the mists. Despite all rational thoughts to the contrary, I somehow suspected— *knew*—that neither was there any longer. We were, in every sense of the word, elsewhere.

The fog billowed before us now and swirled madly in our wake. Horizontal forks of lighting flared along on either side as the tunnel effect closed around us. Visibility dropped to only a few meters ahead. A rainbow swirl cascaded over, through and past us, to the point that I was sure I could not just see and feel but smell and taste the colors. This was the third journey I'd made through this strange between-space in the past couple of hours and it was the worst of the lot. I began to question my very sanity.

I also wondered, for at least the third time, how he was able to do this.

Something happened then that I hadn't expected: the ground beneath us rose slowly into a gentle incline. We were moving uphill. The horses slowed a bit as the slope increased. Istari vanished ahead in the mist. A fear of becoming lost forever here in this realm of oblivion gripped my insides. I started to encourage Comet to pick up the pace—though I could scarcely complain, given how well and how quickly he had adapted to such bizarre surroundings and taken them all in stride—when Istari reappeared directly before us. He had come to a stop. I reined Comet in and called out, "What is it?"

"We have arrived," my pale companion announced.

I turned in the saddle, regarding the fog. The air was strangely dry, not humid as one might have expected. This was not water vapor, I surmised. It represented something else entirely. "Arrived where?" I asked.

"Where we need to be," he said. He leapt from the saddle and took his black horse's reins in hand. I climbed down and did the same with Comet. Together we led the horses very slowly a short distance more in the direction we'd been traveling, and within seconds the clouds parted and revealed a small, shallow, bowl-shaped valley or arroyo. The barren rock surface of the cliff had been replaced by short, rough grass the color of harvested wheat. At the center of the nearly circular open area stood a single tree; it looked to be an ancient oak, currently bereft of leaves. Its spindly, skeletal limbs reached out in every direction. The air around us was cool and smelled of autumn.

Istari regarded the old tree and nodded. "This is the marker," he said. "This is the place."

"What place?"

The pale alien looked at me, impatience clear on his face. "The place where our target should emerge. He has in all likelihood traveled into a pocket universe and is using the sword to siphon cosmic energies from a still-higher plane. When he emerges, he will be somewhat disoriented and vulnerable."

"Oh?"

"Or he should be, at least."

"So—what do we do now?" I asked, leading Comet off to the side and holding the reins firmly so he wouldn't wander into the fog. "We just wait for him?"

"We wait," Istari said.

Reluctantly I nodded. I gazed out at the little circle we occupied, surrounded by walls of opaque mist, and I sighed.

Istari performed the hypnosis trick on our horses again and then moved to stand with his back against the trunk of the tree, facing outward. He gestured. "Take the other side," he told me, an unusual sense of urgency in his tone. "Stand as I am standing. Keep your eyes open."

"For what?"

"For a doorway," he said. "It will be obvious. You will have no doubt if you see it."

I thought—I was absolutely certain—that he was speaking metaphorically.

Of course, he wasn't.

We hadn't been standing there more than four or five minutes, on either side of the tree and with me about to ask why we had been in such of a hurry to get here if we were just going to stand against a tree and contemplate the bleak vista, when something shimmered into view directly before me. Istari had been right—there was absolutely no mistaking what it was.

It was a door. An actual, honest-to-goodness, free-standing door, wooden and ancient-looking and standing right there in the grove, halfway between the tree and the fog, where before there had been nothing but dead grass.

I stared at it incredulously for probably the space of two heartbeats. Then I shouted, "Door!"

Istari was around the tree and at my side in an instant. A second later he'd moved to where the door stood, positioning himself just to one side of it. "Do not move," he told me.

I was starting to ask him exactly what he had in mind, when the door opened.

It was surreal. Not that all the other things I'd experienced since leaving the palace on Victoria hadn't been, but this was perhaps the most surreal thing of all. The door swung on invisible hinges and revealed a rectangular opening—an opening in space, in reality. For a couple of seconds I was looking through the passage into another world, or another universe. My mouth opened and closed but words failed me. I gaped.

And then someone passed through, and out, and into our little valley.

An alien. Another one of the same species as Istari. Slightly taller and heavier-set, he was still freakishly slender and spindly by human standards. He wore a shimmering black tunic of metallic fabric and loose-fitting pants that appeared to be made from the same type of material that Istari wore. His face appeared regal, somehow, with a long, thin nose and arched brows over a bone-white face.

In his right hand he carried a sword.

It was long and somewhat ornate and heavy-looking, and the thought passed through my mind that it might weigh more than he did, leading me to further speculate on how he was so easily able to carry it.

Above all else, though, it was golden. Lord, how golden it was. It gleamed, it shone, it practically radiated *gold*. A very real, visceral sense of power emanated from it.

The alien took a second and then a third step through the doorway and his eyes focused upon me and he halted and stared. He appeared startled at the sight of me, waiting there.

And then his eyes rolled up in his head and he dropped to his knees. The sword fell from his grasp and landed on the cushioning grass with scarcely a sound.

Istari had done something to him. What, I wasn't entirely sure. I saw no wounds, had heard no discharge, and Istari held no weapon. Probably safe to assume it had been some sort of mental attack.

Evidence to support that, a moment later: the air had grown colder, just as it had back at the dome. My breath a cloud, I leaned down and reached for the golden weapon where it lay.

"Stop!"

Startled, I looked up. Istari was moving toward me, his eyes glowing orange.

"The sacred sword is not meant for one such as you to wield," he snapped.

He reached down to grasp the sword himself.

I started to hit him with a retort—or just hit him. I didn't get the chance to do either.

Another shape had come into view behind him, passing through the still-open doorway. It was big and gray and it roared something I couldn't understand as it rushed up behind Istari and drew back its right hand.

"Look out—!" I cried, too late.

The big gray hand swung out and slapped Istari in the back, sending him sprawling.

This time it was anger that swelled inside me. Anger that I had been right—that we were not as prepared for this conflict as my erstwhile companion had believed. Anger that I had told him that, only to have him dismiss the very notion. Mostly, though, anger that once again I was going to have to fight one of these gray giants, and this time I was entirely unarmed—no pistol, no handy surgical lasers, nothing.

As I scrambled away from the giant I saw Istari recover, flip back onto his feet—he was a much more nimble figure now than he had been in the moments after I'd first rescued him—and direct his right hand out in my big adversary's direction. "Kratok," he murmured. "You should not have interfered." His eyes flared orange and the giant emitted a muffled "Ooof" before stumbling backwards, nearly tripping over his feet. Istari motioned again as the big gray guy tried to get up. The giant spun sideways and went down hard.

Okay. Some sort of psychic power, obviously—not just to read minds but to affect the physical world. Call it telekinesis. Istari was more formidable than I'd thought.

Then he flew off his feet and sprawled on the grass, tumbling head over heels.

The other alien—my companion had called him Udasi, I remembered then—had recovered at least somewhat and was climbing back to his feet. His hand was outstretched and his eyes glowed as orange as Istari's had. He turned his attention towards me and I backed away quickly, possibly more afraid of him than I had been of the giant. The giant, after all, represented a very visible, physical force, but the gaunt, slender Udasi did his damage within the realm of the unseen.

Udasi advanced upon me but then an invisible hand smashed him in the back and hurled him to the side and down. Istari stood revealed behind him, both arms outstretched and eyes glowing brighter. The cold now was almost overwhelming; frost covered the dead grass.

Udasi recovered instantly and the two slender aliens squared off, both crouching low, both with arms extended before them, both with nightmarish luminous eyes. The golden sword lay on the ground between them. Each time one would make a move for it, the other would lash out with a violent gesture, and the first would react as though struck with a mighty blow. Then the sequence would reverse itself. They circled one another, trading these psychic bolts and blasts and reeling each time the other's attack got through. It became a dance, almost hypnotic in its bizarre choreography, and it caused me to momentarily forget the fourth player on our little drama. Forget him, that is, until he very violently reminded me of his presence.

Kratok reared up and smashed his massive fist into my back. My golden mesh shirt did little to protect me from the full force of the blow. I was driven forward and down, sent tumbling across the now-crunchy, ice-cold grass, and for a couple of seconds I lost all sense of where I was, who I was, or what I was doing. All I knew at that moment was shock and pain. My vision filled with stars and explosions—and they, incongruously, reminded me of the war probably still going on back home, from which I had abdicated myself for too long now—and I cast about, blinking furiously as my eyesight slowly came back. My hands were splayed out to either side as I tried to rise, and my fingers closed on something. I had no idea what it was but it felt solid and heavy.

A roar of fury. My vision cleared enough that I could see Kratok the giant charging at me, his big, grasping hands reaching out, murder clear in his eyes. My hand clasped firmly the object that lay to my side, and without further thought I raised and swung whatever it was at the oncoming giant.

The roar ceased abruptly. And I was not tackled.

As my swing carried the object around and past Kratok, my vision cleared. I hadn't struck him—of that I was certain—and I therefore couldn't imagine what could've caused him to stop. Then I saw.

Kratok stood only a short distance from me, his expression one of unmitigated shock. His mouth hung open; his dark eyes were wide and they flicked between the object I held and a spot in midair about halfway between us.

The spot in midair drew my attention and I stared at it, puzzled. So strange was it, I nearly forgot my deadly foe and all else that transpired around us. It was a slice, a gash, carved in the very air itself. Within its jagged boundaries I glimpsed, as though very far away, a sheet of flames.

A second later Kratok overcame his distraction and this time as his gaze fell upon me I saw that it contained some small element of—was that *fear*?—along with the hatred and rage. He hesitated, then came at me again. Instinctively I swung what was in my hand a second time.

Another gash ripped open in the air before me, this one larger, wider. A gaping maw, it hung there like a crudely cut version of the doorway through which our foes had arrived. It was filled with roaring flames.

Kratok the giant attempted to halt his progress but his momentum was too great. He stumbled, twisted—and then his great bulk fell through. There came the briefest of screams—a sound utterly at odds with the massive, imposing being that emitted it—and he was gone. The flaming portal snapped closed, along with the smaller one I had opened just before it.

I stood there reeling, not entirely certain what had just happened. Glancing over at the two aliens I saw that they had paused their sorcerous duel and were both unabashedly gawking at me. And particularly at what I held in my right hand.

The sword. The golden sword. I had somehow used it to carve holes in the very fabric of the universe itself. Now I held it out to my side and its weight was as nothing; as a feather in my grasp. It felt as if I'd been born to hold it, to wield it.

Istari was first to recover his senses. He leapt up, came at me, seized the sword from my hand and spun about, dropping lower as he did so. The other like him, Udasi, reacted a second later—a second too late. Apparently a fraction slower to switch from mental to physical combat and action, he was just rising to his feet when Istari brought the golden blade around in a wide arc and took his head—still bearing its look of stunned outrage—clean from his shoulders.

SEVEN

Our relationship changed a bit after the incident with Kratok and Udasi.

Istari retained possession of the sword but he seemed deeply troubled by the revelation that I could use it. He made it very clear to me that such a thing should not have been possible.

I was getting a bit fed up with him leading me around and expecting me to do his bidding—which today had mostly consisted of rushing blindly and unarmed into fights against vastly superior forces. So I put my foot down and demanded answers.

To my surprise, he acquiesced. "That is fair," he said. "I promised to help you with your problem once the sword came into my possession, and now it has."

We climbed back onto our horses, both now awake again after Istari had freed them from his hypnotic spell, and my companion regarded me as if seeing me for the first time.

"There is also the fact that our separate problems are now merging together," he added.

This took me aback. "They are?" I asked. "How so?"

"My enemies—my former associates—are now working with individuals who are your enemies, but whom you still believe to be your allies and associates," he said.

I attempted to parse that out, failed. I was very tired at that point. I'd been up a full day even before the attack on the Victoria moon and the murder of my father, and then add on everything that had happened since then... I had a hell of a headache, to say the least.

"Can you run that by me again?" I asked, rubbing my bloodshot eyes with my fists.

He looked away for a moment as our horses moved lazily about in slow, meandering circles, nibbling at the parts of the grass that weren't still frozen. "Haven't you asked yourself," he said at last, "what my former captor was doing riding his horse away from your world in the first place? Why was he there?"

I shook my head, feeling chagrined to have overlooked such an obvious thing. Of course I had thought about it at the time, but so much had happened since then that the question of that first alien's presence there on Victoria had slipped my mind entirely. And, as I've said repeatedly, I was extremely tired.

"I don't know the answer to that," I told him. "Do you?"

"Of course," he said, flashing me that thin smile I'd seen from him so many times already in our brief acquaintance. Then his look turned more serious. "He was there meeting with someone," he said. "Someone who is in league with him and his associates—my former compatriots."

I stared back at him, a sick feeling growing in my gut. "What are you saying?" I demanded.

"I am saying precisely what you think I'm saying. What you fear most." He chuckled softly. "You harbor a traitor within your ranks."

"Someone on my world?"

"Someone in your family," he replied.

Needless to say, we raced back along the cosmic Paths to Victoria with all the speed I could muster from Istari's mount and my own. I still didn't understand in the slightest how we were doing that, but it worked, and at the moment that was what mattered.

The light had faded to a sort of twilight effect all around us, even before the fog that was our constant traveling companion returned. The ground was firmly packed and Comet moved along its surface easily. Despite all that I'd asked of him since we'd departed the palace, he seemed none the worse for the wear. I suspected it had to do with the sleep spell Istari had placed on both animals twice so far. If only he could do the same for me. But I knew I needed to be alert now—more than ever before.

Along the way, I at last managed to coax some answers out of my reticent associate. Perhaps he believed at that point that I needed to be better informed in order to be a more effective ally. Or perhaps not. I didn't know then and I don't know now, and I don't much care. At that moment, all I wanted was more information. I got it.

How much of it to believe was another question entirely.

Of course, when he pointedly accused someone in my immediate family of being a traitor to the rest of us, I wanted to call him a liar. I wanted to, but I knew it wasn't outside the realm of possibility. For one thing, I remembered seeing that strange, lone figure on the balcony in the palace, seemingly interacting with someone—perhaps one of my uncles—prior to our family meeting. And I could scarcely deny that it might very well have been the same figure that led me along the Path to where I found the captive Istari.

For another, I knew my relatives all too well.

"Who was it, then?" I asked as we galloped along. "Who was it that I saw in the palace? One of your people?" I paused, then, "For that matter, who exactly *are* your people?"

"We are the Immortals," he replied.

"The what?"

"The Cabal of Nine, if you prefer," he added. He looked away for a second, then amended, "Six now, I suppose. Five, if you subtract me from the equation."

"It's looked to me like they've pretty much subtracted you. Every time we run into one of them, they want to kill you. And me."

"I told you before, I am the Renegade. They have rejected my counsel and revoked my membership in their club." He scowled over at me, seemed to think better of it, and smiled again. "Not that I care, because I wanted nothing else to do with them or their twisted agenda."

"Immortals, you say." I thought about that for a moment and snorted. "We've encountered three of them on this trip so far. Not a one of them turned out to be immortal. Pretty darned mortal, every one of them, in fact."

"We have been fortunate." He glanced down at the sword, which now hung from his horse's left flank in a scabbard that fit it perfectly. I hadn't noticed the scabbard before and wasn't sure where he'd acquired it. "Extremely fortunate."

"Tell me about that weapon," I said. "What is it? What exactly did it do to the gray giant, back there?"

"It hurled him into hell," Istari said matter-of-factly.

I blinked. "It what?"

Istari glanced at me and laughed. "I continue to fall back on the colloquialisms I took from your mind when we first met," he said. "I find them colorful and quite useful."

"You're avoiding my questions."

He was silent for a few moments, then sighed tiredly and looked at me again. "Very well. Where to begin?"

"The beginning."

He shook his head. "No. Too far back. Not helpful to the present situation." He pursed his thin lips. "We must begin a bit more recently in time."

And so as we trotted along through the mists, Istari the Renegade began to lay out for me a tapestry of galactic history about which I and the rest of the human race until that moment had known nothing.

BARANAK: STORMING THE GATES

+   +   +

Ages ago, before the human race had climbed down from the trees; before even my own kind, the Dyonari, had risen to become the most advanced and dominant life form in the galaxy, there existed the Machine.

A vast and powerful artificial intelligence, we can only assume the Machine was built by some race now long-vanished. They are gone, but it survived. And the job its creators left behind for it was a simple one: to enforce their vision of peace upon the cosmos.

Some saw the Machine as benevolent and therefore obeyed its laws and prospered, within the strict guidelines it laid down. Others saw it as a malevolent and oppressive force, tyrannical and authoritarian. They refused to follow its laws. They suffered the consequences.

The Machine, you see, had created an army of genetically engineered and cloned warriors called the Hands. It trained them via forced memory download and armed them with the most advanced weaponry ever seen. And it sent them out in sentient ships by the thousands to enforce its laws, its will for all living beings in the greater galactic society.

None could stand before the Hands. Chosen and bred from a race of powerful gray giants, they swept across the spiral arms of the Milky Way and systematically dismantled all opposition.

Were they truly benevolent, or did they represent tyranny and conquest? Who can say? The answer lies in the eye of the beholder. Many races and worlds welcomed them. Some did not.

My own race, the Dyonari, fought back. We were among the last of the holdouts. Our technology had grown and developed to the point that we could fight them more successfully than most. Our warriors became masters of the blade as well as the firearm, because the Hands were proficient with both. Our seers, expanding our people's existing latent psychic skills, developed precognitive abilities useful for early warning. And the most powerful among us discovered how to walk the Pathways of the lower Above, and thus travel from world to world without the need for spacecraft—thereby avoiding the Hands' ceaseless patrols.

Thus we and a few other races challenged the tyranny of the Machine. It was a long and costly war. It raged for centuries and consumed the resources and inhabitants of countless worlds. And, in the end, it was unsuccessful. In short, we lost.

The Hands of the Machine blamed my species above all others for this rebellion. In retribution, they ravaged our home world and all of our colony worlds. Our population was reduced to a fraction of its original size.

Some few of us survived, though. Deprived of our planets, we found or created... *alternate* places to live. And there our people remain.

But a small number of us refused to yield, even then. We formed a secret group—a *cabal*—to work in secret against the Machine. I counted myself among their number. We rallied the people on a hundred worlds. We preached against our enemy's tyranny. We formed insurgencies on dozens of planets. We struck without warning, we sabotaged, we disrupted the Machine wherever possible. Our greatest coup came when we recruited three disaffected former Hands— Dormor, Kratok and Hadog— into our ranks, bringing with them invaluable strategic and technical intelligence. They had lost faith in the Machine's vision, or felt some degree of sympathy for the dominated peoples, or were simply outraged at its growing tyranny.

So—we seven Dyonari and three former Hands set ourselves against the most brilliant intelligence and the most powerful military in the galaxy. For many years we barely accomplished a thing, barely escaped the enemy's traps, barely survived. But then the three former Hands delivered to us a bit of data that turned the tide. We struck at the Machine directly, and we struck it hard. Somehow, against all odds—

and though it cost the life of one of our number— we succeeded. The Machine was knocked offline and its links to the Hands became inactive. In the time immediately afterward, now cut off from their master and from one another, most of the Hands were tracked down by vengeful rebels and insurrectionists, cornered, and eliminated.

That is how my people came to dominate the galaxy, despite our drastically reduced numbers and despite our exile to the great artificial star-cities that drift along the spaceways. That was how we remaining nine of the Cabal—the Immortals—came to secretly manipulate and direct the actions and the fates of the Dyonari and so many other races. And that was the state of affairs at the galactic level at the time when your people, the humans, emerged from your planetary cradle and began to expand onto your Seven Worlds.

For five hundred years, we Immortals allowed that expansion. We saw opportunities and advantages in having the human race become involved in the greater galactic milieu. But then my eight associates changed their minds. They concluded that your species represented a greater danger than we had imagined. They determined to stop your expansion in its tracks—and furthermore, to set you back. I disagreed. I felt your kind could bring a desperately needed energy and vitality back into the greater galaxy. My dissent was noted and ignored, my opinions dismissed. And so, as they moved against your people, I moved against them. I rebelled. I attempted to stop them. For this I was captured, imprisoned, and tortured, just as you found me on—

+   +   +

"Hold on a second," I said, interrupting him. "What is that supposed to mean? The nine of you 'moved against' us?"

"The eight of them," he corrected. "I did not take part."

"In what?" I reined in Comet and we waited there, unmoving, until Istari had to stop and turn his mount around to face us or else leave us behind. "You did not take part in what?"

He regarded me with an expression of annoyance. "Later," he said. "Time is of the essence."

"Now," I countered. "Full disclosure is currently even more of the essence."

He glared at me for several endless seconds, then inhaled deeply, exhaled slowly, and said, "Very well. If you must know..."

"I must."

He nodded. "The Cabal of Immortals—minus myself— determined to pit you all against one another in a suicidal civil war. Better, it was felt, to allow you to expend your violent tendencies and your stockpiles of armaments upon one another than upon the other races of the galaxy." He spread his hands in a sort of shrugging gesture. "And so the ancient interstellar wormholes we had originally made available to your people were shut down, isolating the populations of each of your worlds from all the others."

I nearly fell off my horse. "The Gates, you mean?" I was staggered. "You—you 'Immortals'—were responsible for the Gates closing?"

"We were responsible for you having access to them in the first place. What the Immortals gave, they could take away. And they did."

I ran my hand through my hair, processing this information. I'm sure my eyes were wide as saucers. "Were your associates responsible for their recent reopening, also?"

"They were."

"Why?"

"That was the heart of their plan: Divide your worlds from one another, then manipulate the governments and the populations of each in the direction of maximum suspicion and hostility toward all the others. With that accomplished, reopen the Gates, and..." He trailed off, looked at me and smiled.

"War," I said.

"Just so."

"A war in which the human race wipes itself out," I said, my fists bunching subconsciously, "while your people sit on high and observe it all happening, like gods, laughing as we slaughter one another."

He looked at me strangely, his brows furrowed. "You have heard me state repeatedly that I was not involved in that portion of their plans, and that I disavow such actions. You understand this—yes?"

I nodded impatiently. I had no idea how much of that was the truth and frankly, at that moment in time, I didn't care. Istari was still useful to me. If at some later point I learned that he was lying—that he had participated in the disaster for humanity that he was describing—I vowed I would do everything in my power to make him pay.

And then I understood something more. I gazed at Istari and studied his reactions as I spoke the words: "The Church."

He said nothing in response to that, but I thought I could see him squirm just the tiniest bit.

"When we visited Sarmata," I elaborated, "they had a Church just as we did. The outfits their priests wore were the same; their ranks and emblems were the same. How likely is that over such a long time in isolation?"

Still he said nothing.

"I'll bet all of the Seven Worlds of Man have the exact same organizations, and have had them all along."

His expression remained neutral for another second. Then he smiled; that same sly, evil-looking smile he'd shown me numerous times before.

"Indeed," he said. "You surprise me with your perceptiveness."

If he sought to mollify me with compliments, it wasn't going to work. I continued to glare at him, waiting.

"The Church," he said at length, "was indeed our instrument."

"You infiltrated it?"

"We created it."

I thought about that, nodded. I wasn't surprised, now that I could see it.

"We appeared to its highest leaders on each world in the form of prophets, working miracles and speaking profound words of warning and of guidance," he explained, though I was only half-listening now. "Occasionally we even came to them in the form of the ancient gods of the Burning Stars themselves. From the very beginning, before the majority of our Cabal turned against humanity, we were helping the leaders of the faith. We gave them advice, shared bits of advanced technology with them, and generally shaped their doctrine and encouraged their expansion. They were to be the levers with which we moved your entire race in the direction we desired."

My mind was spinning. So much to take in, to process. I could see it all now. We—the human race—had always been pieces on the board, pieces moved by higher powers with their own agendas. Our free will, our perceived destiny as a people, as preached for a thousand years by the Church of the Burning Stars—all of it was an illusion. I understood that now and it sickened me.

And then the last piece of the puzzle fell into place, and I nearly tumbled from Comet's back.

Istari was still talking but I heard not a word of it. Thoughts were racing through my mind with the force of a stampede. Almost in a daze I climbed down from my mount and approached him. His voice trailed off as he saw me coming. He frowned, puzzled.

I reached up, grasped him with both hands, and wrenched him off his mount before he could fully react. He fell to the ground with a startled exclamation and lay there in the dirt, stunned. Less than a second later I was upon him. My first swing impacted his jaw and he cried out. I raised my fist to swing a second time.

"Wait! Stop! What are you—"

Down came my fist. Pale blood splattered from his nose.

"Control yourself, Gaius," he gasped once he could speak again.

I raised my fist a third time.

His eyes flared orange. "You will stop this now," he hissed.

My fist hesitated in midair, against my will. I growled in my throat, gritted my teeth, felt the anger and frustration and rage sweeping through me, and brought the fist down hard again.

He cried out, as much in shock and surprise as in pain, I think.

I raised my fist yet again. I was lost in my fury.

His eyes focused on mine, and now they flared brilliant orange.

"Stop!"

His telepathic power seized my body. I was flipped head over heels through the air, a ragdoll caught in a storm. I landed hard at Comet's feet; he whinnied and stepped back. He nudged me with his nose but I ignored it.

"Calm yourself and listen."

That last bit came to me not vocally but through his psychic mental voice. It carried with it sufficient force to freeze me momentarily. Istari took advantage of that opportunity and scrambled to his feet ahead of me. As I got back up again and squared off, crouching low, ready to fight, he raised both hands to fend me off. "Stop," he said again, and, "Wait." He scowled, then added, "Please."

I hesitated, surprised. I'd expected a lot of different things from him, but not a polite request, complete with "please."

"What?" I growled, impatient and burning inside. "I get it now."

"Get what?"

"My father," I snapped back at him. "I remember what the thing in the cave told me. I asked it why my father was killed, and it said, 'because he might actually have succeeded.' I didn't know what the thing meant at the time, but now I think I see." I took a step toward him but he held his ground, waiting.

"What do you see?" he asked.

"If my father and his armies had accomplished what he planned, the human race would've been reunited under one single, powerful government. That's pretty much the opposite of what your Cabal wanted, isn't it?"

Istari didn't reply. His gaze dipped down so that he was staring now at the ground instead of at me.

"So now I know."

I waited, but he said nothing. I found his silence infuriating.

"Are you going to tell me again that it wasn't you?" I demanded. "That you hate the terrible things your associates have done? Because that line is growing thin."

"It's true," he said in a quiet voice. "The Immortals used Constantine as a pawn, and discovered almost too late that he was far more formidable than they had guessed. They took action accordingly."

My eyes could have burned holes in him. I felt the impulse to charge at him again, but I resisted it and waited.

He was silent for a moment, then looked up at me. "But set that out of the way for a moment and think. The past aside, we still need one another."

"The past aside?" I snorted. "You want me to just forget what happened to my father?" I glared back at him. "Everything I've done since he was killed was to find his murderer and—"

"And what? And gain justice? Or simple revenge?" He shook his head. "Both of those might make you feel better for a brief time, but they will do nothing to advance his cause, his legacy."

"What would you suggest I do, then?"

146

"I suggest that you *win*," he stated, his sly smile reappearing, then morphing into a broader grin. "I suggest that you carry on that legacy, and see that it prevails."

I took this in and considered it. There was a certain amount of appeal there, I had to admit to myself. Still— "Me? I am no general," I pointed out. "How can I defeat all the enemies of my world? Not to mention your Cabal friends?"

"You do not have to be some great general or warrior yourself," Istari replied. He came up out of his fighting crouch and spread his arms wide as he explained. "Your family and your world already possess the resources and capabilities necessary for victory, even without Constantine commanding them. Your role is different—but every bit as vital, if not more." He moved closer, and all sense of hostility between us melted away. "Your task is to identify and remove the elements that even now seek to bring down your family and your armies—from within."

"The traitor," I said.

"Precisely." He nodded. "You must root out the treasonous element within your family. And you must help me defeat the remaining members of the Cabal of Immortals before they decide to take stronger measures against all your people— against the human race as a whole."

For several moments I simply stood there, allowing the remaining waves of anger toward my alien companion to wash away. At last I felt I could think clearly again. I considered everything he had said and, almost reluctantly, I nodded. "Very well," I said. "We will do as you have suggested." I pointed a finger at him. "But do not think I am absolving you entirely from your role in all of this. By your own account, you spent centuries working closely with these others, doing who knows what sorts of damage."

"I have done much in my time that I am not proud of, human," Istari said. "I seek to redeem myself as well as to help save you and your world."

147

"We shall see," I told him, before climbing back atop Comet.

He mounted his dark horse and together we rode for home.

EIGHT

The grassy slopes of the eastern side of the palace on Victoria materialized before us as we emerged from the tunnel of mists. One last flash of lighting, one last crazed rainbow swirling overhead, and we were there, home, the dimensional portal of the Paths vanishing in our wake.

It looked to be mid-morning—about what I'd expected based on how long I'd been away. I exhaled heavily. My eyes were barely remaining open now. Above all other things, I desperately needed sleep. Even identifying the traitor might have to be deferred for a few hours while I got at least an extended nap.

Istari, however, seemed capable of going on and on with no thought of rest whatsoever. And he'd scarcely shut up since we'd remounted and continued on our way back.

"You know your family far better than I do. Have you experienced any revelations as to who might be the traitor?" he asked as we reined in our mounts and I gazed up at the tall towers and gray ramparts of the palace. We had discussed that issue a bit along the way, and determined that while Istari had known of the Cabal's interest in my relatives, he had never been privy to the identity of our target. As far as he could tell, he'd been a prisoner and cut off from all information well before his former associates had managed to subvert a member of my family. I chose to believe him, at least for now. I certainly didn't trust him, though.

That meant we had nothing to go on whatsoever. We would have to investigate beginning at square one.

I thought of my relatives all side-by-side then, and went down the row, considering the possible motives and likelihood of each of them being involved.

"We can go in order from oldest to youngest, and begin with Justinian," I said. "If he's the traitor, we're all done. Finished. Because he's the only true military commander we have left."

"Wouldn't he have the most to gain, though, by seeing your father killed?"

I thought about that. "True," I said. "He took over the family and the military with scarcely any real objections." I thought back to the conversation in the library before my departure. "But he could have gained the same things without falling in with enemy powers."

"Possibly. Who is next?"

"Aurelia. She is very religious—very connected to the Church."

"That would be a mark against her, I should think."

I nodded. "She's always been the most mysterious of the bunch. I wouldn't put it past her to be involved. She might even see herself as being the only one of us doing the right thing—if that's what the Church told her to do, or to think."

Istari grunted. "Next?"

"Aunt Octavia," I said. "I haven't seen or heard from her in quite some time. She wasn't at our family meeting before I left."

"That seems suspicious," he said.

"But if one of your Cabal was indeed here to meet with the traitor that night, and Octavia was that traitor," I pointed out, "it wouldn't make sense for her to be absent."

He frowned at this but nodded. "A fair point. Next."

"The twins— Jerome and Alexius." I scratched at my goatee. "I can't see what they would have to gain from—"

"You consider them together," Istari noted, interrupting me.

I was taken aback by this, but realized quickly that he was right. "Yes—I suppose I've always thought of them as a pair—as a set."

"Need that be the case in this instance?"

"No," I said after a moment's reflection. "No, I suppose that one of them could be the traitor and the other innocent. But it's hard to imagine one being that involved in nefarious dealings and the other not knowing about it at all."

He nodded. "Anyone else? Isn't there a young one—?"

"Stephanie," I said. "Youngest by far—younger even than me, though she's technically another aunt. I can't imagine Stephanie being involved in anything like what we're talking about. She wouldn't have the slightest clue, or the wherewithal to—" I trailed off as I recalled her uncharacteristic talkativeness at our family meeting. Could little Stephanie be mixed up in all of this? Surely not, I told myself. And yet...

Istari gave me a curious look as I stood there, thinking. I came back to myself and shook my head. "No—not her."

"It has to be one of them," he reminded me.

I yawned again and stretched. "There's no way I'm figuring it out right now," I told him. "I can barely keep my eyes open."

"If not for me," he said, "you wouldn't have made it this far."

I blinked as this statement penetrated my gauzy brain. "What?"

"I have subtly stimulated your mind for the past few hours. It was plain to see you were fading."

I whirled on him, anger flaring past the walls of sleep. "I warned you about messing with my mind."

"I didn't 'mess with' anything," he said. "I merely stimulated your brain activity such that you could stay awake and alert longer."

"Even so—"

"If I had not," he went on, "you would already have been killed. At least once."

I simmered for a moment, then looked away and nodded once. "All right," I said. "But you should have told me. At the time you did it." I jabbed a finger at him. "And you will ask in the future before doing anything involving my mind. Anything."

He nodded his head once.

The horses carried us across the grassy field at a trot.

"Be warned," Istari said after a few moments had passed and I'd calmed myself, "that time runs differently in each layer of reality. We spent no small amount of time on other planes. I cannot judge offhand how much time might have passed here on your world."

This took me aback.

"You mean—this morning now..." I sought to find the right words. "...*this* morning might not be the one after the night when I left here?"

"That is correct. We are surely further along in time now than otherwise would have been the case had you remained here."

"Are we talking a day?" I asked, a mild concern deepening within me as I thought about it. "A week?" I frowned at him. "More?"

He shook his head. "I cannot say," he replied. "We will know soon enough."

I wondered how the war was proceeding. Was it over? Had I missed it entirely? And—if so, who had won?

Shaking my head to clear it, I put such thoughts aside. No point in getting all worked up before I had to. I pointed toward the far corner of the palace just ahead of us and to the right. "The stables," I said. "Let us drop off our horses and then—"

"You cannot mean to take me openly into the palace," he interrupted, frowning. "That could precipitate things before we are fully prepared to deal with them."

I squeezed my eyes closed, yawned, and looked back at him. "No— no, of course not. Not yet, at least." I hopped down from Comet and took him by the reins, then reached out and grasped the reins of Istari's dark horse. My companion dismounted and stood there as I gazed up the hill in the direction of the stables. The area appeared deserted and idly I wondered where the family's retainers were.

"What will you do in the meantime?" I asked him.

"I will be nearby. Have no fear of that. I will be watching and waiting for the proper moment."

I wasn't sure what to make of this so I shrugged and led the horses up the slope toward the stables. After several steps something occurred to me and I turned back.

"You never told me the name of your horse—" I began, but he had vanished.

I looked from the now-empty grassy field to the black horse. The animal seemed to regard me with curiosity bordering on dislike. I patted it on the nose. "Hmm," I said. "I think we'll call you 'Sneak.'"

The horse didn't visibly react to that, though I'd half-expected it to. I had no idea what Istari's kind might have done to their horses over the years.

So I led Comet and the newly-named Sneak up to the stables and there I found a lone retainer—an elderly man with sparse, white hair, clad in dark blue overalls—cleaning the place with a hose. I nodded to him and he shut off the water and greeted me. I recalled his name was Roger.

"Lord Gaius," he said as he set the hose aside and came up to take the reins of the two horses. He stroked Comet's nose and then gave Sneak a look of mild surprise, before leading them to open stalls. "They've all been wondering where you'd gotten off to," he said.

"Something unexpected came up," I replied. I hesitated, then, "Can you tell me how long it's been since I left?"

He was in the process of lighting a pipe. He puffed on it for a moment, pursed his lips and thought. "Let's see— you took Comet out on the evening of the twelfth. This is the morning of the sixteenth."

"The sixteenth?" I took this in and shook my head. More than three days had passed while I'd been off gallivanting about the cosmos with Istari. How much could have happened in such a long time? I looked around and reassured myself that the palace still stood—it wasn't a smoking crater overrun with Verghasite troops—and breathed a sigh of relief.

"How goes the war, then?" I asked him.

Roger puffed on his pipe again, a cloud of smoke billowing about his head. "I'm sure your uncles could give you a much more detailed answer to that question, my lord," he said.

"Are we winning or losing? In general."

He spread his hands. "More winning than losing, I'd say. They've pushed the battle lines back in the direction of the enemy, from what I've heard. But don't quote me on that," he added with a smile.

So Victoria wasn't in imminent danger of being overrun by Verghas. Presumably neither was the larger world our moon orbited, Majondra. That was a relief.

"Thank you, Roger," I told him. "Please see to the horses. I may be back for them before long."

"I will, my lord." He looked over at Sneak again and stroked his chin. "This is a mighty fine animal, if you don't mind my saying so," he added. "Might I inquire as to how you came by him?"

"He belongs to a... a friend," I answered hastily. "Take good care of him. But," I added before I rounded the corner, "keep a watchful eye on him. I'm not entirely sure I trust him."

Roger started to laugh at this, then saw my grave expression and the laughter died in his throat. The last I saw of him, he was turning to look upon Sneak with a wary expression. Then I came to the stairs and started up to the landing and the side entrance to the palace.

All was a blur from the moment I entered the palace until Aunt Aurelia awoke me. I sat up and looked around. My eyes were crusty and I generally felt as if I'd been partially mummified, but the crushing weariness was gone. I was sitting on a couch in a corridor outside the kitchens—but how long I'd slept there, I couldn't yet say. Clearly I hadn't even made it to my bedroom, but had passed out on the first horizontal surface I'd come across. Aurelia was standing over me, clad now in a tight-fitting black outfit of some synthetic material or other, her red hair tied up atop her head. She was gazing down with a troubled look on her face.

"Where have you been?" she all-but-demanded.

"What time is it?" I countered.

She looked annoyed that I'd deflected her question but replied, "Nine in the evening."

Nine. So I'd slept at least nine or ten hours. Good.

"It's a good thing Stephanie found you lying here and told me," she was saying, "or else you might have slept through the whole rest of the war."

"Stephanie?" I asked, rubbing my eyes.

"She didn't have the heart to wake you. Fortunately, I don't share that limitation." She rested her hands on her hips and repeated, more forcefully, "Where have you been?"

"Right here for quite a while, it sounds like," I said. "Since before noon."

"I've only just arrived from Tolkar," she said, referencing the world that lay next to us along the line of Gates, in the direction of Earth and the opposite direction from Sarmata and Verghas.

"What were you doing on Tolkar?"

"Meeting with the Church leaders there. Discussing an alliance against the Verghasites."

"You mean Justinian hasn't already whipped them?" I asked facetiously.

She gave me a sour look. "He's done a fine job thus far. Our forces have beaten the enemy back through the Gate and across the Sarmata system to their own Gate."

"Sounds like a new operation is being planned," I said, "if he has you off making deals with the other worlds."

She looked as if she were going to make a smart remark to that, but then changed her mind and nodded. "Justinian wishes to secure alliances with Tolkar and Earth, at our backs, so that we can more confidently prosecute the war against Verghas in front of us. We don't want to face a two-front war."

"Makes sense." I smiled at her. "Glad things are going well."

She looked even more annoyed.

I stood, stretching and yawning. "So what else is new?"

"The morning after our meeting in the library," she said, "Justinian asked everyone to meet in the dining hall. There he assigned each of us a task to help win the war. But you, alone of all of us, were nowhere to be found."

I looked at her innocently. "Oh? So you mean Aunt Octavia finally showed up?"

She frowned. "No," she admitted almost reluctantly. "Octavia has yet to make an appearance."

"Well," I said, "I don't know where she is or what she's doing, but I know what I was doing."

"And that was?"

"Exactly what I told you and the others I would be doing: Investigating my father's murder."

She looked bored by this. "And did you find anything?" she asked in perfunctory fashion.

"I did," I said—as much to gauge her reaction as anything.

I was rewarded for this decision. Her eyes widened and she took a step back.

"What?" she asked, her voice soft but filled with tension.

"I found the... *people*... generally responsible," I said. "And I also found a very interesting connection that leads back... *here*."

She appeared taken aback by that. Her eyes widened and she tried a couple of times to speak before words actually came out. "Back—back *here*? You mean..."

"I mean someone here is involved," I said. I knew this violated my arrangement with Istari about not spilling any beans too soon, but I felt that I was onto something with her and wanted to draw it out before she had a chance to recover and mask herself.

"Someone here," she repeated, staring back at me. "You mean—someone in the family?"

I shrugged. "There are indications that might be the case," I said. "But I can't be sure yet."

She looked away for a long second, then back at me, and now her face was set in a grim, determined manner. "Tell me where you have been and who you've talked to, Gaius," she said. "No more teasing."

"Not just yet," I said. "I have a few more bits of information to gather and then I'll speak to everyone, all at once."

I scooted out of there before she could object further. I did have other investigating to do, but before that, I wanted to check up on the two priestesses I'd left behind. They had almost entirely escaped my thoughts during the journey with Istari. Knowing now that they'd been here for almost four days without me... I was concerned.

On the way there I passed the armory. There was no attendant present, so I stepped inside and took a quick look around. Most of the drawers and cabinets were locked, but I did spot a fancily-decorated set of components of deflector armor that lay on one table where a servant had been polishing them. They gleamed golden and possessed almost a medieval look, though their advanced materials and construction meant they would provide a decent amount of protection in battle. Certainly more than I had enjoyed up until that moment. I didn't know when I'd have the chance to acquire something different or better so I donned the breastplate, boots and other pieces, tucked the gloves in my belt, and hurried back out.

Up the nearest stairs and down a long hallway I traveled, moving about as quickly as I could get away with, amid all the statues and vases and whatnot that lined the walls. Coming at last to the room I'd given to the two women, I knocked.

Nothing. I waited and waited, and no one answered.

I knocked again, and got the same result.

I tried the knob and the door opened. The room was in good order, but it was entirely empty.

Walking back out into the hallway, I ran my hands through my hair and looked around. Perhaps they were at dinner, I thought. That would mean the others were aware of their presence but, given how long they'd been left here alone, I could hardly blame them if they'd revealed themselves eventually.

I hurried down the main stairs, rounded a couple of corners and entered the main hall. And nearly ran into Jerome coming the other way.

He looked at me and his eyes widened. "Well! There you are, at last."

I stepped back and regarded him: Tall, bald, and almost— but not quite—as imposing as my father had been.

"It's good to learn everyone's been so concerned for my welfare," I said. "Something came up. It kept me busy longer than I expected."

He looked me up and down, seemed to evaluate me, and nodded. "I see. Any progress with your investigation?"

"I believe so," I told him, watching him closely. I made the decision on the spot to do the same with him I'd done with Aurelia—to throw out a few tidbits and see if I got any bites.

"Oh?" he asked, looking surprised. "Such as?"

"I believe I know who was responsible, at least indirectly," I said.

Now he looked even more surprised. "Let us bring them to justice, then," he said. "Do you require a detachment of troops, or—?"

"The process of apprehending the guilty parties likely will prove a bit more complicated than that," I replied. "And I have yet to identify all of them."

Jerome frowned at this. "It sounds as if you're describing a conspiracy, not just a single assassin," he said.

"There was a single assassin," I replied. "His name was Corindar Jeras. He was my father's friend and religious counselor. Dad trusted him. But Jeras worked with certain individuals who apparently had a hold over him greater than his bond of friendship with Dad. They ordered the murder." I gazed back at him, studying his every tiny reaction. "I now know who most of them are—but not all. Not quite all."

He nodded slowly. I could see no guile, no deception. Either he was very, very skillful or he was entirely innocent. I didn't remember Jerome as particularly skillful at anything.

"Very well," he said. "Anything else you need to conclude your investigation, or to bring the guilty parties in, just let me know. All right?"

I nodded. "I will." I paused. "Say—what are you doing here? Shouldn't you be with the fleet, and with Alexius?"

"Normally I would be," he said, "but Aurelia has been off negotiating with the leaders on Tolkar and we were to meet here to discuss what she accomplished. But I haven't seen her yet. She's late."

"I just saw her," I told him. "She woke me up."

"She's here?"

"She was a short time ago. Down by the kitchens."

He blinked. "You slept by the kitchens?"

I laughed. "I was pretty tired."

"You must have been."

"That old sofa there is pretty comfortable."

He smiled. "Oh," he said then, "before I go looking for my dear sister." He gestured behind him, toward the dining room. "I have a couple of your friends here."

"What?" I started to ask—but then I saw what he meant.

Seated at two spots along the big dining hall table were the two dark-haired women I'd left behind when I'd ridden Comet off into the night, now four days past—the two priestesses from the Church on Sarmata. Sister Halaini and... I still couldn't recall the name of the other one. Neither now wore the brown robes of a corinda; they were both dressed in the relatively comfortable daily-use blue uniforms of our family's personal guard. Each had her hair tied back in a ponytail and each now gazed up at me with what looked to be a combination of surprise and anger, from what I could tell.

"They came to me two days ago," Jerome was saying as I strode around the big table toward them.

"You never came back," Halaini said as I approached. She was clearly not happy at all. "We were stuck in that room for two days."

"And then we decided to forget you and your secrecy and take matters into our own hands," the Sister Superior interjected. "Fortunately Jerome here was present and was good enough to see to us."

"Something I am very grateful for," I replied, giving Jerome a solemn nod. He smiled affably back at me. As I said before, taken individually, my two younger uncles are not so bad.

"Two days," Halaini repeated, glaring at me, clearly wanting explanations I was not really in a position to offer.

"I apologize," I told them both instead of attempting to explain. "But I assure you it was unavoidable." I offered them as sincere a smile as I could conjure. "And it's safe to say that the events that detained me also shed a good deal more light on exactly what has been happening on both our worlds."

The two looked at one another, then back at me.

"And what exactly—" the Sister Superior began.

Then all hell broke loose.

They came out of the dark recesses of the room. They moved fast, darting from cover to cover. I saw them immediately and yet my brain didn't—or couldn't—process exactly what I was seeing for a full two seconds. By then it was almost too late to react.

They wore black robes and they carried long knives and they slid across the room like shadows crossing the lawn in late afternoon. Their lower faces were masked with black as well and only their eyes were visible. The blades flashed out and up and they were upon us, and it took all my years of military training to deflect and dodge the two who came for me.

I spun aside and came up in a crouch, taking in the broad scene in a flash. Jerome had his blast pistol out and was giving ground as three of the shadows stalked him. His other hand clasped at something at his belt; I trusted it was a signal that would call the house guards. I certainly hoped it was, and that they were paying attention this fine evening. On the other side from me, another attacker had leapt onto the table and was menacing the women.

"Stop," shouted Sister Halaini, as she stood and raised both hands before her, facing our attackers. "What is the matter with you? These are not our enemies!"

One of the figures in black backhanded her and she went down with a cry.

Jerome was firing now; I decided he had his situation in hand and so I dove for the guy on the table.

The Sister Superior was already up and out of her seat before I could get to the table. She spun to her left and her right foot lashed out, the toe pointed sharply. She caught her assailant in the throat and sent him hard to the floor, choking.

I was impressed. I gave her a nod before turning back, just in time to be tackled by two more of the attackers in black. They drove me to the ground and I felt a blade bite into my upper leg. Not deep, I guessed, due to the exotic material the pants I was wearing were made from. But bad enough. All I could see as I went down, before the spinning stars supplanted my actual vision, was Jerome being swarmed over by a horde of them. He was still firing as he vanished from sight, and at least two of the guys in black lay dead or severely wounded on the floor before him.

I couldn't feel the real pain yet from the knife that had stabbed me but I knew it was only a matter of time—probably very little time. And even less time before one of the two guys that currently lay on top of me found a more vulnerable spot and got in a killing blow. If not for the golden armor I'd put on a short time earlier, I was sure I'd be dead already.

I squirmed beneath them and fought to gain any small bit of leverage. With all my might I kicked up with both feet, pushing, shoving at one of them while with my arms I fought to fend off the other one's dagger.

I managed to kick the first one away but the other was in my face now, holding me down, pinning me. His fierce, burning eyes hovered but a few inches above mine and the tip of his blade came down slowly, slowly as I fought to push it away; it descended so slowly yet so quickly, and was mere millimeters from my chest. And then a dark boot kicked that masked face and he flipped backward and off of me.

I made it to my feet in time to see the Sister Superior taking down the attacker she'd just removed from me with a quick volley of deadly kicks. Impressive. I looked behind her and saw that the other corinda, Halaini, appeared to be okay. She was certainly not the fighter that her colleague was; but then, based on what I had seen in the past few seconds, few were. Then I looked the other way and saw that Jerome had vanished entirely beneath a scrum of black-clad assailants. I crossed the distance between us in a flash and grasped the robes of the figure nearest to me, jerking him back. As he looked around and into my face, I decked him with a right cross.

Now I could see the bottoms of Jerome's legs. They were still moving, still kicking. That, at least, was a good sign. I cursed when I realized I'd been in the armory earlier and hadn't been able to acquire a weapon, since they'd all been locked away. Now I had to deal with what looked to be half a dozen remaining bad guys and I had nothing but my fists with which to fight. Frantically I looked around, seeking anything that could be improvised into a weapon. Nothing of any real use presented itself.

But I had to do something. Jerome was still fighting, fending off at least four of the killers—the Sister Superior, I could see, was currently fighting the other two—while I stood useless. Cursing, I roared and grasped the next guy down on the pile atop Jerome, pulling him back and punching him hard in the face before he could react or defend himself.

Something changed then. I can only imagine it was that they felt Jerome was done for. The others began to rise from the pile and turned to face me. I could see my uncle then, lying there unmoving, either unconscious or dead. I wanted to feel badly for him but I didn't have the time, because the assassins now clearly wanted to put me in the same state. I glanced quickly behind me and saw that the Sister Superior was thoroughly engaged with the two still on their feet over there. This was all on me—live or die.

I raised my fists, ready to go down punching. The assassins in black charged.

And then a new shape emerged from the shadows, and a golden light appeared and swept out. I saw that light and I knew it instantly. It was the sword, radiant and gleaming, and Istari the Renegade, my traveling companion of late, wielded it.

And wield it he did, like a scythe, like he was the Grim Reaper and for my four assailants the time had come. The golden blade swung back and forth and the figures in black robes screamed and fell, and blood fountained as they did.

As I watched him I thought once again how peculiar that such a slender, frail-looking figure could carry and use such a heavy weapon. Yet Istari wielded the golden sword as easily as if it were nothing more than a small knife.

Mere seconds later, all the assassins were down, some in pieces. I turned from staring at their bodies to address Istari, but before I or anyone else could say a word, all of the felled killers erupted in flames.

A mere moment's shock and hesitation and then I leapt for Jerome's unmoving form and began dragging him away from the fire. The Sister Superior joined me quickly, helping to move him, while Istari merely looked on, frowning. The flames roared hot and fast over the bodies but for some reason didn't catch on the carpet or walls—something for which I was grateful.

The taller corinda was staring up at the wraithlike, alien Istari, her eyes wide, even as I began to check my uncle's vital signs. He was alive, though I could see he had sustained multiple stab wounds.

At that moment, and seconds too late to actually be of any use, help finally arrived. Six men and women in the royal blue uniforms of the house security guards charged around the corner from the stairs, pistols drawn. They came up short as they saw the situation. All the black-clad attackers were down, their bodies now almost entirely disintegrated. The fires were going out.

As the guards rushed over to Jerome's side and I stepped back from him, I started to demand what had taken them so long. Then I saw their condition and I bit my tongue. They were worse off even than we were. Their uniforms were disheveled, bloody in spots and cut in places almost to ribbons. Every one of them looked as if he or she had gone at least a dozen rounds in a top-ranked boxing match. I absorbed this information and I reeled; clearly we here in the dining hall hadn't been the only targets of these attackers. How many more of them, I wondered, had suddenly appeared in other areas of the palace? And how many of our guards were now down—wounded or worse?

I cast another quick glance at Jerome and saw that two of the guards were acting as medics now; they'd brought emergency response equipment with them in anticipation that one or more of us would be needing it. The near-frantic way they were working on him indicated to me that he was still alive—a fact that seemed nigh-miraculous, given what he'd suffered. Then I turned to our tall alien guest and fixed him with a look that, I hoped, carried with it all the anger I felt at the moment. "Who," I demanded, "were those guys?"

"Assassins of the Church," the Sister Superior answered before Istari could speak.

We both looked at her. She was bruised in places and still catching her breath, but she appeared to be intact. "You know them?" I asked, surprised.

"I know of their kind," she said.

Sister Halaini, who alone among us all had come through the crisis unscathed, stepped up next to her. "They are Purifiers," she said. "Secret warriors of the Holy Church. They arm themselves with the sacred daggers of the high sept, and nothing more. It is their tradition."

I looked at her and something in my mind pinged. "You called them 'we.'"

The two women looked at me. Halaini nodded.

"I did. They were part of our Church. I thought I could warn them that no legitimate targets of their wrath dwelled here—that their assignment must have been a mistake."

"Assignment?" I asked. Now the Sister Superior was looking at her, too.

"I assumed they were assigned by the Church to come here—to kill you all, and I wanted to stop them," Halaini explained, blushing now. "But they didn't listen to me."

I could see the bruise on her cheek where one of them had hit her and knocked her down.

"She meant well," the taller woman said. "But clearly these were not from the Church on our world. They were rogue elements, perhaps, or from your own planet, or—"

"I think there's less of a difference among the Churches of the various worlds than you might guess," I told them both. "I just wonder how they got in here." I looked around, then, "That ties into what I've been learning in my recent travels with my new friend here." I nodded toward Istari. He bowed.

They stared at him unabashedly. Meanwhile I leaned in and inquired as to Jerome's condition. I was informed that he had lost a lot of blood and was unconscious but stable.

I exhaled deeply and gritted my teeth.

Then I began to wonder where Aurelia had gotten off to. Jerome had said he was to meet her here, but instead of my aunt, he'd encountered an assassin squad armed with daggers. Interesting.

Quite a few members of the house's staff had come out now into the dining hall and were gathering about. Some were buzzing about Jerome's injuries—particularly his chief adjutant and intelligence advisor, a colonel by the name of Markos—but most were gawking at Istari. At least, I saw, he'd put the sword away. I turned to him and started to address him—I cannot tell you what I was going to say, though—when a shrill, nearly deafening alarm reverberated throughout the hall.

The guards that weren't directly involved in assisting my uncle stood and drew their pistols once more, instantly on guard. I looked about wildly, wondering what could possibly be happening now.

"That's the attack siren," the nearest guard told me, shouting over the sound of it.

"Okay, well—it's a little late," I shouted back. "Turn it off."

He spoke a few very loud words into the mic at his collar and a second later the wailing ceased. I shook my head, my ears still vibrating. I could see that he was listening to a report coming back from the other end of the line.

"What was that?" the Sister Superior asked, scowling.

I held up my hand to hold her off for a moment and turned back to the guard, whose name badge read LOHANDAR. He was nodding as he spoke into his mic and his face grew ashen.

"What?" I demanded.

"It wasn't about this—whatever it was—my lord," he reported, gesturing to the blackened spots on the floor where the assassins had burned. "It was the orbital sensor warning."

I blinked at this. "Orbital—?"

Another trooper, this one with eyes wide and nearly hyperventilating, rushed in and informed me, "The defense platforms in orbit have detected a ship passing through the Sarmata Gate and firing an array of missiles, my lord. They are hyper-velocity warheads, and—" He looked away for a moment, his hand to one ear, indicating he was receiving more information, probably from the same source as the first guard. His eyes were wide as he looked back at me. "They are quantum warheads," he said.

"Quantum—?" I frowned at this and looked past the man to where Jerome still lay on the floor, the two medics working on him. I really needed his expertise and guidance at the moment. Unfortunately, those things were unavailable because of his current condition. That also meant everyone would be looking to me to make the decisions. And I wasn't even entirely sure I understood what they were talking about.

"Quantum warheads," I repeated, frowning, not linking the sound of those words together. I stepped up to the first trooper and looked him directly in the eyes. "What exactly are we facing here?"

He looked about ready to jump out of his skin. He pulled himself together and managed, "Hyper-velocity quantum missiles are something your father has been working on for some time; long enough for our sensors to recognize the type of weapon when it encounters them."

"So what does that mean for us?" I asked, growing impatient.

"It means that, if they are targeted on this palace, or this city around us—" He paused, shook his head. "We are all dead."

"Can't our defense screens deflect them? Or the weapons platforms shoot them down?"

"No," he said, shaking his head slowly. "They're quantum-state and hyper-velocity. They can't be blocked or targeted by defensive systems."

"And there's a whole swarm of them inbound," the other guard added, swallowing with difficulty.

I started thinking about evacuation methods—ways to get out of the palace, out of the city, out of the general area before it was too late. We had spacecraft and aircraft and a few other high-speed vehicles down in the basement facilities...

"How much time do we have before they arrive?" That seemed the most pertinent question I could ask at the moment, so I asked it.

The second trooper was listening to something on his earpiece again. "Less than five minutes," he reported.

"Five minutes?" I felt the ground sliding out from under me. That was barely enough time to even get down to the hangar bays of the lower levels of the palace, much less fire up a vehicle or two and fly it anywhere. And how many people were currently in the palace? I looked around and could easily count a hundred, maybe more, now milling about in the dining hall and adjoining areas. I felt truly sick inside, because I knew they and I were all about to die and there wasn't a thing I could do about—

My eyes settled on Istari then. He was looking right back at me. And he was offering that same sly smile I'd seen so many times already on our travels.

Of course.

A glimmer of hope made its way through the gloom pervading my mind and brightened me. *The Paths*.

But—could he lead so many people through behind him? Could he open the way here, inside the palace? If not, did we have time to get everyone down and out onto the lawn or beyond? I had no idea how it all worked. But I didn't see that we had any other options.

These and more thoughts were running through my head when I heard a whispering voice. It took me a moment to recognize it as Istari's voice, because I was looking directly at him and his lips weren't moving. He was speaking to me telepathically, so that only I could hear.

"I believe," he was saying, "that it is time for the two of us to leave this place."

NINE

I nearly punched him.

"Time for the *two of us* to leave," he'd said.

With the clock ticking down and no other way to avoid the oncoming storm of destruction, my alien companion was suggesting that he and I simply run away.

That was *not* happening.

I wasn't about to abandon my family members and the house staff to that fate. Not if one potential avenue of escape remained.

"They're all coming with us," I told the alien who stood before me, and I jabbed him in the chest with my forefinger as I said it. "We're not leaving anybody behind."

For a second he looked as if he would object, but then he nodded ever so slightly in acquiescence. "Very well," he said, "but we must hurry." He raised the golden sword and pointed it at a shadowy alcove across from the stairs. "Have everyone pass through that doorway. But I must go first, to open the Path."

"Doorway?" I frowned. "There's no doorway over there—" And then I looked more closely and my eyes bugged.

An old, weathered door occupied the center space of the wall, almost hidden in the shadows. It looked nothing like any of the hundreds of other very elegant, carved doors that could be found throughout the palace.

I rubbed at my eyes, very certain that no door at all had stood there previously.

"Oh, it's been there for some time," Istari said, as if reading my mind—something I didn't consider outside the realm of possibility by any means. "But it was hidden. Hidden, you might say, in plain sight. By another of my associates. The one who has visited here and met with one of your family members on numerous occasions, I would imagine."

I didn't like the sound of that.

"Fortunately," he added, "I noticed it immediately."

I nodded. "Where does it lead?"

"Somewhere not about to be struck by quantum warheads," he replied.

I didn't like the sound of *that* either, but there was no time to discuss it now. "Fine. Go," I told him, pointing toward the newly visible door. "Lead them on. I'll bring up the rear and round up all the stragglers."

I ordered the guards to access the house PA system and call everyone there as quickly as they could possibly come, leaving anything and everything behind. Fortunately the earlier alarm already had drawn many of them out into the hallways or down to our location, so they didn't have as far to go. Within a matter of moments we had quite a crowd assembled there in the main hall.

Getting their attention, I told the palace staff and others present to follow my strange friend to safety, and not to worry about his rather outlandish appearance along the way. I gave them my assurance that all would be well.

I honestly had no idea if what I was telling them was true at all.

Istari opened the door and passed through. I couldn't see what lay beyond. The two medics carried Jerome's limp body through next. A line of people, four wide until they reached the doorway, piled through behind them. They all seemed confused. Why wouldn't they be? Why would they think that following a strange alien through an old doorway in the palace could possibly lead them to safety? I kept reassuring them to just trust us and go.

Within about ninety seconds most of them had passed through. Meanwhile I was racing about the areas immediately surrounding the dining hall, shouting for anyone else to come on and come on *now*. Another half-dozen responded—mostly older people looking confused and afraid—and I bustled them toward the doorway, where they caught up with the last few waiting to pass through. Then, concluding that I'd rousted out as many as reasonably possible, if not all, and in any case that I had lingered long enough, I sprinted for the doorway. The last clump of staff members was waiting to go through; probably a couple dozen men and women.

Aurelia, I thought then. Where had she gone? And—hadn't she mentioned Stephanie having been there, too? I had seen neither of them, and certainly Aurelia at least would've spoken up in the last few minutes if she'd been present. I hesitated for an instant, then ran over to a house communications panel on the wall to my right and activated the PA system.

"Aurelia," I shouted into the mic, and heard my voice booming out of speakers throughout the palace. "Stephanie. If you're still here, get to the dining hall now." I stood there waiting for a few seconds, but no one responded and no one came running.

I glanced back at the doorway and the last two or three staff members were passing through it. The last one, a woman of about fifty, looked at me and beckoned. "Lord Gaius," she called. "You must come!"

"I'll be right there," I told her. "Go on!"

Reluctantly she followed the other two through the black rectangle of the doorway.

I clicked the PA once again. "Aurelia! Stephanie!"

Nothing.

VAN ALLEN PLEXICO

A glance at the doorway chilled my blood: The opening and the door itself were fading away.

I cursed. All I could do was hope they were no longer in the palace. Even if they'd run outside onto the surrounding grounds, or jumped into a surface transport vehicle, they were about to be dead; that was scarcely enough distance away to avoid the effects of a quantum blast. If for some unknown reason they'd taken a spacecraft away from Victoria, they might survive.

My time was up. I ran for the doorway. It had almost vanished from sight when reached it. Passing through it was like walking through quicksand—like feeling hundreds of grasping hands trying to catch me, to hold me, to shove me back. I gritted my teeth and leaned forward and pushed my way into and through and out the other side—

I tumbled out onto a grassy surface.

"Lord Gaius," someone shouted, and hands reached down and helped me up.

The others were there. I'd made it through to where they'd gone—wherever that was. I looked up, taking in the sight.

The stables. We were, all of us, on the lawn near the stables. Just outside the palace.

I frowned. This was not what I had expected. I'd been thinking the doorway would lead us to some alternate dimension or pocket universe. Not just a short distance beyond the building.

"We are out of time," Istari said as I climbed to my feet and saw him mounted on Sneak.

"Just what I was thinking," I replied, involuntarily gazing up at the sky as if I could make out the warheads bearing down on us. "So why are we standing here—"

"This way," he said, gesturing ahead. "The Path opens here. We go. *Now*."

I nodded, relieved. "By all means."

One of the guards held the reins of Comet and I took them, then climbed into the saddle. Istari had his horse moving forward across the grass at a slow trot and we followed.

"My lord," the guard who had handed Comet over to me said. His nametag read CEVELAR and I saw that his expression was frantic, almost wild. "This—what will this accomplish? Dying here instead of in the palace?"

"Trust me," I told him, offering a confident smile. I nodded toward the other horseman and added, "Trust *him*."

And that thought nearly made me sick, because I certainly didn't. But he was the only chance we had.

"Warhead impact in twenty seconds," one of the guards shouted.

Istari spurred his horse and I did likewise. The mass of people behind us hurried along in our wake, and the world around us began to change. The last I saw of the environment of Victoria was what looked like the sun rising and the sky turning red. Then that world was behind us and we were elsewhere in the cosmos.

Istari raised a hand and brought his horse to a halt. I reined in Comet and looked at him, waiting.

We had traveled over rolling hills with tall green grass and short yellow weeds, over a patch of desert with copper-colored sand, and along the shore of a lake that fairly radiated indigo. In all, our journey had taken a bit more than two hours, as we felt the passage of time, and the surprise and relief of the others had slowly given way to a growing sense of wonder at our strange surroundings. Now we stood on a flat, wind-swept plain with only a few sparse weeds growing here and there. The sun looked much larger and redder than usual, where it hung in the sky directly overhead.

I rode up next to Istari. "Is this the best place to stop?" I asked.

"We do not stop here," he said. "But it is the best place to make the transition to a higher plane."

I had no idea what that meant so I merely watched and waited as he climbed down from his horse and unsheathed the golden sword. Behind us, more than a hundred human beings in the livery of my family's house stood and watched as well. Most of them were still buzzing about the fact that they had somehow avoided death and destruction—that following the strange, pale alien on his black horse as he led us across a bizarre combination of landscapes had somehow resulted in their living through an attack of such magnitude. I could also hear a few of them commenting on the likelihood that the palace and a good portion of Victoria around it were now gone. I assumed they were correct, and that many more people had been vaporized in the areas beyond the palace. There had been nothing I or anyone else could have done—I had saved as many people as was possible for me to save. I did not wish to dwell on that. There would be time later. Time to find those responsible and see that they tasted swift and terrible justice.

For now, our mission was at last clear to me. The family traitor could wait. Even the Verghasites could wait. At the moment, I wanted those ultimately responsible for all of this. And none of them were human.

I climbed down from Comet and stood a short distance away, watching, as Istari raised the golden sword, dropped himself into a fighting stance, and then brought the blade around in a broad, single cut.

The air—and the very fabric of the universe—parted before him, as it had done for me when I fought the gray giant. It split, opening a horizontal rift in reality, and continued to expand until it had formed an oval-shaped portal hovering there in midair, leading someplace else.

"Through here," he called out to the crowd behind us. "You will be safe enough in this place for now."

"We aren't taking them to Majondra?" I asked, surprised.

"There are no Paths that lead directly there," he replied. "It would be a much longer journey, and time is of the essence now." He hesitated, then, "Also, given that your world's enemies have just done what they did to your moon, would you rule out their doing the same to your homeworld?"

I blanched at this. For some reason the attack on the palace and Victoria itself had struck me as a one-off, though now that I considered it directly I couldn't imagine why. It might very well be the case that the Church, acting through the Verghasites and surely the instigators of the attack, would next assault Majondra itself. If they hadn't already.

"Fine," I said, growing more agitated by the moment. "I agree that time is of the essence. Because this entire thing has gotten ratcheted up too many levels now. Too many have died. It has to end. Now."

Istari nodded. "And there is only one way to effectively end it."

"The Immortals," I said. "We have to confront this Cabal of yours directly."

He nodded again. "Five remain now. One more former Hand of the Machine—Hadog—and four of my kind. Understand, though: they are the strongest, the most treacherous, the most dangerous of all."

"I never doubted it."

His wry little smile returned. "One way or another, my human friend, it should make for a rousing tale when it is done." He paused, then, "If anyone remains alive to tell it."

I was in no mood to laugh. I moved away from him and gathered up twenty of the best troops that had come through the doorway with us. That seemed adequate. The rest I directed to pass through the portal Istari had just created with the sword. On the other side lay a virtual paradise: waterfalls, fruit trees, grassy slopes, and a beach with gentle waves rolling in. The sun was yellow and not too hot, and I could hear the call of birds from somewhere in the distance. I had to fight the desire to remain there myself. Alas, there was work to be done.

I borrowed a blast pistol from one of the guards that was going through with the others and for the first time in too long I felt that I could adequately defend myself in a fight. Holstering it, I turned back to Istari. Twenty men and women who had little left to lose stood at my back.

"Where do we begin?" I asked him.

He smiled again, and this time it took the form of a predatory leer. It gave me the creeps.

"Most of them are likely gathered in the Great Nexus," he said. He pursed his lips, thinking. "But not, generally, Orondi. Let us begin with him. Remove him from the board; carve him from the bone, so to speak. So that when we assault their main gathering, there can be no surprises from other quarters."

I didn't ask about that new term he'd casually thrown out: "Great Nexus." I figured I'd find out soon enough—and before it mattered that I knew. I simply nodded. "Fine."

He turned and leapt into the saddle.

"There may be other advantages, as well, in beginning with that one," he added.

"Such as?"

"Orondi is the Oracle." He chuckled. "Perhaps he can share with us the outcome of this endeavor." He laughed again. "Before we hurl his broken body into the Abyss."

I didn't reply to that. In earlier days—or hours—I might have objected to such talk. Not now. At the moment, hurling bodies into some metaphorical or metaphysical abyss sounded perfectly fine to me.

We rode.

In retrospect, I probably should have guessed that someone called "the Oracle" would be expecting us.

Fortunately, Istari took that into account. Either that, or he got extremely lucky. Or both.

Orondi was certainly prepared. As we burst through the portal Istari had carved for us, rending the dimensional walls and storming into his dome of a base, the frail Immortal gazed down solemnly from his broad, throne-like seat atop a raised dais of concentric rings and barked orders to the dozens of heavily-armed warriors that surrounded him.

They were human, or at least looked that way from a distance, but upon closer inspection they scarcely resembled any humans I was familiar with. Savage, they were—yet quite competent at wielding the advanced-design energy weapons with which they were armed. It was as if this Orondi had dipped into the ancient past and recruited a tribe of Neanderthals to serve him. They charged at us, firing madly, and several of my troopers went down immediately.

I cursed. In addition to the mere thought of losing more good men and women to these arrogant bastards, the Cabal, I hated seeing our ranks cut down so soon, with four more "Immortals" still at large. I was sure we'd need every fighter at our disposal before the job was done.

Istari didn't waste any time, though. The golden sword held high, he shouted something in a language I didn't understand and then he charged directly into the mass of Orondi's protectors. The sword sang its deadly song and the Oracle's savage guardsmen fell before him.

Gun in hand, I followed him in and blasted away, and the rest of our band came behind us.

We fought on two sides of a circular pool that occupied the center of the chamber, directly in front of the Oracle's dais and at the foot of the stairs that led up to its top. Istari and I and some of our men fought our way around it on the left side, while others of our number curved around to the right. We converged again at the base of the steps once the enemy had been beaten back and laid low. As we passed by the pool, I couldn't help but look down at it and my stomach turned upside down, my equilibrium for a moment lost.

What upon first glance had seemed to me a basin of water now revealed itself as a window unto the greater universe. Stars and constellations sparkled across a black velvet background, glowing nebulae of purple and red and blue streaking diagonally from left to right. It took my breath away and it very nearly got me killed.

As I gawked, one of the enemy warriors screamed a bloodthirsty cry and lunged for me. He probably would've had me, as well, but Istari saw what was happening, swung the long blade around behind himself, and took the savage's head off.

I exhaled and realized once again that I was in the alien's debt. I didn't feel any better about that now than I had before, because I still did not trust him and still suspected his motives. There comes a time after someone has repeatedly saved your life, though, that you have to give them at least a tiny break.

We fought on.

I will not bore you with the grim details. We battled and we battled and no small number of our own ranks were killed or wounded. Of the enemy, though, we left none alive save the Immortal himself, the one called Orondi.

Istari bounded up the steps, extended his right arm and directed the sword at him. Its gleaming tip almost touched the alien's scrawny neck. Frail Orondi was indeed; frail and small and quite ancient. Obviously he was of the same race as Istari—the *Dyonari*, I believe he called his kind—but he appeared older, smaller, and very frail. He hadn't risen from the big vertical bowl of a seat he occupied, and as we drew near I began to wonder if he even could. Then I saw the multitude of tubes and wires that led from the sides of the clamshell seat to his body, where they plugged into sockets set into his flesh. Here was one so aged in appearance that I could imagine him having lived for centuries, for millennia before. But "Immortal" implied he'd go on living, and nothing about his appearance now suggested he'd be around for another week, much less another millennium.

"So," the elderly alien croaked, ignoring the blade that hovered in the air before him. "You have come, as I knew you would."

"If you knew we would defeat your guards," Istari hissed, "why did you bother sending them against us? Or recruit them at all, for that matter?"

Orondi laughed; a painful-sounding, wheezing laugh. "I still believe in the mission of our Cabal," he managed once his breathing had returned to normal. "I want them to succeed, even if I won't be there with them at the end."

"What does that have to do with—?"

"Your ranks needed thinning," he continued. "My role, as I foresaw it, was to remove as many of your pawns from the board as possible, before I met my own fate. That I have now done."

Istari and I both glared at him.

"You have always carried with you an overinflated sense of your own importance, and of the significance of your visions," Istari growled. "Seeing the future is not interpreting the future. Glimpsing isolated moments as you do is not comprehending the full course of time and destiny. Context is everything."

Orondi leaned forward such that the point of the sword was now actually jabbing him in the neck. A thin trickle of blood ran down from the puncture. "Spare me your lectures, Renegade," he said, spittle flying from his wrinkled mouth. "Do what you have come to do and begone." He sneered. "Your own reckoning draws near as well."

Istari glanced at me; I exhibited no reaction. This, as far as I was concerned, was all his show.

"What do you see of me in times to come?" he asked the one whose title was Oracle.

"What do you care? You don't believe it."

"Call it an academic interest."

The old Immortal glared back at him for several seconds, then brushed with his clawed hands at the sword blade. "Then let me up from here and I will show you," he said.

Istari moved the blade away but kept it ready. He backed up a step and I did as well.

Orondi rose from his seat and slowly and carefully made his way down the steps until he stood before that circular pool. The tubes and wires pulled loose from him as he moved, spilling oily-looking fluids across the dais, but he ignored them. We followed him, while our troops all trained their weapons on him, in case he tried anything.

A comet, blazing bright orange, was burning its way across the face of the basin as we looked down at it. The stars behind it had faded somewhat, washed out by the magnificent manifestation.

"Look into the Well of Eternity," Orondi intoned, "and witness your fate."

Was it some sort of trap? I couldn't imagine so. In a way, however, I sort of hoped it was. Because if he actually could show us our own futures, and what we saw revealed there turned out to be horrifically negative... I shook my head. I didn't want to think about it. Call me an optimist, but I'd always believed that seeing the future would reveal to me the best possible outcome for my life and my work. I doubt that I'm alone in thinking that. Being able to show someone a dismal, depressing future—whether true or not—would therefore be a powerful weapon in this being's hands. It could potentially undermine one's entire self-confidence and belief system. The more I thought about these things, the less I wanted to look into the Well.

Istari seemed to have no such compunctions. He leaned over the edge, gazing into the cosmic waters.

Orondi sneered as he watched Istari looking into the Well. Then he turned to me and instantly he frowned.

"Who are you?" he asked, his bravado melting away. "How did you come to be here?"

This puzzled me; I'd gotten the impression he had seen me, and had been addressing me, since we'd entered. But now it was as if he were encountering me for the first time. I started to ask what he was talking about when his clawlike hand darted out and grasped my own.

"Hey—" I began.

He gasped, released me and staggered back a step. His bloodshot eyes stared back into my own. His mouth opened as if to speak but no sound came forth save a series of short gasps. Then he stared down at the floor, mumbling something unintelligible.

Istari had been staring into the Well during the entirety of this exchange and caught none of it. Now he looked up, grunted, nodded to himself, and looked away for a moment. Then he turned to me.

"Are you satisfied?" he asked.

I hadn't looked into the Well. I had pretty much decided not to, anyway, and then I'd been distracted by the Oracle's reaction to me. I thought about it one more time, looked back at him, and nodded. "Yeah. I've seen all I want to see here."

Istari nodded back, then turned to Orondi. He smiled. "It would appear your usefulness has reached its ending."

"Wait," I interjected. I faced the Oracle and asked, "What was that all about? What made you react that way to me?"

"I...what?" The Oracle had still been contemplating the floor. Now he looked up at me, and again it seemed as if he were noticing me for the first time. This time, though, he exhibited no sudden reactions. He merely peered back at me dully.

Istari gave me an odd look; he'd missed it all and had no idea what I was talking about or what was happening.

Orondi blinked, shook his head, and replied, "...Nothing. It was nothing."

I gave him another second or two to acknowledge and explain, but he merely frowned and looked off to the side, as if utterly confused by it all.

Istari gave me a quick look. I shrugged, not certain what was happening or what to say. Istari took this, however, as an indication from me that I didn't care what became of the old guy. He nodded back.

Then he ran the elderly Immortal through with a lightning strike of the blade.

I recoiled, surprised.

Before I could say anything, Istari had kicked Orondi off the impaling weapon and allowed the Oracle's dying body to stumble backwards. Gasping, he staggered back until his lower legs met the rim of the Well. He tripped, head over heels, and tumbled into it. There was no splash, no impact of any sort. He merely fell, and fell, and fell, and eventually he was lost to view.

Istari leaned down and gazed into the Well. "He claimed Eternity," the alien said. "Now he belongs to it."

I looked up from the dark depths of the void to the darker depths of my companion's eyes. They were now cold and hard.

"Why did you—?"

"I told you I would hurl him into the abyss," he said, his voice flat. "And I did."

I started to respond but couldn't decide what to say. I exhaled slowly and nodded, and together we walked around the Well of Eternity and helped our wounded troopers to their feet. Then we made ready for the next phase of the operation.

How had it come to this? I had never considered myself a proper soldier, a warrior of any sort. Unlike my uncles—and perhaps even my father himself—I had never dreamed of the glory of battle.

No. What I was doing was not out of love of combat and desire for victory over my foes. It was something much less glamorous, less exciting, less thrilling.

It was simply *duty*.

That was it. That was what I clung to, for the longest time. I was merely doing my duty. Duty to my father, to my family and to my homeworld. Nothing beyond that.

At the time I refused to even entertain the idea that some part of me, deep inside, had been awakened by it; that I might actually be enjoying it.

Later I would want to blame Istari for that change within myself. But I know now that he was not at fault—at least not in that way. No, there had been in me since birth, I believe, a potential for violence, for battle, that had lain dormant, like dry kindling awaiting a fateful spark. Istari, Prometheus-like in so many ways, provided that spark. But he was not the fire. The fire was within me all that time, awaiting its opportunity to blossom.

As for Istari?

"Four down," he stated flatly, wiping the blade of the golden sword on the outfit of one of the Oracle's fallen savages. "Four to go."

I didn't like Istari. I found him entirely too enigmatic and not at all trustworthy. I certainly didn't condone all of his actions.

But I couldn't argue with his math.

TEN

We rode along the Paths between the worlds and the surviving dozen of my soldiers, shocked and staggering but resolute, followed along.

Istari had told me that the remaining four of the Cabal were likely to be all gathered in one place now—the so-called Great Nexus—and that we should strike them immediately and hard, before they had further time to prepare for our coming.

"What did you see in the Well?" I asked him as Comet and Sneak carried us at a trot.

"Nothing of any importance," he replied offhandedly.

"So Orondi lied, then? His Well didn't show you your fate?"

"No," he said. "It did."

I looked at him, taken aback. "And?"

"He could show me nothing I did not already know," the alien answered. "My fate is sealed; I have known this from the beginning. Nothing he or I or anyone else could do can change that. I am the closed loop, the Alpha and the Omega. My destiny is my own—it does not answer to one such as him."

I tried to comprehend what he had said but most of it eluded me. The gist of it, though, seemed to me to be, *He didn't show me anything that surprised me.*

And hearing that, I looked back at my companion of these last couple of days and I realized with a start that I could tell he was lying. I'd gotten to know him well enough as we'd charged from crisis to crisis that I could see the signs of his deception. I wanted to press him on it, but decided not to. Not yet. We still had major work to do—and very powerful beings to fight—and I wanted nothing to interfere with that mission.

Even so, I was convinced that he had seen something in the Oracle's little pool that had taken him unawares.

We traveled on for a short while with each of us lost in our own thoughts. The tunnel of mists that comprised the usual transitional phases between the worlds had given way now, and we found ourselves on actual, non-metaphysical dry land. A slanted, rugged, rock-strewn piece of landscape, to be specific. The sunlight was a pale violet and the breeze was warmer than I would have liked and the air was filled with strange, birdlike creatures that circled far overhead and screeched and cawed. The horses had to pick their way carefully down the invisible path that Istari directed them along, and the soldiers behind us were slowed by the terrain as well.

I took the opportunity to raise a question that had puzzled me.

"Immortals," I said, and Istari glanced my way. "Why that name? The impression I've gotten so far is that none of you are particularly immortal."

He shrugged. "We have all lived a very long time," he said, "but your point is a fair one. We have found ways to prolong our lifetimes by drawing upon the cosmic energies of the Above that we have been able to access for many centuries. But each of us yet faces a finite span followed by inevitable decline and death." He smiled that evil smile at me. "Our plan, however, included overcoming that limitation."

"Overcoming?" I repeated, raising one eyebrow, the skepticism evident in my voice. "Overcoming death? Entirely?"

"Indeed," he said. "We had a plan—the other four still do, I'm sure—for attaining true immortality."

I couldn't quite believe this but I went along for argument's sake. "If that's so," I said, "then why would you turn against them—and against your chance for immortality?"

He chuckled. "You haven't been paying attention," he intoned. "I told you—my fate is sealed. Nothing those four wretched creatures do can alter it in any way."

I nodded slowly. I had no intention of debating that topic. My thoughts turned instead to the more practical question: "So how do they think they can achieve immortality?" I wasn't really expecting him to answer. To my surprise, he did. Or, at least, he attempted to.

"That is actually something you need to know now, before we arrive," he said. "For it bears directly on what will happen once we begin—"

I never got to hear the rest of that sentence, because that was when the bomb detonated in our midst.

The brass band was winding down its medley of greatest hits inside my brain as I came back to wakefulness and looked around. Instantly my mind rebelled at what it was seeing, for it simply couldn't be.

I sat in a hard metal seat centered at one end of a chamber twice as long as it was wide. The ceiling curved far overhead, descending on either side to straight, fluted walls of stone and metal, all gray and white. Enormous columns of stone spiraled with silver and gold braced those walls in rows along both sides. Seated stadium-style on each side were hundreds of gray giants; giants of the same race as the two I had encountered—and helped to kill—earlier. They were all dressed in long, loose robes of black with gold metal trim, and they eyed me with what appeared to be unmitigated hostility.

This, you might understand, concerned me greatly.

At the far end of the room, a bright ball of shimmering light hovered in midair above a gray circular pedestal. The ball oscillated from red to orange to yellow to green to blue to violet to red again. I had the strangest sensation—I know not why—that it was a great eye, scrutinizing me in the finest detail. It gave me chills.

Directly ahead of me, at the center point of the room, stood another of the giants—but this one wore a skintight suit of metallic red and blue that covered all but his face and hands. Traces of gold wound here and there along his torso and arms and legs in a manner similar to the detail on the columns.

As I took all of this in and began to formulate the most obvious questions within my mind, the figure in red and blue took two steps toward me, frowned, then turned back to the assembly and to the hovering ball of light and cried out—in a language I could actually understand—the words, "He is awake!"

A general murmuring from the audience. A flaring of bright orange from the light.

The figure in red and blue strode toward me in a deliberative manner, his head down and his hands clasped behind his back.

"What is this?" I demanded, rising to my feet. "Where am I?"

The giant halted in mid step, now three-quarters of the way toward me, and raised his head up high, eyes wide, as if thoroughly shocked by my question. Then he slowly turned, meeting the gaze of most of the others assembled on either side, before completing his turn by facing me once more.

"He wants to know where he is," the deep voice intoned, a hint of laughter about the edges. He paused for effect, then, "Better that he ask *who* he is!"

General laughter from the galleries. It died out quickly.

"I know who I am," I called back. I leaned out against the waist-high railing that circled in front of my chair, placing my hands against it for support. At that moment I noticed two things. One was that I no longer wore the golden armor I'd donned earlier; they had been replaced by a simple shirt and pants of some rough, gray, natural fabric. The other thing I realized was that my hands were shackled by heavy metal cuffs and chains. How I hadn't noticed that until this moment baffled me.

"He thinks he knows who he is," the figure before me called out, ridicule in his tone. "But I seriously doubt that he actually does." He faced me again and met my eyes. His burned with an almost manic intensity. "Who are you, then? Tell the court who you believe yourself to be—that we may disabuse you of that notion."

"I am Gaius Baranak, son of Constantine and lord of—"

"No," the giant boomed out, cutting me off. "You are none of those things. Not any longer, if ever." He strode closer. "You forfeited the right to be any of those things when you transgressed the law. Now you are one thing and one thing only," he declared. "You are the accused. The defendant in this trial."

"Trial?" I realized then what I had found myself in the middle of. A trial, indeed—with this giant who stood before me as the prosecutor, obviously. I looked around with a newfound understanding and decided that the audience must be the jury. That begged the question, though—who or what was the judge?

"Trial," the prosecutor repeated. "That is correct. You are the defendant here. You are accused of heinous crimes against the galaxy. And you will be tried and found guilty."

"That's already been determined, has it?" I asked, still trying to gain my mental footing.

"It is a verdict that I am quite certain the judge will reach," he replied.

The judge. So. There was a judge—somewhere—and he or she would decide my verdict rather than any jury.

"Where is this judge?" I asked.

The prosecutor looked back at me, seemingly dumbfounded, for more than a couple of seconds. Then he laughed. "You mean you do not recognize the presence of the Machine?"

"The what?"

I looked around, trying to figure out what he meant and what or to whom he might have been referring. I saw no one else present save the gathering of gray giants.

"The Machine! The great bringer of law and order to this galaxy. He whom we all serve."

I shrugged and shook my head, perplexed.

"I don't serve any machine," I tried to point out. But no one there was listening.

The prosecutor turned so that his left side was to me and his right faced back down the chamber. He raised his right arm and directed it, palm open, toward the hovering ball of shimmering light.

"The Machine!"

I frowned. The light? The thing I'd taken as their mood lighting for the room? *That* was this Machine he was speaking of? That was my judge—the decider of my fate?

Then something Istari had said earlier came back to me. He'd said a great artificial intelligence—a Machine—had once ruled over the galaxy, but it had been overthrown. In part, I seemed to recall him saying, by the actions of his Cabal of Immortals. And what was more, I remembered with a start, the agents of that Machine were the same species of gray giants I saw before me now.

So—had I gone back in time? Or had the Machine been restored somehow, along with its servants? Was it now "alive" and well and doing its thing again—and deciding to begin its new campaign of galactic domination by removing me from the board?

Why me? What was I to it? What threat to it or to anyone else could I possibly represent?

The prosecutor was addressing me again and with effort I managed to direct my attention away from my churning thoughts and back to him. He was saying something about the charges that I faced.

"I'm sorry," I said, "but I was... too overwhelmed with the grandeur of this court to hear the charges. Would you mind repeating them?"

He appeared annoyed but he straightened and read them off again: "You, the accused, are hereby charged before this gathering of the Hands and before the Machine himself with the following crimes. One, that you did trespass within the bounds of the Above. Two, that you did aid and abet your accomplices, the so-called Immortals, in their efforts to aggrandize themselves while destroying the galaxy. Three—"

"Destroying the galaxy?" I interrupted. This had taken me aback. "Who is destroying the galaxy?"

The prosecutor regarded me with a dubious expression for a moment, then spread his hands. "It is entirely plausible that you, a mere human and doubtlessly a thrall to their sinister will, do not know the full extent of their schemes," he said. "Perhaps you are not aware that this Cabal has detected an oncoming wave of ultra-destructive energy traveling toward our galaxy from some point in the distant future. Perhaps you do not realize that their intentions are not to deflect it away but to encourage its arrival in the mortal realm of spacetime, where they plan to harness much of it to their own ambitions—while allowing the rest of it to crash into the stars and planets themselves. They would wreck the galaxy in order to magnify their own petty powers." He shook his great gray head. "It is all utterly shameful."

I was reeling at this information. If true, it meant that my mission with Istari was even more critical—far, *far* more critical—than I had known.

"This is all news to me," I said. "But—wait—you said I have been aiding and abetting the Cabal?" I laughed at this. "You have that exactly backwards."

"Oh do we now?" the prosecutor snapped, putting on an exaggerated performance of recoiling in shock at my words. "So you deny assisting that member of the Cabal of Immortals called Istari?"

I blinked. "Well of course I've helped Istari," I began.

"You see?" he cried, turning back toward the ball of light, which was reddening as he spoke. "He doesn't deny it! He helps the worst of them all. He is no victim, no hostage of the criminal Istari. He is a willing accomplice!"

"But Istari and I have been working *against*—"

"Silence! By your own words are you incriminated." He turned back to the light. "The prosecution moves for immediate judgment and sentencing."

"Wait," I shouted. "Don't I get to make my case? Doesn't the defense get a turn? What sort of unfair, illegitimate court are you running here?"

The prosecutor stalked the remaining length of the hall and stopped only inches away from me. He towered over me and bent down such that his blunt gray face was directly before mine. It was unnerving; in the previous instances in which I had been anything like that close to one of his kind, they had been trying with all their considerable might to kill me.

"Disrespectful words directed toward this court will only make your punishment come more swiftly and in a more painful fashion," he barked.

"This is no court," I replied, anger filling my voice. "A court is a place where both sides in a dispute are allowed to make their case and then an impartial judge and jury decide based on the facts presented. This is merely a *performance*, based on some imagined slight I've caused that has no basis in reality."

The prosecutor made to interrupt me again but I continued, overriding him.

"Is the Machine nothing but a petty tyrant, condemning all who dare speak the truth?"

"Certainly not," the prosecutor snapped.

"Does he fear to hear the truth from a lowly creature such as myself?"

"Never!" he barked, his expression defiant. But then he frowned suddenly and turned back toward the light, not quite as certain that he accurately spoke for his master as he had been seconds earlier.

"Are you so sure of that?" I asked.

The prosecutor's expression twisted with fury and he started to speak but then the Machine took an active role in the proceedings for the first time.

"*Let the human speak*," it intoned in deep, resonant waves of sound that swept down the length of the chamber like waves crashing on a beach. "*I would hear his account.*"

I smiled at this. Finally.

"O great Machine," I began, "I know not how I came to be here, but I know that any honest and fair being who defends the law and fights against chaos—as I understand that you do—will understand my recent actions and support them." I then sketched for him in very brief terms the series of events that began with my father's murder. I paid special attention to explaining the role Istari had played in helping me.

When I had finished, with my last words still ringing off the stone and metal walls and then fading, the courtroom fell silent. The ball of light floating at the far end of the chamber continued to pulse, but as I had spoken its color had oscillated from red through orange and now it radiated a bright yellow. The prosecutor eyed me now in a different manner than before, with less anger and more puzzlement. Then he shifted his gaze to that pulsing light. We all waited.

"Human, your story matches the evidence brought before me," the rumbling voice from the light said at last, *"and I detect sincerity and honesty in your voice and in your vital signs."*

The prosecutor scowled and looked as if he wanted to leap over the railing and strangle me before his master could say more.

"However," the voice went on, *"your admitted association with the outlaw Istari, whom you have labeled Renegade, and your participation in his schemes, incriminates you by association."*

"But—"

The prosecutor's expression changed instantly into one of relish and glee. "Sentence him, master!"

"I am willing," the Machine said after a pause, *"to suspend your sentence and grant you temporary release if you will continue in the mission you have already begun—if you will track down and destroy the remaining members of the Cabal."*

"Such was my intention before I was brought here," I replied, "but—what of Istari?"

"The one called Istari has already been found guilty by this court and will be executed."

"No," I called out. "No—I can't do the job without him. It would be impossible."

"He is a criminal, tried and convicted many times over in absentia by this court."

"He works against the Cabal now," I told them, "and without him I have no chance whatsoever of succeeding."

Even as I spoke passionately in my companion's defense, a tiny voice in the back of my head raised the question once again: Had I honestly come to trust Istari? Did I believe all—or any—of what he had said to me? If such great power awaited the Cabal in the form of this 'wave' approaching us, might he merely wish to destroy his old associates in order to have it all for himself? I had no answers to these questions.

But I knew I spoke the truth when I said that without him there was nothing I could do.

"*It is impossible,*" the voice of the Machine stated flatly.

I looked around the courtroom, thinking fast. "What about all these Hands?" I asked. "You have so many at your disposal. They are great warriors, yes? They once enforced justice across the entire galaxy. Send some of them with us. Just a few. Surely they would be enough to guarantee Istari's good behavior at least through the completion of the mission—and they could be of great assistance to us in bringing justice to the Cabal."

"*It is impossible,*" the Machine repeated.

"Why?" I was leaning against the railing, almost shouting now. "If justice is your aim—and if you wish this Cabal to be brought down—then surely dispatching a few of your Hands to assist—"

The prosecutor rushed up to me and the answer that came booming out at me came from both his own lips and the glowing sphere of light at precisely the same time. "*IT. IS. IMPOSSIBLE.*"

I staggered back from the sheer force of this rejection. It nearly bowled me over. Recovering quickly, I leaned out once more, addressing both the Machine and his assembly. "Then I question your claims to be the great keeper of the peace and enforcer of law and order. No—I don't question those claims. I *reject* them outright."

"How dare you?" the prosecutor bellowed. He stalked towards me, fists bunched. "How dare you make a mockery of this—"

"This is a mockery!" I shouted back at him. "If you refuse to help, you forfeit the moral authority to judge me or anyone else!" I was jabbing one finger at him and realized with a start that it was no longer impeded by the weight of the chains. The manacles were gone, as if they had never been, though their marks remained on my wrists. Placing my hands on the railing, I leapt over it and confronted the prosecutor directly. I drew back a fist, preparing to punch him.

"*STOP*," called the Machine and the prosecutor, again speaking as one. "Stop," the prosecutor said again, this time alone. He retreated from me, his expression morphing very rapidly now from righteous fury to surprise to what almost looked like fear. He dropped to one knee before me, his head in his hands, and moaned.

Utterly confused now, I looked around at the courtroom—and was dealt yet another shock.

The room itself was fading from view. The ranks of black-clad giants had already vanished and the pulsing light that represented the presence of the Machine had now dwindled to a tiny firefly speck. Then everything went away—everything except myself and the prosecutor.

Then he looked up at me and screamed, and I woke up.

I came awake suddenly and sat up. I occupied a cold gray slab of a table in a small, domelike structure. I wore the same golden armor I'd had on since we'd left the palace. The chains were still gone and there were now no marks on my arms whatsoever from them. Some sort of mechanical arms were positioned on either side of the space where my head had lain.

I looked around quickly and saw two more slabs. Tall figures lay on each, and both of them were moving, awakening. One I recognized as the prosecutor from the courtroom—something I now realized had been a sort of imposed dream; a virtual reality experience, played out entirely within my head. Instead of being big, muscular and powerful and wearing a gleaming red and blue metallic suit, though, he was thin—emaciated, almost—and wore the tattered remains of what once might have been such a uniform.

On the other slab lay Istari. He sat up and looked over at me, then at the prosecutor. Then he saw the golden sword where it rested against the wall nearby.

In a flash he was up, off the slab, and grasping the sword. He leapt over my table to the space between it and the giant, and the sword flashed out.

"Wait," I called to him, starting to understand a bit more. "Don't hurt him!"

The sword tip halted just millimeters before the neck of the prosecutor even as he sought to rise.

The emaciated giant halted his motions, looked wide-eyed at my alien companion and then at me.

"How—how did you—?"

"It was all in our heads, wasn't it?" I asked him. "It was all a trick."

"Not a trick, no," he said, blinking rapidly and shaking his big head. "It was merely all I have left."

Istari frowned at this and glanced at me. I held up a hand. "What do you mean?" I asked.

He sighed heavily. "I truly am a Hand of the Machine," he intoned. "Possibly the last one."

I glanced at Istari to gauge his reaction.

"I did not know even one remained," he said.

The giant nodded. "Only me, as far as I can tell. I am called Aucari."

"And the Machine?" I asked.

He shook his head. "I have heard nothing from the Machine in ages. I fear him destroyed forever. What you saw inside the simulation was my representation of what the Machine was like, during his glory days." He gestured around the inside of the dome, and I saw that it was unkempt, untidy, dirty. "But those days are long gone now." He shook his head tiredly and then gestured toward himself. "My equipment has kept me alive this long, but with no new bodies into which to download my personality and my knowledge, I have had to make do with this poor frail thing." He groaned. "My time is nearly done," he said, "and then the galaxy will be without the last of its defenders."

"Such a tragedy," Istari said, his voice dripping sarcasm.

I gave him a reproving look but he ignored it.

"These Hands have been nothing but tyrants for ages," Istari said. "I don't regret helping my former associates undermine them and their Machine."

The giant—Aucari—gave Istari a dirty look but said nothing. Gone was the bravado of the trial. He seemed utterly defeated now. Despite everything, I felt bad for the guy.

Istari must have sensed that, too. He stepped back, moving the sword tip away so that Aucari could move into a more comfortable seated position on the slab. Then he looked at me. "You did well," he said. "You continue to surprise me with the depths of your resourcefulness."

I snorted. "I thought you were dead, and that I was about to join you."

Then more of the memories from the trial came back to me and I looked at my companion sidelong. "Did he speak the truth?" I asked. "Are the Immortals truly attempting to harness some energy wave—and to destroy the galaxy in the process?"

He looked back at me, then away. He didn't answer.

"It is true," the giant murmured, his head down. "A god told me."

"A god?"

"Solonis," he said. "He visited me, not long ago." He looked up, met my eyes momentarily. "He's a god. A god who travels in time." At my expression of skepticism, he hunched over again, mumbling. "He wanted to warn me. To warn the Machine. He didn't realize the Machine was no longer active in this time." He made a sound that could have been a laugh or a sob, or both. "So I recreated the Machine, as best I could, within that simulation. Along with the legion of Hands." He made a choking sound. "I fear now it was all for nothing."

Solonis. That rang a bell. I thought about it a moment and it came to me: it was the name of one of the soldiers in the household guard—one we'd left behind with the others in the pocket universe, to keep them safe, after the evacuation from Victoria. I didn't know the man—not well—but he scarcely seemed to match the description Aucari had given.

"A god who travels in time," Istari repeated. He looked at me. "I think our friend here is too far gone for us to rely on anything he says."

I couldn't argue. The big gray being sat hunched over, not looking at either of us. He seemed somehow... *broken*. I ignored his nonsensical words and turned my attention to my companion.

"But is he telling the truth?" I asked.

Istari looked at me, pursed his lips, appeared to be considering a variety of responses, and then simply nodded. "Yes. I hadn't wanted to burden you with the additional weight of our mission, but there it is. That is why they must be stopped—beyond your simple quest for revenge or your desire to protect your Seven Worlds."

I looked at him still closer, and I went ahead and asked him the main thing that bothered me now, just to see what he would say. "And if we defeat them," I went on, "did you plan to try to deflect this wave, or to allow it to strike so you could take that power all for yourself?

Now he looked back at me and offered that same wry, evil smile. "You think I would turn down the opportunity to gain such power?" he asked.

I felt my pulse quicken. He still held the sword and my pistol lay at the far end of the slab I'd occupied. I knew I had no chance in a direct physical confrontation with him. The giant would be of little help; he seemed near death now.

But then he shook his head and laughed. "Oh, my dear Gaius," he said. "You continue to wrong me."

"What?"

"I have told you that my fate is sealed; that my destiny is a closed loop. Nothing you or I or anyone else does can change that." His smile was no longer the evil thing it had been moments earlier. "I will never have that power, much as a part of me wishes it could be so. That, my friend, is not the destiny that awaits me."

I took this in and tried to accept it. I needed him. I needed our alliance to endure, at least a bit longer. I wanted to trust him, though every part of me screamed that I should not. Blast it—I *liked* the guy. I didn't want him to be the villain of the piece in the end.

"I do wish you had looked into Orondi's Well when you had the chance," he added. "It would have made everything so much simpler." He paused as though considering those words, then, "In some ways, at least."

I waved this off. I was sick of metaphysics, tired of what *might* be and what was *destined* to be. I wanted to *act*.

"Where are my soldiers?" I asked him, suddenly realizing their absence. "And how did we all come to be here?"

Aucari explained that he had caught us unawares with a concussion bomb as we passed through an area he regularly patrolled. He had dragged our unconscious selves to his headquarters. My troops were held in an adjoining building, safe and sound, pending the outcome of the trial. We walked outside and waited while he freed and rearmed them. They were a bit disoriented and angry at first but I managed to settle and refocus them as quickly as possible.

"Let's get moving," I said when we'd all been reunited. "This little side excursion has cost us precious time—and now I know that a lot more rides on our actions than just the fate of the Seven Worlds of Man." I smiled at Istari. "You said it yourself— four down, four to go."

The giant explained that we were currently on a moon of a gas giant far out beyond human space—but in a place where the layers of reality were thin enough that Istari could easily find a Path and guide us almost anywhere. That pretty much went over my head but Istari seemed happy enough to hear it.

As we walked out of the dome and rejoined my confused but now relieved soldiers, Aucari nodded to us. "Go with the blessings of the Machine," he said, "and find victory."

"The Machine can go to hell," Istari said.

The mists gathered, and my companion led us into them once more. I told myself it was purely my imagination that they seemed tainted now with the lingering scent of brimstone.

ELEVEN

It was not in fact hell but a sort of alien heaven into which we stepped, as it turned out.

We fourteen—the twelve remaining soldiers from the palace on Victoria, plus Istari and myself—pressed on along the Paths, with my alien companion leading the way, the sword held out before him as if it were some sort of cosmic tracking device or divining rod that told him the direction to travel. Occasionally he would halt our procession, then step away from us and swing the blade back and forth a few times, powerfully, through the space before him. Once this was accomplished, he would lead us on again—and the terrain over which we passed would take on some new form, from rolling grassy hills to desert flats to craggy mountains. I assumed this meant he was cutting a new and unseen Path through the layers of reality among which we walked. But I was not entirely certain.

In truth, it mattered not whether any of us understood it. All that mattered was that we reached the proper destination at the end. And, as it turned out, we did.

We had been marching for some time up a steep incline, with the familiar waves of fog forming on either side and above us, swirling about. Forked lightning traced its way along the perimeter. Our world contracted, became nothing but the immediate view before and behind us. The ground was soft and damp and the smell of richly turned earth nearly overwhelmed us.

At last we leveled off from the climb and marched through grass that stood ankle deep. Within a very few steps the grass had lengthened to knee height and beyond, presenting us with a legitimate obstacle to further progress. We pressed on, Istari now using the sword like a traditional blade, hacking away at the now-man-high grass and carving us a way through.

Then the grass abruptly vanished and we found ourselves in a darkened forest. Branches of alien trees pressed in from all around. Istari was clearly growing tired from all the work he was having to do, cutting an actual, physical path as well as a metaphysical Path. But he would not allow anyone else to touch the sword—not even me.

Then, abruptly, he stopped, and the rest of us came up short behind him. He turned and motioned us back a few steps, then grasped the hilt of the golden weapon with both hands and swung it around hard, like an axe. Instead of the forest rending aside, the air itself seemed to split open and fall away, leaving behind a shimmering oval that hovered there, facing us, like a doorway into another world.

Which is precisely what it was.

Furiously he motioned the troops through as he stood off to one side. When I made to follow, he stuck out a hand and held me back. "Wait," he said.

"What? But—the men—?"

He held me back for one more second, then, "Now," he said, and together we leapt through the portal.

The soldiers were scattered about, guns out and ready, but no one fought them or shot at them. They looked to us as we appeared through the doorway in reality Istari had cut for us. For his part, he brandished the sword, ready to do battle with any comers. I had my own pistol in hand, but my attention was focused mostly on taking in the strange environment we had just entered.

"Where are they?" Istari demanded of anyone that might be listening. "Where could they have gone?"

Clearly he had expected someone to be waiting here when the soldiers emerged, and it dawned on me relatively quickly that he had expected some portion of them to be dead now, having secured for us a beachhead. Instead everyone was still alive, no gunplay had ensued, and the quarry he'd expected to catch by surprise was not where it was supposed to be.

This all passed through my mind in a mere instant, even as I was looking around and taking in our new and drastically different environment. We were inside an enormous hollow sphere, probably a couple hundred meters across, its curving walls all of gleaming silver metal. The dome of the ceiling loomed high above us and the bowl-like bottom was lost in darkness below. I could see these two directions because I and the others stood upon a ring that circled the equator of the spherical space. A walkway—the one we'd run out onto—led to it from an actual, physical doorway behind us. We had bypassed that doorway by coming here to this spot directly, via the Paths. The ring on which we stood, which seemed to my eyes to hover in space with no visible supports, formed a walkway that circled all the way around the perimeter, and was itself never wider that twenty meters.

Up through the center of the chamber came a bright pulse of coruscating crimson energy every ten or twelve seconds, floating up from the depths and blinding us all momentarily. Each time, it floated up to the ceiling of the sphere and then vanished like a soap bubble popping. I was sure it held some great cosmic portent but its meaning and purpose were entirely lost on me.

"They should be here," Istari was saying, his voice betraying his anxiety. "Where could—" He frowned, then, "Quickly," he shouted, motioning to the others. "This way. They must be this way. Hurry!"

We all raced around the ring in the direction he pointed, thankful that it took us around the perimeter and therefore kept us always well away from the center of the sphere and the occasional mass of energy that flared up through it. We reached the opposite side and saw ahead of us a large opening in the smooth, silver metal wall, identical to the one behind us. As we started towards it a lone figure strode out of it. He held a data slate and was gazing down at it and had not seen us yet. His features were wreathed in shadow.

We stopped in our tracks and our guns were out and at the ready. Istari had the golden sword up and prepared to swing.

The figure stepped out into the light and we could see his face.

I staggered. I nearly fell.

"Alexius?" I blurted, astonished to find my uncle there.

He wore his dress blue uniform with gold and red trim. His shaven head gleamed in the pale light. His expression portrayed at least as much surprise as I myself felt.

"Gaius?" he whispered, incredulous. Then, louder, "What is this? Why is our palace guard here?" He glanced at Istari and frowned even more deeply.

I looked from Alexius to Istari, very confused. I didn't know where we were, and therefore didn't truly know if it was a place Alexius should or should not have been found.

Istari laid this question to rest for me immediately. "We have identified the traitor in your ranks, Gaius," he said softly.

"What did he say?" Alexius demanded, stepping forward.

"Are you sure?" I asked, keeping my eyes on my uncle, feeling my stomach twist.

"This is the stronghold of the enemy," Istari answered. "And he is here."

Cursing, I started toward Alexius, my gun still up and ready.

"Gaius—what are you doing?" he asked, frowning and moving back a step.

"Don't move, Uncle," I warned him. "We are here on business of the most critically important sort and I'm afraid we will have to detain you for a short time, until—"

At that Alexius threw the data slate at me, spun about and started to run.

"Wait," I called after him, knocking the crude projectile away.

He was shouting words I couldn't understand at someone back down the way he had come.

None of the soldiers moved or took any sort of precipitous action. They all knew my uncle at least as well as they knew me. Most of them had served him for years. None of them had much more idea what was happening than I did. It wasn't as if they were going to strike him down in cold blood.

Istari didn't share that concern. He hurled the golden sword and it flew across the short open space and speared Alexius straight through the torso.

My uncle was bowled off his feet by the force of the blow and fell.

The troops were shocked, of course. They looked from Alexius to Istari, uncertain how to respond.

I was already running. I got to him before anyone else. He lay on his side, gasping, one end of the sword protruding from his front and the other end from his back.

I knelt.

"Alexius," I said in a pleading tone, "what is all of this? What were you doing?"

His eyes were unfocused; the words he spoke next were meant, I believe, more for himself than for me.

"So close," he gasped. "So close to ultimate power..."

And then he died.

Staggered, I fell back. I caught myself with my hands and looked up in time to see Istari lean down and draw out the sword. Its blade was red with blood—the blood of my own family.

Jerome lay there in a pool of that blood, lifeless.

"You knew there was a traitor," Istari said quietly. "Are you so surprised now that his identity has been revealed?"

I didn't answer. What could I say? Somehow I must have hoped it would all turn out to be a mistake.

Little did I know far bigger shocks had yet to be revealed to me.

"Come," Istari said, reaching down with his left hand. "We have work to do."

I allowed him to pull me back to my feet and together we passed through the doorway into what lay beyond.

Four gods awaited us.

We emerged into an even larger open space. Another dome towered far above us. I reflected that these people really liked domes. The floor was a pale white tile that stretched off into the distance. A dim light filled the room. At the far side, we could see banks of unearthly machinery. What seized our collective attention, though, were the four luminous figures that floated directly ahead of us.

Gods indeed.

They towered over us, each at least four meters tall even if their feet had been touching the floor. Three of them were of the same race as Istari, slender and gaunt, one of them female and the other two male. The fourth figure was of the now-familiar race of gray giants. The four gazed down at us with naked arrogance and contempt. Shimmering with light and energy, they appeared to be gigantic ghosts or holographic projections.

A moment later, they proved themselves to be quite solid indeed.

As Istari and I walked into the huge room, the soldiers fanned out behind us. One of them circled around, attempting to outflank the four cosmic beings. The gray giant saw him, swept out with a massive hand, and swatted the man; he flew head over heels across the chamber and when he came to rest at last he lay very still.

"Stay back," I called to the others.

"So," Istari called up to the four. "You've done it, then."

"The Renegade," boomed the voice of one of the three Dyonari figures. "You have returned, as we knew you would—but entirely too late. Our apotheosis is at hand."

Istari shook his head. "You do not fool me, Elendi. The wave has not fully reached our place and time yet."

"Its leading edge washes over this point in spacetime even now, Renegade," replied the one he had addressed. "Our power grows moment by moment."

Istari looked to one of the other Dyonari specters. "You have seen what will be, Farseer," he called. "Tell him, Yadrui. Tell him of the defeat you will shortly experience. Tell him that you and he and these other two are no gods, not yet—and never will be."

This one, Yadrui, scowled at Istari. "The future is a malleable thing, Renegade," he said. "I have seen conflicting signs and portents and—"

"I have looked into Orondi's Well," Istari shouted back. "I have seen—"

"Orondi is not infallible," Elendi boomed.

"Orondi is not anything now," Istari snorted. "I tossed him into the sea of fate. And he has drowned in it."

The four of them frowned down at us.

"We know you have slain the others, Renegade," the female specter stated, contempt dripping from her over-amplified voice. "Your crimes are almost unimaginable, and soon you will pay for them."

"You are quite correct," Istari said, nodding. "But you will all die first."

"We will never die," rumbled the gray giant. "We are now truly immortals in more than name. This galaxy will bow to our will for the rest of eternity."

"Such delusions," Istari said. "Perhaps godhood only magnifies one's false assumptions." He laughed. "And makes a mortal fool into a godlike fool. And mortal mistakes into truly divine ones."

The ghostly giant roared and lunged forward, sweeping out with his massive hand. Istari leapt out of the way just in time, but the giant was fast—faster than either of the ones we had encountered previously—and his other hand came around and struck Istari, sending him sprawling. The golden sword clattered away, coming to a stop behind the four apparitions.

My troops looked to me. I had no idea what to do or say. This had been Istari's play, and now he lay insensate on the cold stone floor. What chance did we thirteen mortals have against four alien gods?

"Gaius!"

That voice, calling to me from the far side of the chamber. I knew it.

"Aurelia?"

I ran, dodging the ghostly hands of two of the beings that reached for me. Their attention had remained focused on the one who had so enraged them, despite his being apparently unconscious, and they hadn't been paying the slightest attention to the rest of us. I made it past them and saw my eldest aunt standing there, just ahead. She wore an elegant black dress and her red curls were down, a cloud about her pale features.

"Aurelia?" I repeated. "What are you doing here?"

"She is one of us," boomed the voice of the first Dyonari god who had spoken—Elendi.

I looked at her, and I'm certain my expression was a combination of shock, horror, and regret.

"Your family has been of much assistance to us, human," the alien apparition went on. He had turned about and gazed down at the two of us now. "Yes—we know you, Gaius Baranak. Long have we known of you, and long have we worked in secret with members of your family."

"The Church," I breathed, looking back at Aurelia. "Of course. You have always been closer to the Church than any of us, and it—"

"It was entirely our creation and our instrument," Elendi stated, his voice overflowing with arrogance and contempt. "As was she."

I looked back at Aurelia and met her eyes, but what I saw there suddenly changed. Instead of glee or shame or anything else I might have expected to find in the expression of my family's second revealed traitor, I saw the dawning of a smile. A pure, untainted, and very encouraging smile.

Elendi's massive apparition hovered now between myself and my aunt. His back was to her as he gloated to me. But before he could speak again, Aurelia suddenly dashed over to the fallen sword and lifted it.

"I was never part of this, Gaius," she called to me as she ran with the sword toward the far wall of the dome. "They brought me into it through the Church, but I never accepted their offer of immortality in exchange for betraying my own." She reached the far wall, where the massive banks of machinery stood, even as her words registered with the four apparitions.

"What?" boomed Elendi. "What are you saying, woman?"

"I am what we humans call a double-agent," she declared. "And I have waited a very long time for the moment to strike." As she spoke, she raised the sword over her head and then brought it down into a very specific spot in the machinery. Electricity flared out, massive bolts of lightning flashing across the chamber. Aurelia screamed and her hair stood on end. She shook violently, apparently unable to let go of the sword.

"*Noooo!*" wailed Elendi, and his cry was echoed by the other three.

And then the four ghostlike images flickered, enlarged even more, filled with static, and vanished.

Smoke filled the dome. Aurelia groaned and slumped to the floor.

I ran to her side.

Blood trailed from her nose and mouth. Her eyes were unfocused. I could tell instantly that she was dying—was near death even now.

I knelt and cradled her head in my lap. The soldiers of my house ran up to half-surround us.

"Gaius," she said. Her eyes were unfocused and her voice a harsh rasp. "Gaius—you need to know..."

"Don't try to speak," I told her. I could see how much it was costing her. "We will get you to a medic—"

"Too late," she gasped. Her voice was faint now and fading further as she spoke. "But listen—you need to know what happened to Octavia."

"Octavia?" The one family member not at our meeting back on Victoria—the only one I hadn't seen in months. I leaned in closer. "Yes?"

"She discovered... what Alexius and the Cabal... were doing." Aurelia coughed, blood splattering out. "She believed... I was part of it as well. But—" Another horrific coughing fit. When she'd stopped, she tried to continue: "They captured her... and were going to kill her. But I used my influence... within the Cabal... to convince them to send her... into exile instead."

"Octavia is alive?"

"Yes, she lives—but they carried her to a far distant dimension." Her voice was nearly inaudible now. Blood flowed freely from her nose. "You must find a way... to go and... bring her back. She is—"

The voice faded out entirely and Aurelia collapsed, limp and lifeless.

I breathed in deeply and exhaled. Another member of my family dead, and this one not deserving it. I cursed. Then, out of the corner of my eye, I saw Istari. He was up and moving. He reached out, grasped the sword by the hilt, gritted his teeth at the current that must still have been passing through it, and drew it out of the machinery. He held it up, inspecting it; it appeared no worse for the wear.

"We aren't done yet," he said to me then. "Two things yet remain."

"Two things?"

Frowning, I watched as he strode over to the far end of the banks of machinery. I lowered poor Aurelia's head to the floor—two of the soldiers knelt down and began to examine her for vital signs— and I stood, curious.

"They were not transformed into those forms," Istari said. "The wave of energy coming toward us from the future—the energy that would grant them actual godhood—has not yet reached this time and place in full."

I took this in and tried to process it.

"Those ghosts we saw were merely semi-holographic, semi-solid transitional bodies this machinery created," he went on. "Their mortal bodies still exist—here."

He pulled back a long sliding panel and revealed four tall figures—three of them Dyonari and one a gray giant—each sealed inside a separate transparent, liquid-filled cylinder, each covered in wires and cables and tubes. Colorful lights flickered and danced along the tops, bottoms and sides. A soft hum filled the air.

I moved closer and peered at the cylinders. Inside them, I could see the four beings staring out, eyes wide, with bubbles floating up around their faces. As with their faux-godlike apparitions, one of the Dyonari appeared to be a female, the other two male. They were alive and awake but presently trapped within their tanks.

"They are pitiful," Istari intoned, shaking his head. "They know the danger they now face. Their mortal bodies stand vulnerable before us. Yet they have waited so very long for godhood, they simply cannot bring themselves to disconnect from the equipment now—not even to try to protect themselves—when the moment of their expected apotheosis is so near." He laughed. "And thus do they condemn themselves."

He drew back the sword and plunged it into the first tube, which contained one of the male Dyonari. The transparent material yielded easily to his thrust, as did the alien on the other side of it, and thick, viscous fluid sprayed out as the cylinder cracked vertically above and below the spot where the sword had entered. The liquid turned a pale red and I saw then that the blade had skewered the figure dwelling within. Arms and legs thrashed frantically for a few moments. Istari then withdrew the sword and the disgusting mixture of fluids fountained out through the hole. By the time it had all drained away, the figure inside—Elendi, by the look of him—hung forward on his tubes and wires, limp and unmoving.

Istari nodded in satisfaction and moved on to the next cylinder.

"You're just going to butcher them, then?" I asked.

"Certainly," he replied. "Just as they were going to butcher the galaxy, due to their own selfishness."

The other three had gone berserk the moment Istari stabbed the first. Lights above each of the cylinders were in the process of changing from blue to orange and the liquid in each tank bubbled furiously and began to drain out. I took that to mean they had decided perhaps it was time to emerge from their cylinders after all.

The machinery wasn't fast enough. The other three were still trapped. Istari moved to stand before the second cylinder. He struck again, impaling the male Dyonari who thrashed within it.

"A very cold-blooded performance," I observed, feeling extremely uncomfortable watching what he was doing. I wasn't exactly stopping him, though.

He looked back at me, his eyes burning. "They tortured me," he growled. "They held me for ages, making me suffer for my crisis of conscience—for daring to stand up for *your* worlds and *your* race. They are unthinking, uncaring, soulless creatures, and I am quite happy to bring their miserable, eons-long existence to a very sudden end."

What could I say to that? I held out one hand toward the remaining two, as if to say, "Then be my guest."

Istari was not the least concerned as to whether or not he had my permission. He turned back and moved down to the third cylinder. The liquid had nearly drained out of it and the fourth one by now. The seals on each of them popped open and the front halves of both cylinders angled out and away from the figures contained inside.

The female Dyonari, her eyes wild and her movements frantic, tried to climb out, her fingers scrabbling against the smooth metal and plastic surfaces. Istari didn't hesitate. He skewered her just as he had done the first two. She cried out something unintelligible and she died, her body dangling out of the open tube, suspended by the web of wires and tubes and cables. I later learned she had been Aleuvi, called the Assassin, one of the deadliest killers the galaxy had ever known. At the time, she was simply another being cut down by Istari, right there in front of me. I gritted my teeth and wanted to look away, but I dared not.

The fourth tube was fully open. The gray giant inside reached up and ripped the wires and tubes away from himself and leapt out onto the floor. Fluids dripped from his limbs and his eyes were filled with fury.

Istari swept the sword around at him.

He jerked his upper half backwards with a swiftness and a fluidity that belied his massive form.

Istari missed.

The giant lunged for him, grappled with him, knocked the sword from his hand.

Istari spun about but couldn't break free. The giant seized him, wrapped his massive arms around his neck and started to squeeze. Istari gasped as the big creature roared in fury.

I picked up the sword where it had fallen and ran the giant through with it.

His roar changed drastically, morphing into to a cry of pain. He released Istari and staggered back, in the process wrenching the hilt from my hands. The blade remained protruding through him. He spun about and glared down at me and reached out with his huge hands, meaning to murder me. The hands moved far more quickly than I could have imagined. They grasped me by the neck, lifted me up, and began to crush my windpipe. I couldn't breathe. I kicked and flailed frantically.

From the corner of my eye I could see several of my troopers rushing forward. The nearest one fired, the blasts from his pistol impacting the giant but scarcely affecting him.

And then the golden blade that protruded from the giant's torso vanished. It had been drawn back out from his back, and it reappeared in midair, sweeping around.

The giant's head separated from his shoulders and fell to the floor, followed a moment later by the massive, headless body.

Istari stood over the slain giant and frowned. "That's odd," he said.

"What's odd?" I gasped, desperately trying to catch my breath. *What* isn't *odd here*, I was thinking.

Istari shrugged. "I didn't expect to end up decapitating *all three* of the giants," he said.

"This is not good," Istari called out to me from where he was almost entirely engulfed in the innards of the dome's futuristic machinery. Only his lower legs and feet protruded from beneath the wide gray console. A constellation of colorful lights danced across its surface, though several had gone dark moments earlier as Istari worked underneath.

"What?" I asked, afraid to hear the answer.

Slowly he withdrew himself from the depths of the machinery and sat up. His expression dour, he shook his head and looked up at me.

"The oncoming wave of cosmic energy cannot be stopped," he said.

I felt my heart sink in my chest. I shook my head, moving quickly into denial, and looked away for a moment. Then I turned back to him.

"You mean they—the Cabal—created this power wave, but their equipment can't *un*-create it?"

"They did not create it," he said. "They merely learned of it and were attempting to take advantage of it."

"Then where did it come from?"

"Not *where*," he replied, meeting my eyes again. "*When*."

I recalled what had been said earlier. In all honesty, I'd happily allowed the details to go right over my head. Now, though, with all that had happened, and all that yet could occur, I found a renewed interest in the subject.

"The future," I said. "It's coming back to us here and now from some point in the future."

"Correct."

"But—how is that possible?"

"I do not know," he said. "I suspect none of my former compatriots of the Cabal did, either. But they didn't allow that to dissuade them. They detected—or were told of—the wave's approach long ago and resolved to harness it for their own purposes. In order to do that, they sent out certain *signals* and *emanations* into the various layers of the multiverse, redirecting and channeling its course as it drew near." He sighed heavily. "Those changes cannot be undone. The wave is coming, and it will sweep across the mortal plane, wreaking untold carnage over the greater portion of our galaxy." He paused, looking away. "Unless..."

"Yes?" I said, seizing on the slender hope his last utterance had promised. "Unless what?"

"It just might be possible that sending out a new set of signals, while unable to stop or reverse the oncoming wave, might be able to divert it... shall we say... *vertically*."

"Vertically?" I stared back at him, utterly mystified.

He smiled flatly. "Understand that we are speaking of multi-dimensional phenomena while we ourselves are constrained within only three dimensions. So by 'vertically' I mean into a higher realm; a higher level of being."

"You mean into the Paths?"

"Not precisely, no," he said, shaking his head. "The Paths are but connective passages between various levels of reality. They do not constitute a dimension unto themselves. But," he added, his smile growing sly, "there are many actual dimensions available to us. It just might be possible…"

"I'm all for it," I said. "What do we have to do?"

"We would have to…" He paused, frowned, and his eyes grew unfocused for a few seconds. I assumed he was mentally working out formulas and equations. When he was finished and he looked at me again, his frown deepened and he shook his head.

"I had forgotten a few very basic properties of the higher planes," he growled.

"What does that mean?"

"It means it is not so simple," he said, clearly disgusted. "If we did succeed in redirecting the wave into a higher dimensional realm, it wouldn't just remain there and fade away. It would in all likelihood echo across that plane, doing just as much damage there—whereupon it might very well re-energize and re-emerge into this plane, at least as powerful as before."

I took this in, blinking rapidly. "Okay," I said after a couple of seconds. "You're saying if we do nothing, it will destroy the galaxy—"

"Yes."

"—But if we do redirect it away, it will destroy *other* dimensions, and then come back down and destroy this galaxy anyway."

He brought his slender hands up to his pale white face and rubbed at his reddened eyes. "Yes," he repeated. "In all likelihood, that is so."

"Then—" I looked away, staggered. Was this the end? "—is there anything we *can* do?"

He met my eyes again and offered a sort of resigned shrug. "I'm afraid there is."

At first, given his tone, I was sure he had answered in the negative. Then I realized what he had said, and I looked up. "Wait—there *is* something?"

"Yes."

"You don't sound confident it will work."

"Oh, it should work," he said.

"Then what—?"

"But it will definitely cost one of us our lives. Both of us, quite possibly."

I absorbed this, considered it for perhaps three seconds, and nodded. For some reason I found the potential price we would have to pay didn't much surprise me. It would cost us our lives? Of course it would. Anything else—anything less—would've been the real surprise.

"What do we have to do?" I asked.

His evil half-smile returned one last time. "You are so prepared to sacrifice both our lives for the greater good," he noted with a snort. "That has *never* been my favorite of your qualities."

According to Istari's plan, he was to remain in the dome, burrowed deep inside the machinery, manipulating circuits and controls on the fly, moment by moment, regulating and directing the flow of the oncoming wave of cosmic energy as best he could. By precisely managing the wave at the micro level, he believed he could blunt its impact and shape it so that it remained in the higher planes and never blasted back down into our universe. Such a task could not be left to the existing machinery the Cabal had possessed, and there was no time to go and find, procure, or create new equipment for that purpose. Only he could process the changes made to the flow of energy in real time, as they needed to happen, using a combination of his telepathy and precognition to anticipate the fluctuations in the oncoming wave.

Unfortunately, the wave was going to strike the dome at the same time it struck wherever else we managed to make it go, and there was no combination of factors that could cause it to do otherwise. In other words, Istari would be here when it hit, and he would die.

He didn't seem terribly upset about this fact. I assumed that meant it was what he had seen in the Well of Eternity, and that he had been prepared for it for at least that long.

I assumed that, but I wasn't certain of it.

The rest of the plan, of course, involved me, as he explained:

"You must move quickly. Go back to where we left your people, in the pocket universe. Lead them home." He paused. "Not to your palace—I doubt it exists any longer. Take them back to Majondra. Then follow the Paths back to that same pocket universe, and—"

"Wait," I said, holding up a hand to interrupt him. "If you remain here, how am I supposed to travel the Paths?"

He lifted the golden sword and pressed it into my hands. I was surprised, to say the least.

"Take this. I know that it will work for you. I have seen it."

I accepted the sword and held it up before me. Its golden form gleamed in the pale light. It looked marvelous and terrible.

"You can take my horse, as well," he said. "He will lead you back to the others, and along the Paths. He knows the ways almost as well as I do."

"Your horse? Sneak is here?"

"What?"

"Never mind. How did your horse get here?"

"I called to him," he said. "He awaits you outside this chamber."

"Very well," I said, surprised and impressed. "I will."

"As I was saying. After you have taken them to Majondra, go back to that pocket universe, which—if you have done your job properly—will no longer contain one hundred and twenty-seven of your soldiers, retainers and other employees."

"One hundred twenty-seven?"

"I counted them."

"Huh."

"May I continue? Or is there anything else of no importance you must ask?"

"By all means," I said.

"Go back to the pocket universe. Find its center. The sword will help with that, too. Then use it to punch a hole in the ground."

I simply stared back at him, dumbfounded.

"Yes?" he asked.

"I punch a hole in the ground."

"Yes."

I thought about this for a second, then nodded. Why not? It made about as much sense as anything else, at this point. "And then what?"

"You get the hell out of there, as quickly as you can."

I nodded. "Because...?"

"Because you will have just opened a new path for all the energies of the oncoming wave, and—if I have done my part of the job properly, which of course I will have—that energy will be directed up through the hole you have created and into that pocket universe."

"Ah," I said, able to at least visualize what he was saying if not fully comprehend it. "And will I need to return at some point and seal the hole, somehow, so that it won't escape?"

He shook his head. "No. The energy will not work that way. It will have resonated down through the time stream from the far future, and it will continue to flow for ages to come. The energy will never drain back out—it will always be flowing into the pocket universe, through that hole in reality."

"Always?"

"For all intents and purposes." He shrugged. "I imagine there will be some bleed-over, of course. Traces of the energy will probably radiate outwards from that pocket dimension and throughout all the layers of reality for eons to come. But not in any sort of harmful levels."

I thought about that.

"And what will happen to me if I don't escape the pocket universe in time?"

Istari looked back at me, pursed his lips, and smiled.

"I have no idea," he said. "Quite possibly the same thing that will happen to me, here." He paused, then, "Or possibly something entirely different."

"I see," I said. "I think."

"That is the beauty of the plan, my human friend," he said. "You don't have to think. Just do as I say."

I chuckled, then nodded once to him.

He offered me a smile, and for once it wasn't an evil one. "Good fortune to you," he said.

"To you as well," I replied.

"Now hurry. Time grows exceedingly short."

I turned, raised the sword before me, and strode out of there. I never saw Istari again.

TWELVE

The blast came from nowhere. Sneak went down with a cry of pain and threw me clear. I rolled across the soft surface of the Path and came up with my pistol drawn.

No one was there.

I looked around, furious. Time was my enemy now. I had none to waste. Who could have wanted to stop me?

I glanced over at the black horse where he lay on his side, unmoving. Dead, I was pretty sure.

This was bad. Without Sneak, I wasn't certain I could find my way to the pocket universe, much less lead the men and women who waited there back home. Even if I could—even if the sword would do it all for me—I would be traveling so much slower now. Would there still be time?

Wary, on constant guard, I ran.

The waves of mists parted before me and lighting flared along beside me. I wasn't entirely sure I knew what I was doing or where I was going, but it felt right.

I knew the situation had grown critical now; that much was certain. I had to take my best guess, rely on my instincts, and go.

Another blast, a few seconds later. This time I leapt out of the way, tucking and rolling, and when I came up I was in the mists and no longer on the Path.

Panic struck at me. What if I couldn't find the way again? How long would I wander in this nightmare of nothingness before—what? This attacker killed me? I died of thirst? Or some strange creature out of shadow and nightmare devoured me?

I felt the sword still clutched tightly in my right hand and I held it up before me. The radiant golden glow it threw off seemed to penetrate the gloom and now I could see the course of the Path again off to my left, clear as day. Relief flooded over me, but mixed with fear: I was in all likelihood broadcasting my precise location to my invisible assailant. But I had no choice. I hurried back to the Path and started forward again. Where was my assailant? Who was it? Why did they want me dead?

Another blast. Again I hurled myself down, rolling off to my left, but this time I kept the Path in sight. I looked around quickly, seeking any sign that might betray the location of my foe.

Nothing.

I was growing extremely frustrated, to the point of recklessness. The clock was ticking; I needed to be moving. Without Sneak to carry me along, every second was precious.

Fed up, I sat up and shouted, "Come out, whoever you are! Let's settle this like men and not like children hiding in the shadows!"

"Like men?" came the response in a familiar female voice.

As I looked on in utter astonishment, my young Aunt Stephanie emerged from the fog and walked slowly towards me, a blast pistol in one hand aimed at my chest.

"Fancy meeting you here," she said, a wry smile crossing her face.

"I have to admit, it's a bit unexpected," I replied. My own pistol was still in its holster but I held the sword in my right hand and experience had taught me over the past couple of days that it might be the deadlier weapon.

She glanced over at Sneak's body, frowned, and looked back at me. "Aren't you upset that I shot your horse?" she asked.

"It's not my horse," I told her.

"Oh."

"But yes—pretty upset. He was what you'd call a key component in what I'm trying to do."

"That's a shame," she said. "I didn't really want to. But you were going to gallop right past my position."

She'd been waiting out here? Waiting for me?

"Why did you do it?" I asked. "That and, you know, shooting at me, too."

She laughed. It was a sweet, carefree laugh; wholly out of place here and entirely creepy. "I needed you to slow down. I'm on foot, you see. A horse gave you an unfair advantage."

"Ah," I said by way of reply. "You could have simply asked, you know. I've always been partial to my aunts over my uncles."

"You hate all of us," she said. "Not that I blame you."

"But it's a relative thing," I told her. "No pun intended, of course."

She scowled. "I should kill you for that alone."

"Why would you want to kill me at all?"

"Because you know too much," she said, growing serious. "And because I want that sword." She chuckled. "That makes two very good reasons. I tried to kill you the first time just for the first reason."

"The first time?" I edged to my right, attempting to get back on the Path. She raised her pistol and fired a warning shot just past my shoulder. I halted.

"Yes," she said then, as though nothing of consequence had happened. "Didn't you wonder why someone suddenly targeted the palace on Victoria with quantum missiles?"

My jaw dropped. "That was you?"

She shrugged. "If someone hadn't come along and awakened you from your long nap, you'd be taking a much longer one now," she said.

"Aurelia," I murmured, thinking of my eldest aunt. "She woke me. And she told me she'd seen you there earlier. I never put it together like that, though. I never would have."

She smirked. "It would have been Aurelia. She claims to be one of us, but I've never trusted her."

"She's dead," I stated flatly.

"What?"

Stephanie blinked and lowered the gun a couple of inches. I considered making a break for the path—or attacking her with the sword—but I dared not risk it; not just yet, anyway. She was distracted, but not enough.

"Aurelia was killed saving Istari and me from the Cabal."

"I knew she wasn't truly committed," Stephanie growled. Then her frown deepened. "Cabal. Huh. I don't like that name," she said. "We are the Immortals, and soon we will be gods."

"No," I told her. "You won't."

Quickly I sketched for her what had recently transpired within the dome of the Cabal.

"I don't believe you," she said at length. "I don't believe you could have killed all four of them."

"Istari actually killed them," I said, "but in hindsight I think I could have given a pretty decent accounting of myself, if necessary." I held the sword aloft. "Especially if I'd possessed this."

"You think you can use it? The only reason I am willing to try is that I've spent years studying it, working with the Immortals, learning to master such artifacts and powers. But *you*—what do you know of it? It will destroy you."

"I can use it," I replied coldly, holding it up before me. "As you can see."

Her eyes glinted with desire as she looked upon the golden weapon.

"I will have to," I added, "since you and your friends have left me no other choice." I gazed at her with contempt. "To think that you would have been willing to see the entire galaxy destroyed, just for your own selfish reasons."

"You know nothing," she spat back at me. "And you'll never be able to stop the wave."

"I know," I said, smiling flatly at her. "Fortunately, that's not the plan."

She continued to regard me for a couple of seconds in silence, and a tiny frown passed over her features. Then she scoffed and shook her head. "I don't even know that I believe you about the others being dead," she said offhand. "But—whether you're telling the truth or not, my priority at the moment is that sword." She moved closer. "The rest I can find out for myself once I possess it."

"Then come and get it," I said, holding it out before me, hoping she was agitated enough now to actually try it, and not just shoot me down from there.

Sure enough, she took another step closer.

A whinny sounded from behind her. Sneak wasn't as dead as I'd thought, apparently.

She glanced back, surprised.

I tossed the sword to her.

She reached out for it, the gun forgotten, tumbling from her fingertips.

I lunged, punching her in the stomach. She grunted.

The sword fell to the ground.

She started to rise. I punched her again. "Stay down," I shouted, furious with her.

She reached for her fallen gun.

I brought the sword around and down and sliced the gun in half. Sparks flew from it in a golden cascade.

Cursing at me, she got to her hands and knees and scampered into the fog on the far side of the Path. Gone. To where, I couldn't say—but there was no way, even if I'd had the time, that I would have pursued her into the depths of the mist, away from the Path. She was unarmed now. Let her come back and try something.

I checked to be sure my own pistol was safe in its holster. Then I got to my feet and went over to take a look at Sneak.

He was in a bad way. I knew I had to do something about it, and so I did. Then I walked away and back onto the Path, sick to my stomach.

I was beginning to question my career choices.

I had trudged along the Path for what felt like half of eternity when the little black creature trotted up beside me and struck up a conversation.

"Hi. What are you doing?"

The monotony of the journey had nearly lulled me into a state of hypnosis, and it took a moment for the creature's voice to get through to me. When it did, I looked down.

It was black and furry and went on all fours and was about the size of an average dog, but it wasn't a dog. To be honest, I wasn't certain what it was. It gazed back up at me with a pleasant enough expression on its all-too-human face, and its blue eyes sparkled in the dim light.

Considering several possible answers including a couple of smart-assed ones, I settled on the truth. "I'm traveling to a pocket universe," I said.

"Ah," the creature said. Its eyes shifted to the sword I carried ahead of me for a few seconds. Then, "That's a lovely item. May I ask where you found it?"

"I didn't find it," I replied somewhat testily. "It was given to me. By a friend."

"Ooooh," it said. "A friend. Nice."

I trudged on in silence and the little creature kept the pace, trotting along next to me. I looked for all the world, I'm sure, like someone taking their dog out for a walk. Except, of course, dogs didn't look like this. And they didn't talk.

"Do you think you'll be in time?" it asked a few seconds later.

I looked down at it again, surprised. "What do you know of that?"

"You seem in quite a hurry," it replied. "I'm wondering if you think you'll be on time, or late."

I stared into the mists ahead of me for a moment, then shook my head. "I don't know. I don't think so. But I'm going to try."

"Commendable," it said. "Most commendable."

We walked on together silently for a short way.

"I know the answer to that question," it said suddenly. "Would you like to hear it?"

"To what question?" I asked, confused. My entire focus was on moving forward, following the Path, finding the entrance to the pocket universe as quickly as possible.

"Whether you make it or not."

"How could you know that?" I asked, not taking the creature seriously.

"I have powerful friends," it squawked. "I know a lot of things."

"Then why ask me?"

It chuckled; the sound was curious. "I don't know. I just wanted to hear your perspective on it all. You don't seem terribly confident, if you don't mind my saying so."

I looked down at it and frowned. "Actually," I said, "I think I'd make better progress without you here, distracting me. If you don't mind," I added.

"Of course, of course," it said. Then it moved in closer. "But I have to tell you—you won't succeed. There isn't enough time."

"Is that so?" I asked, growing angry. "You know that for a fact, do you?"

"I do," it said. "But that's okay. You tried. You tried very hard. No one can fault you for effort." It looked off to the side.

"Now it's time to lay down your burdens. Time to lie down and rest."

"Lay down my *burdens*?" I held the sword up and nodded toward it. "Like this one, for instance? You'd like that, wouldn't you?" I snorted. "You aren't the first being I've encountered that wanted to divest me of this weapon."

"Oh, I'm not interested in your sword," the little creature replied. "I simply took something of a liking to you, the last time we met, and I didn't want to see you needlessly killed when the wave comes through."

I frowned at this and looked back down at the little being.

"We've never met," I said.

"Oh, you wound me, sir," it said. "How soon they forget. And here I was considering offering you a shortcut by way of my cave."

"Cave?" My forehead creased even deeper as I thought about what it had said. Then the light came on, metaphorically.

"No," I said. "You don't mean you are—"

"One and the same," it replied.

The creature in the darkness of the cave. The one that had allowed me to ask a couple of questions, and had let me depart in peace—something that had initially surprised Istari.

It was only *this* big?

"If you truly could provide a shortcut, I would be very grateful," I told the little beast, not at all sure how serious to take it.

It made a sort of shrugging gesture with its forward shoulders and replied, "Why not? It could prove diverting for a time, at any rate." It nodded forward. "Keep going a short distance more—my, but you do cover a lot of ground quickly with those long legs—and... now, turn right."

I turned.

The mists and fog and the Path itself vanished from around me.

I panicked at first. Was the creature leading me astray—removing any last vestiges of hope I had left? Was it planning to strand me forever in the mists between universes?

But then darkness swallowed me, and I actually felt better about things. For this darkness seemed familiar to me. It was the darkness of the cave I'd entered and exited after meeting Istari.

About that much, at least, the little beast had spoken the truth.

"Straight through and out the back," it was saying. "When you come out, you'll be very close." It regarded me, its head turned partway to the side, now reminding me more strongly of an actual dog. "Of course, you'll still be too late," it added—and now its voice was deepening, growing smooth and resonant, and much more familiar. It was the voice from our previous encounter, without a doubt. "But at least now you can say you came close."

Ignoring these last words, I called back a "thank you" and ran for the far end of the cave.

"Good luck," I heard it say, its voice now grown very deep, harsh and rough. "Glad I didn't eat you."

"Me too."

The creature's cave opened out onto another nearly identical segment of the Paths. But this time I could see a standard, run-of-the-mill door—the same sort mankind had been building for ages— standing there before me, upright and unsupported. It wasn't the first of its kind I had encountered, and by now I knew the drill. I could only assume my own subconscious made me see it that way, and I suspected that others would see something entirely different—something that fit within their own point of reference.

I felt strange, suddenly. My head hurt. The light that until now had been pale, dim, diffused, now seemed too bright, too intense. I chalked it up to having just emerged from the darkness of the cave, but I knew that was only part of it. Something was happening. I feared I knew all too well what it was.

The wave had arrived. The little creature had been right—I was too late. Based on what Istari had told me, when it became physically noticeable, the wave of energy had arrived. In the universe I called home, somewhere at the far end of one of these Paths, the wave front was poised to break. I knew that, back at the Nexus, Istari was laboring intently even now to aim the bulk of the wave toward this place. He had lived up to his part of the deal, and would likely be dead in moments. For myself, I had only seconds before the point of no return—the moment the massive energy could no longer be diverted.

My people from the palace were no longer a factor in this. They couldn't be. Despite my best efforts and desires, they had moved firmly into the category of collateral damage. There was nothing to be done for them now.

I reached out, grasped the copper-colored knob, turned it and pulled. The door swung open on invisible hinges and I stepped through.

It was a paradise. Rolling green hills stretched into the distance. Trees and flowers and hanging fruit and colorful birds soaring by. And in the foreground, standing or seated in little groups of three or four or more, all busily engaged in conversation or eating or just lying back in the warm sunlight, were the hundred-plus members of our household staff.

One would have scarcely guessed we all teetered on the brink of the apocalypse.

A couple of them looked up and saw me then and they called out to the others and next thing I knew a whole crowd of them was rushing up to me.

I was sick. I didn't have the heart to tell them what I had come to do.

But, for the galaxy to survive, they—and I— would all have to die.

The plan had been for me to lead them all back home, then return and do what I had to do here. But Stephanie had utterly ruined that possibility. Now all I could do was save every other living being in our galaxy except for them.

I pushed past them, shoving them aside, racing toward the center of this universe.

As I ran, I saw Jerome out of the corner of my eye, sitting up, being tended by the intelligence officer, Markos. I was glad he had survived the earlier attack in the palace and was sorry he would live no longer, after what I was about to do.

Brushing aside their multitude of questions—mostly about where I had been, what had happened, and when they could go back home—I hurried out into the grassy field beyond their campsite. Was I anywhere near the center of this tiny little pocket universe? I had no idea. Somehow, I doubted it. Was that vital to the plan's success? I didn't know that, either.

But there was no more time even to try to find it. My vision was growing blurry—it appeared as if everyone around me was streaked with lines of light, and illuminated by some inner glow. They could see it too; they stared openly at one another, some of them staggering around aimlessly, some falling to the ground as if drunk or dying.

I felt a burning in my gut. It was as if I'd swallowed a small star, and now it was preparing to go nova inside me.

The wave. The wave was upon us. Even through the walls that divide the universes, I could feel the pressure wave striking hard. I could only imagine the damage being wrought on the greater universe back home.

The deed would be done now, or not at all.

I waved my arms frantically, shouting for them to get back. Then I raised the great golden sword above my head, grasped the hilt firmly with both hands, and drove it down into the ground before me. It sunk partway into the surface and stopped there.

Nothing happened.

I waited for a long moment, uncertain what to do next. Finally I decided to do what came instinctively. I tightened my grip on the hilt and drew the sword back out of the ground.

A rumbling.

An earthquake.

A cataclysm.

Out in its wake spewed a geyser of blinding, coruscating, raw energy. The force of it hurled me back, knocking the sword from my grasp.

The others backed away, shocked and astonished, while I fought my way onto my feet, sought the sword, found it where it lay and lifted it again. When I did, I saw that my hands, my arms were... *bigger*, somehow. More muscular. The golden armor I wore had begun to morph into a heavier, thicker material of the same color.

This all seemed meaningless to me. I ignored it and regarded what I had wrought.

A plume of pure, elemental power jetted up toward the sky from the hole I had punched in the ground with the sword. That energy, I knew, was not coming from under the surface of this strange world we now occupied; it was coming from some other plane, and if all was going as Istari had planned and predicted, it was now being siphoned away from our universe and here instead.

Enough energy to obliterate those of us who currently occupied that universe a thousand times over. A million times over.

Yet still we lived. I raised my left hand—the right yet clutched the sword—and I looked at it again. It was big, powerful, luminous. I could not understand what that meant.

Looking around at the others, I saw that each of them now stood transfixed, arms out wide and heads thrown back, as shimmering waves of cosmic energy washed over them. I recognized the Sister Superior, and at last her given name came back to me from our first meeting on Sarmata: *Karilyne*. Her name was Karilyne.

I knew her name again, but now I only barely knew her by her appearance. Her stature had grown even beyond what it had been, her bearing had become more regal, and she now wore gleaming silver armor that sparkled beneath her mantle of jet black hair. She looked at me and her blue eyes glinted and my legs, strong as they now were, felt for a moment very weak indeed.

All of the others around me were as affected by the flood of energy pulsing into our little pocket universe as I was. They were changing—metamorphosing—before my very eyes. Into what, I did not know. Part of me feared to know. Another part reveled in it.

The flame within me—the flame of battle—had fully ignited, and the energy wave was pure oxygen breathing upon it, nurturing it, causing it to flourish.

I sensed something then. I realized I now possessed a greater native understanding of the forces at work here. My consciousness was expanding even as my body did. I looked at the geyser of energy and then at the little world around us and I simply knew on an elemental, fundamental level what was happening, and what I had to do.

The energy wasn't killing us. It was changing us. *Sustaining* us. And if I did nothing, it would continue to erupt, uncontrolled, and to escape away into other dimensions, leaving us bereft of its gifts.

I turned and saw Comet standing to my left. He appeared changed for the better, as well—bigger, stronger, and radiant with power. I called to him and he trotted over.

Yes. I knew what had to be done—what only I could do.

I climbed aboard Comet and raised the sword high and we rode. I spurred him forward and we crossed the grassland like his fiery namesake.

When I felt the moment was right, I brought him up and turned him to the left, and as we began to move in a long, broad circle with the plume of energy at the center, I stretched out the sword and willed its blade to carve into the very fabric of this universe's spacetime. A glowing line of yellow-white remained etched in the very air as we passed, as the blade cut through the walls of reality.

Everything began to change.

I gazed upward as we rode. I gasped.

The sky filled with stars, and stars rained down from the sky.

The heavens wheeled about me, wheeled again. Day to night, night to day, in endless cycle—and yet so quickly. Days passed—or was it seconds? I no longer knew.

Sleet blew strong against us one moment, blazing heat the next. The ground became a treacherous sheet of ice, then a morass of warm swamp water. Comet pressed on, undeterred.

The sky overhead was all black velvet, then bright white, then crimson, then azure. Then it divided in half, glowing gold on one side and deep purple on the other. Then it split like a pie into eight triangular segments, each a different luminous color. I gazed up at this happening as I rode and I felt I would lose my now-tenuous grip on sanity.

Another part of me, though, seemed to almost expect these strange phenomena; to take them in stride. I tried very hard to lean on this part of my expanding persona.

Space and distance became abstract concepts, and time no longer had meaning. All the ages of the universe passed me by as I rode, and yet it all happened in the blink of an eye. Comet and I traveled the length and breadth of a universe, even as we rode a circuit no greater than the distance around a small city.

And that was what we were doing, of course. We were inscribing the perimeter of a city. A great city. A Golden City. The greatest city there had ever been or would ever be, existing there in its own universe, on a higher plane of reality than almost any other.

We were in the Above. Our City would be the capital of the Above.

I apologize. I told you before that I am no poet. Would that I could describe for you in more evocative language what I experienced that day. Of course, I know that you were there, too—but I have to believe the experience was somewhat different for me there, at what amounted to the heart of the storm.

After a timeless time that paralleled a new morning's dawn and the lifespans of galaxies, I completed my miles-long circuit about the plume of energy and halted Comet, then hopped down and strode back over to where my people waited. They were scarcely recognizable now; they had been utterly transformed.

I could feel what they felt. Our old lives, our old identities were falling away, moment by moment, bit by bit.

Was this the apotheosis—the rise to godhood—that the so-called Immortals of the Cabal and my traitorous relatives had longed for, had planned for and been willing to throw away the lives of every living being in the galaxy to attain?

In shame I must admit some part of me understood that now. For this was worth almost any price. This was power indeed—power to reshape the cosmos. Power to create our *own* cosmos.

I looked about at the glowing circle in the air and I willed that there be walls there instead. And lo, great walls a hundred feet high and forty feet thick rared up from the ground and positioned themselves to precisely match my vision. The others looked upon them and declared them good, and the walls in turn reflected in their nature the esteem that the new City's inhabitants felt for them, and they became strong and smooth and beautiful to gaze upon.

Then I envisioned buildings, palaces, towers—and those took form from out of nothingness, and they radiated beauty and glory.

And last of all we gathered in the center of our new Golden City, surrounding the great geyser of energy—that elemental Power that now invigorated us all. And we beheld it and imagined that it should be channeled, regulated, contained. It should be not just a wild, raw geyser. It should become a great fountain—the Fountain of the Golden City, the source of our might and the seat of our very beings, spouting suns and stars and constellations of energy into the heavens and then back down into a great basin at its foot.

We imagined that, we envisioned it, we willed it— and that, too, came to pass.

And we gods looked upon it, and we said that it was good.

Sometime shortly thereafter, we made our presence known to the universe that we had by our sacrifice saved. Our sacrifice, of course, was to transcend humanity—to become beings of awesome might and majesty, wise and powerful and terrible in our wrath. We were determined to acquaint our former world's enemies with that fact.

The great Verghasite fleet had assembled in high orbit above Sarmata and was making ready to strike at Majondra through the Gate when a dozen of us emerged from our own portal—a gate we created ourselves. The cold, the vacuum, the void; none of that mattered to us, none of it could harm us now.

We flew in like angels of death and descended upon them like the wrathful gods we had become, and they never knew what hit them; they never stood a chance.

Vashtaar led the way. He blazed with cosmic fire and his flames lashed out across the empty distances, caressing numerous elements of the Verghasite fleet with overwhelming power. Those ships melted at his touch.

Korvak, glowing vivid indigo, unleashed bolts of lightning that fried all the electronics systems aboard a dozen more of them, leaving them to tumble away into the night.

Burly Turmborne brought down his axe and battlecruisers before him were cleaved in half, showering the dark cosmos with debris and the remains of enemy soldiers.

Goraddon whispered a suggestion here, a command there, and in response the Verghasite ships turned on one another and opened fire, no longer perceiving their comrades as anything other than what he told them they were—enemies.

And I? I swept the great golden sword back and forth, and as I did so the ships that closed in on me were shredded, their forward compartments disintegrating under the onslaught.

The battle lasted scarcely twenty minutes. When we were done, the power of Verghas had been forever shattered. Majondra faced no other serious challenges to its dominance of all of human-occupied space.

We turned about, opened a new portal, and returned to our City. Even as we did, our mortal concerns for Majondra that had spurred us to that action were fading. By the time we reached the City, we could scarcely comprehend why we had acted at all.

And so the battle above Sarmata was the first time the new gods had meddled in the affairs of human conflict, and it would be the *last* occasion for a very long while to come.

At least, as far as I then knew.

That is the story of how we, the gods of the Golden City, came to be. I am glad that I told it to you, my friend, while I still remembered it. For I find the details slipping away from me moment by moment. Soon, I fear, our mortal memories will evaporate and all we will be is what we are now. And you knew very little of how this all came to be, because you experienced only a fraction of these events as they occurred. One moment you were a military aide to my uncle, the next you were a god.

One last trip down memory lane, before that road is ripped up forever.

We never did learn the source or the cause of the potentially galaxy-shattering wave of energy that came back to us from the future. It changed the galaxy, though—and it changed us. It transformed us from mere mortals into the gods we have become. Perhaps, if we live long enough, one day we will discover the cause of it first-hand. Perhaps there is even some sort of divine benefactor that, on that occasion, we will be able to thank personally. For now, though, we accept the gift of the Power and are grateful for it.

What, you ask, of the rest of the war for the Seven Worlds?

I had nearly forgotten it. But yes, the story would be incomplete without some mention of how things turned out on Majondra.

I heard later that the war was won by my family's side. Justinian's forces stormed the Gates of the other six worlds and subdued them. With their attack fleet destroyed and with the Cabal and its Church no longer supporting the Verghasites and the other hostile regimes, their armies collapsed quickly. To Justinian I'm sure all the credit must have gone. He was the hero; he was carving out a Second Empire of Man, and doing it in the name of my late father.

That was fine with me. I no longer cared what transpired on the Seven Worlds. Aurelia and Alexius were dead; Octavia and Stephanie were missing, and Octavia might well be dead also; Jerome was here with me, and was now someone else— as was I. In truth, Justinian was the only one of my family left in that universe. Even his home, our palace, had been annihilated. He deserved whatever solace he could find.

I thought that he, now master of an interstellar empire, must be an extremely lonely man.

As for us, here we stand now, before the Fountain of the Golden City, and we gaze out at what we have wrought and we celebrate.

Our old identities, our old selves are falling away. New identities, new Aspects consume us and shape our natures. I, for one, find myself transforming from the mortal known as

Gaius Baranak to *Baranak*, the god of battle. At first I found this incredibly ill-fitting. Now, though, the new me warms to the role. Perhaps the Power understands us better than we understand ourselves.

Yes, my friend—I am aware that you disagree on that point. These new Aspects that we wear along with our new, brightly colored raiment, in your opinion, do not necessarily represent our true natures. You see them as artificially forced upon us.

Perhaps. Time will tell.

So I turn and greet my new peers—no longer members of some aristocrat's household staff, but equals in divinity and power. I exchange a portentous look with grim, cold Karilyne in her silver and her black that promises interesting times to come. I nod to the old blacksmith, Voras, who now appears much bigger, much stronger, his bald scalp gleaming in the glow of the Fountain, and who radiates an almost palpable aura of confidence and power. And lastly I shake hands with you, my new friend. For I have sensed something within you—something special—that I believe will become extremely important to our kind in the ages to come. For good or ill, I cannot yet say, as your own Aspect has yet to fully manifest. But let us be optimistic and trust that it will be all to the good.

I clasp your hand, my friend, and I think upon the glorious city, the perfect society we will build here, together—a society free from strife, from conflict, from disorder.

I clasp your hand, Lucian, and I know that our friendship will endure down through all the ages to come.

THE END
OF
BARANAK: STORMING THE GATES

THE SAGA OF THE SHATTERED GALAXY BEGINS IN
HAWK: HAND OF THE MACHINE

THE STORY OF THE MURDER OF THE GODS
AND LUCIAN'S QUEST FOR THE KILLER
IS TOLD IN
LUCIAN: DARK GOD'S HOMECOMING

THE CAUSE OF THE GALAXY-SHATTERING
BLAST-WAVE FROM THE FUTURE
CAN BE FOUND IN THE LEGIONS TRILOGY,
BEGINNING WITH
LEGION I: LORDS OF FIRE

Thanks and appreciation this time around to:

Ami, Maddie and Mira, as always.

Mark Williams, for his continued artistic excellence.

The late, great Roger Zelazny, gone twenty years and more now, whose spirit I once again strove to channel as I worked on this book. Anything that strikes you, dear reader, as somehow familiar here, should be seen for what it is: Inspiration, loving tribute and homage.

The usual crew of early readers of my books. Your acclaim for this series kept me going through thick and thin, and I appreciate each and every one of you tremendously.

A whole slew of good friends who, at my request, offered suggestions for a plot point I was struggling with. Mark Bousquet, Sean Ali and Ken Akamatsu in particular nudged my brain in just the right direction to work it out, and I thank them (and everyone else who took the time to make a suggestion).

The several hundred people, at last count, who have listened to the White Rocket Podcast episode where I talked about writing these books. I'm delighted that so many are interested.

My regular retinue of friends, fans, readers and commenters on Facebook and Twitter who seem to appreciate my occasional updates and comments about this and my other books.

And last but not least, all the members of the Pulp Factory who nominated LEGION III: KINGS OF OBLIVION for the Novel of the Year Award, and all the folks who then voted it the trophy. My gratitude knows no bounds.

The Shattering saga will return!
Next up: THE LEGION CHRONICLES 2: RED COLOSSUS!

ABOUT THE AUTHOR

Van Allen Plexico writes and edits New Pulp, science fiction, fantasy, and nonfiction analysis and commentary for a variety of print and online publishers. He won the 2015 Pulp Factory Award for "Novel of the Year" for *Legion III: Kings of Oblivion,* the 2015 Pulp Factory Award for "Anthology of the Year" for *Pride of the Mohicans,* and the 2012 PulpArk Award for "Best New Pulp Character." The first volume in this series, *Legion I: Lords of Fire*, was a finalist for Novel of the Year in the 2014 Pulp Factory Awards and the New Pulp Awards. His best-known works include *Lucian*, *Hawk*, the *Assembled!* books, and the groundbreaking and #1 New Pulp Best-Selling *Sentinels* series—the first ongoing, multi-volume cosmic superhero saga in prose form. In his spare time he serves as a professor of political science and history. He has lived in Atlanta, Singapore, Alabama, and Washington, DC, and now resides in the St. Louis area along with his wife, two daughters and assorted river otters.

Van Allen Plexico's Sentinels
Super-hero action illustrated by Chris Kohler
    The Grand Design Trilogy
    Alternate Visions (Anthology)
    The Rivals Trilogy
    The Order Above All Trilogy

TheShattering
    Lucian: Dark God's Homecoming
    Baranak: Storming the Gates
    Hawk: Hand of the Machine
    The Shattering/Legions Trilogy

Other Great Novels and Anthologies
    Gideon Cain: Demon Hunter
    Blackthorn: Thunder on Mars
    Blackthorn: Dynasty of Mars
      By Ian Watson
    My Brother's Keeper
      By David Wright

Nonfiction:
    Assembled! Five Decades of Earth's Mightiest
    Assembled! 2
    Super-Comics Trivia
    Season of Our Dreams &
    Decades of Dominance (Van Allen Plexico and John Ringer)

All are available wherever books
are sold, or visit
WWW.WHITEROCKETBOOKS.COM